MAD SWINE
THE BEGINNING

D1730831

MAD SWINE
THE BEGINNING

STEVEN PAJAK

Permuted Press
The formula has been changed...
Shifted... Altered... *Twisted.*
www.permutedpress.com

Acknowledgements

This book is dedicated to my brother Brian for allowing me to use his likeness in the novel and for his contributions to the storyline.

I'd also like to thank the members of AR15.com, Zombie Central, and Essential Survival Guides & Fiction forums, as well as those at SKSboards.com who took a chance on reading this in its early stages of development and encouraged me to finish this for publication.

A PERMUTED PRESS book
published by arrangement with the author
ISBN-13: 978-1-61868-001-3
ISBN-10: 1-61868-001-3

Mad Swine: The Beginning copyright © 2012
by Steven Pajak.
All Rights Reserved.
Cover art by Richard Yoo.

PROLOGUE:
THE BEGINNING

No one really knows how or why it started. What we do know is that the H1N1 virus—or the damn vaccinations that everyone so anxiously lined up for hours to get—mutated in a bad way. Whether this mutation happened naturally, like the seasonal influenza virus does every year by changing its signature protein, or if it was the work of some mad dictator bent on bringing hell into the world by unleashing the bastardized disease, no one can say for sure. Even now, information about the origin of the disease and its spread across the continents is sporadic at best and filled with guesses, assumptions and fiction.

If there was an official name to the disease I never knew it. Most people called it "Mad Swine" because it was derived from the original "Swine Flu". I know that "Mad Swine" doesn't really come close to properly describing what the damn virus truly is—we're still not sure and we may never know—but I can't think of a better or more descriptive title.

Although it's not a truly accurate term, people started to refer to the infected as "zombies" from the very beginning. The word "zombie" implies that the infected person has died and been reanimated, but those

1

infected with Mad Swine didn't die. They're still alive; they even breathe. They're just not…human anymore.

The infected didn't resemble zombies, at least not in the beginning, and not like any movie zombies that we all reference when we hear that word. In fact, by all outward appearances an infected appeared as ordinary as any other person. They're not pale or gray, nor do they resemble anything we'd describe as dead-looking. And except for the stupid, confused look that's apparent on their face when they're not trying to tear at someone's flesh, you wouldn't know they were some fucked up dreg of humanity until they turned on you with teeth bared, seeking your flesh.

Their seemingly normal appearance worked in favor of the disease and helped spread Mad Swine quickly. I'm sure by now we've all heard tales—some of you may even have firsthand experience—of someone sitting at a bus stop minding their own business and reading a paperback when a man in a suit and tie, looking like he's ready for day trading or on his way to court for a deposition, walks up to the unsuspecting traveler and takes a bite out their cheek. The infected, the "crazies" as I tend to call them, looked so completely normal in the beginning that you let them get close, but by then it was already too late. By then you were either dinner or worse, part of the horde.

As time progresses, the infected begin to look more like what we think of as the classic zombie: tattered clothing, sunken faces, blood stained, and mottled flesh. Some of them end up looking like road kill after a few months. They become dirty and crusted with blood, brain matter, and other fluids. Some of them sustain severe bodily damage, too, and look like demons crawled forth from hell before their bodies have time to repair. Their advanced and deteriorated state just adds to the Halloween effect.

Once I saw an infected that looked like he'd been hit by a garbage truck, dragged for a mile over a cobblestone road and then loaded into a meat grinder. His face was literally ribbons of old flesh that dried like jerky. In the socket where his left eye had been, dark flesh and spots of white bone were exposed. His legs were torn and tattered but must have healed a great deal to allow him to walk. His appearance was so shocking and horrific that I killed him instantly rather than trying to evade him. Perhaps my actions were born out of the desire to give him peace, but more likely my reasons were selfish. I just couldn't bear witness to such an atrocity walking through my world. After I blew his head off with the shotgun he still looked the same as he did before I pulled the trigger. But he no longer walked among us.

Over time, the stink of them becomes unbearable. The scent of their diseased and deteriorated flesh and the stench of their fetid breath are not the only aromas that cling to them; the world is their toilet. The crazies urinate and defecate as they walk the streets, like guinea pigs trapped in a cage. Their clothes or the tattered remnants that adorn their disgusting bodies become soiled with their body's excretions. I witnessed an infected man who had shat his pants so many times that the seat of his trousers was distended. Although much of it had seeped down his legs, enough of the excrement had accumulated that he appeared to have an enormous hemorrhoid.

An important difference between zombies and the crazies is that those infected with Mad Swine sleep, at least they did in the beginning. The infected would fall into a deep coma-like slumber at sundown, or shortly thereafter. Casual sounds would not wake them, but loud rackets would rouse them. Although this is speculation, I believe this slumber was an effect of the disease, allowing it to infest the entire circulatory system, to take full control of all organs and tissue. I also believe that during this time the healing process began for the wounded creatures; skin, bones, muscle, and tissue would regenerate while their bodies lay dormant.

Mad Swine was like nothing we've ever seen before. I'm not a scientist and I'm not going to get technical, so don't expect that I can fully explain this. And don't think that everything I tell you is the truth, because the fact is, I don't know everything about it, nor am I truly interested in the how and why. At least not anymore; right now I only care to survive. But here's what I know: Mad Swine spread through bodily fluids, by contact with infected blood, and through sexual intercourse. Some believe that the disease must have also been airborne for some time in the beginning for it to have spread so quickly, but that has been neither confirmed nor denied. There is probably some truth in that theory, but I spent little time studying the origins of Mad Swine, and instead set my goal on survival.

Whatever the method, once infected, the host initially showed no outward signs of changing during the first twenty-four hours. However, in the case of the elderly or the very young, newly infected have been known to turn in as few as eight or nine hours. Once Mad Swine took hold in the body, the infection spread with such quickness, perhaps because of their weaker immune systems. In rare cases some infected with Mad Swine continued to survive for as much as seventy-two hours without showing symptoms.

After infection, the disease first attacked the memory. At first they'd forget the small things, like picking up that roll of toilet paper on the way home from work or telling a coworker that the boss wanted to see them when they were done with their phone call. As the infection continued to incubate, to lock its tendrils into the circulatory system and nervous system, memory loss became much more severe and complete deterioration of the mind occurred rapidly thereafter. Soon the infected couldn't remember their children's names or recognize family members and close friends; the mind deteriorated to the point of total devolution, and the infected would forget everything except the most basic of instincts of the human animal—the need to eat to continue to survive.

One thing those infected with Mad Swine do have in common with the conventional zombie is that a headshot will kill them. Chopping off the head or severely caving in the skull and damaging the brain will do the trick. Aside from these methods, the crazies are hard to kill, because, as a side-effect to the H1N1 vaccination's mutation, their wounds heal over time. The damn things actually regenerate flesh and broken bone actually re-fuses with frightening speed. A gunshot to the thigh will slow an infected down a bit but within three days the wound will heal. Surprisingly, blood loss, even severe blood loss, does not kill the crazies. The mutated virus drastically increases blood regeneration to a matter of minutes.

Since the day Mad Swine began to decimate our way of life, I have seen infected hit by automobiles, thrown and dragged, with legs disabled, who still kept coming, crawling their way toward human flesh. Even legless or armless, they continue to live, driven by their mindless hunger. Without fear or pain to inhibit them, the infected were unstoppable. Within a week, small towns were completely overridden. In two weeks large cities fell and entire states were overrun by the infected. With a mere three percent immunity to the H1N1 vaccinations and the overwhelming ratio of infected over humans, there were pathetically few of us left after the first six months.

CHAPTER 1: EGRESS

The morning that the world changed started like any other. I was running late again because of the traffic on the Jane Addams. The road crews were working on the same stretches of road they worked on last year. Although to my untrained eye the road looked to be in good repair, it was obviously in need of professional care. Traffic cones, blaring horns and insane-angry drivers had become as much a part of my day as getting that cup of morning coffee and kissing my wife on my way out the door.

The kids were late to school and received tardy slips again. My daughter complained about it as I accompanied her on her walk of shame down the hall to her classroom. She tried to find a place to hide the pink slip before anyone saw it. Katie thinks our record for most tardy slips in a week reflects badly on her second grade social life. Mark on the other hand was a trooper and simply collected his pink slip from the office attendant and swaggered down the hall like he owned the joint. As a kindergartner, he obviously didn't yet share his sister's social awareness.

Next, I made the commute to work, which was pretty uneventful after the stressful journey on the Jane Addams. After consulting my wristwatch and realizing I was already running twenty minutes late, I skipped my planned detour to Dunkin Donuts. I strode into the office just over a half hour late, but I had the advantage of being the man in charge and no one even lifted an eyebrow at my untimely entrance. I greeted the front desk staff, who kindly buzzed me in, and then I worked my way through the maze of halls and cubicles, nodding a good morning to whomever I passed. I poked my head into the vice president's office and discussed the usual morning statistics and attendance logs. That was just small talk leading up to a more serious discussion about the latest professional sports games. I had picked my teams well this year and my bracket was the envy of the office.

When I finally made it to my own office I found my staff in good spirits. We were caught up on projects and there was so little tension that everyone was able to breathe a little easier. I was even able to extend our admission deadlines a month without the usual groans, protests, and eye-rolling. I passed the student worker desk and was greeted with an assortment of pastries, cookies and fresh banana bread. We'd celebrated Mary's birthday last week, and everyone in the office had pooled their money and purchased a set of cookware and a bread maker for her. Mary had obviously put our present to good use. I grabbed a napkin and snagged a chunk of the banana bread.

When I finally reached my desk, I set down my messenger bag, travel mug, and morning sweets. I slipped out of my vest and hung it on the coatrack in the corner of my cubicle. Today I was dressed casually in jeans and a checkered button down shirt. After a long month of attending meetings where almost nothing seemed to be accomplished and the same old arguments were rehashed, I'd finally been able to clear my schedule for a day. With no appointments on my calendar there was no need for my usual shirt and tie.

After sitting in my chair, I pulled up behind my desk and turned on my computer. As it booted, Mary, my trusted assistant and resident Betty Crocker, appeared in the doorway of my cubicle. Mary's straight brown hair and fashionable glasses portrayed her as a moody or artistic.

She wore a smart white blouse and charcoal gray slacks with light gray pinstripes. Her makeup gave color to her otherwise colorless face.

"Good morning, boss."

"Good morning, Mary," I replied. Indicating the bread on my desk I said, "I see you've been busy this weekend. Did anything exciting happen or was baking the highlight?"

She chuckled. In ten years I'd never known Mary to be anything but perky and accommodating. Her sense of humor in this horde of cynics in our office was commendable.

"Just the same old boring stuff, as usual. My weekends are filled with exotic chores and sinful errands," she said. "I also spend much of my time driving the kids to their various events. Their calendars seem so full these days and they're just teenagers. By the way, your calendar is wide open today. How did that slip my radar?"

"You're slacking." I smiled at her. Mary, being responsible for scheduling the large majority of my meetings, was certainly aware of my free day. In fact, I'm sure this anomaly was the result of much planning rather than good luck. "I guess I should thank you for the free day."

Mary winked conspiratorially. "I have no idea what you're talking about. I know you may think you won the lottery, but I'm sure something will pop up any minute now. You're going to feel silly sitting down with the Provost wearing that lumberjack shirt."

"Don't jinx it," I said, logging onto the network. "And I'm sure the Provost would be very jealous of my lumberjack shirt."

"Whatever," she laughed, waving a pale hand at me. "Anyway, coffee's done. I'll save you some." And then she was off to put out some fires before the heat could get to me.

After logging into Microsoft Outlook to check my email, I finally turned to my banana bread. Having skipped breakfast I was close to ravenous. My appetite was awakened by the sweet smell of nutmeg and other spices. Just as I was about to bite into the moist treat, the office was unexpectedly rent by the harsh and tremendous buzzing of the fire alarm.

Startled by the intrusive alarm, I dropped the bread onto my desk, watching as crumbs jumped up and spread onto my blotter.

"For Christ's sake."

More than just a little aggravated, I pushed back from my desk, stood up, and grabbed my messenger bag. Sometimes these drills could last for up to half an hour. My bag was full of things that would keep me from suffering of boredom. The buzzing of the alarm was making my eyes water. I plugged my ears with my fingers and the sound, although still loud and obnoxious, was almost tolerable. In three long strides I exited my cubicle and stood in the aisle.

"Everyone gather your personal stuff and move to the nearest exit, just like we practiced," I said loudly, although my voice was dominated by the damn alarm. I turned to Nate and with a bit more gusto added, "Get your side of the room moving! Follow the egress plan. No stragglers, okay?"

Last year, after another senseless act of violence on another college campus, our university finally decided to launch a safety campaign. The decision was more political than altruistic, but as a result, fancy new egress placards were placed on walls near every office door outlining the best way to exit the area in case of an emergency. Each hallway, elevator and staircase was also outfitted with the crisp white placards with blue lettering. As designated building coordinator, I held a few drills with my staff as part of a larger scale mock emergency that our Public Safety Office had insisted on. I was confident everyone would remember the drills and follow the egress path like cattle.

With my ears plugged and my sinuses still aching, I watched without amusement as everyone vacated their maze of cubicles and started moving. I could see in their faces that they were displeased that they had to evacuate before morning coffee. Nate was leading our group as planned. As the last of the employees left the office I brought up the rear, peeking down the aisles and into cubicles, making sure there were no dawdlers. Soon we all formed up at the door, like schoolchildren, and in single-file moved out of the office and through our side exit that led to a main corridor and eventually out of our building.

Our route of egress led us southward toward where Building D and E met, about one hundred feet to the nearest exit and then out into the courtyard immediately adjacent to our office where we'd have a clear view of the quad, the library and the Science building. There we would stand and wait until given the all-clear, at which point we'd file back into the building and get back to business. As we neared our designated exit, a commotion drew my attention. Raised but unintelligible voices could be heard above the din. Someone screamed loudly enough to be heard through my plugged ears.

Nate stopped fifteen feet shy of the exit, bringing the whole line to a halt with him. Moving swiftly to avoid colliding with Maureen at the tail end of our line, I strode angrily around the group until I stood beside Nate.

"Why the hell are we stopping?" I asked him. We were supposed to keep moving regardless of what was going on. Leave the rescue to the professionals. Turning to my group I shouted, "Keep moving! You know where to go!"

"There's something going on up there," Nate said.

He was always one to state the obvious. I was in no mood for incompetence. The damn buzzing was driving me nuts. I felt like the fillings in my teeth were rattling, and the buzz made my skin feel like thousands of flies were walking all over me.

"Forget that," I said. "Keep moving! Get them outside."

Nate nodded and started the line moving again, although only half of his attention was devoted to his task, while the other half was worrying over what the hell was going on down the hall. We finally reached our exit and Nate resumed his place at the head of the line. He held the door open for the staff to file through, his lips moving silently, taking count as each person passed. The last of my crew exited the door when the sound of the crowd swelled behind me. Another loud scream rose above the sound of the alarm, and more screams followed, screams like those you'd expect to hear from an audience at a horror movie. Screams that prickled the hair on your neck.

Nate, still at the threshold holding the door open asked, "What the hell?" He let the door fall closed behind him and started walking toward the crowd. A nervous feeling started to work its way up from my stomach and into my chest. This was no drill. Something real was happening, something bad. I moved forward, too, my curiosity getting the better of me. I shoved some people out of the way in an attempt to get a closer look at what was going on.

As I traversed the mob, a group of onlookers suddenly turned as one and started to scramble away from the scene, confirming that this was no drill. Something was wrong...majorly wrong. Nate and I neared the center of the ruckus. I winced as an elbow struck my ribs and a knee dug painfully into my thigh. For as many people as were fleeing the scene, just as many crowded forward, flooding it. Faces whirred past me, some recognizable and some strangers, most masked with fear. In the crowd I spotted James Harrington, our VP of Finance and Administration. Jim wore a navy blue suit with a cornflower blue tie. His coat was still buttoned but his shirt was disheveled and un-tucked, hanging out from his waistband. His tie was loosened and pulled askew, and his hair was a mess. In the ten years I'd known Jim I'd never witnessed a hair on his head out of place. He'd always been a sharp dresser and concerned about his appearance. Seeing him in this state was surprising.

"What the hell is wrong with him?" asked a voice to my left.

"I don't know," I shouted without turning my head to see who raised the question. I stumbled forward as someone banged into me from behind. If not for the crowd I would have fallen. Instead I was jostled and shoved and elbowed. I lost track of Nate for a moment before finally spotting his balding crown behind me and to my right.

"Did you call campus police?" another person asked.

Ignoring the startled questions and throwing a few elbows of my own, I resumed my push through the crowd, now determined to get a look at what was going on. My determination waned quickly and I halted suddenly as another series of bloodcurdling screams rose up around me. Having made my way to the front I had a good enough view to now see what was going on. I wish I'd minded my business and exited the building per the egress plan. In the center of our ring of curious onlookers, Jim turned in a circle, eyes wild and teeth gnashing. Strange noises came from deep within his gut. The crowd of stunned people stared at him with wide eyes and curious faces, which turned fearful when Jim unexpectedly jumped on one of the onlookers and tried to bite the guy's face.

The crowd surged with this new turn of events, and this time I was knocked backward, losing my balance. I hit the tile hard with my butt, feeling pain shoot up into my lower back. A series of knees and feet pummeled me as the frightened crowd made their mass exit. A sharp pain tore at my ear when I tried to gain my feet. Another knee smashed into the back of my skull; that hurt like hell. I shifted to my hands and knees, attempting to stand, and someone stomped the knuckles on my left hand pretty good. The nervous feeling had turned to downright fear now. Desperate to get to my feet, I grabbed onto someone next to me. I was dragged a few feet and then my grip loosened and I fell again.

I crouched on the floor doing my best to cover my face with my arms to avoid serious injury from flying knees and pumping feet, and I felt hands pulling at the collar of my shirt. With the assistance of the tugging hands, I pushed up off the ground and got my feet back under me. I stumbled a few steps as I tried to catch my balance and swayed for a moment before the hands at my back grabbed me firmly and steadied me. I looked over my shoulder, trying to catch my breath and get my bearings. Nate stood behind me, his own breath hot against my neck.

"I got you, boss," he said, his lips trembling under his thick mustache. Worry stole over his face. His graying blond hair looked windblown and sweat trickled down his temple.

Without thinking, reacting to the stimuli around me, I grabbed Nate's arm, leaned in close and shouted, "Get outside now! We have to get out of here before we get trampled!"

At that moment I couldn't give a damn about Jim or this situation. Whatever the hell was going on would have to sort itself out without my assistance. Although I was designated floor coordinator during times of emergency, I wasn't expected to step into a violent situation. My job was to get people out of the building and to safety until first responders arrived and gave further instruction. Let the authorities deal with this mess.

Nate and I struggled and jostled and moved with the flow of the stricken crowd and within seconds we were at the door leading to the courtyard that was our designated meeting place. Together we slammed through the door and stepped out into the cool air, taking deep gulps of oxygen. I realized I was sweating when the cold air stung my temples and neck. Still among a crowd of panicked students and staff, I shoved my way forward about twenty or so feet before I found my staff. As they gathered around Nate and me, I was grateful to be free from the horrible buzzing of the alarm. I felt lightheaded and my ears were ringing from the residual effects of having my fingers jammed in tight. My right cheek was tender and I felt other places on my ribs and back that were sore and would probably bruise by morning.

Everything was happening so quickly I felt like I couldn't get my head wrapped around the situation. This was all so unexpected and I was unaccustomed to having to deal with such pandemonium in my civilian life. Before I had time to recover from my thrashing everyone was crowding me, asking what was going on and what was happening. They were now becoming aware of the fact that this was not a drill and more than likely the alarm had not been sounded because of a fire. This was something totally different.

"Calm down everyone!" I shouted. "I can't hear when you're all talking at once."

"What's going on in there, Matthew?" Mary asked.

Her voice was higher than usual, and she was clearly scared. Ordinarily, Mary was calm, cool and collected. As my assistant, she was faced with irate students and parents on a daily basis that were sometimes downright scary, but she never showed any fear. Now, though, she looked panicked. All of them looked as though they were about to bolt any moment. I had to say something to calm them down, to let them know everything was okay.

I shook my head to clear my thoughts and said, "I don't know yet, but I will find out. In the meantime, I need everyone to remain calm and alert."

Nate looked at me and raised his eyebrows. I don't know how much of what happened in there he'd witnessed, but I was honest. Regardless of what I saw, I had no idea what was going on. Why Jim was going crazy in the middle of the Student Union and trying to bite onlookers was still a mystery to me.

"Nate, keep them all here until I give you the all clear. Don't let anyone start wandering."

"Maybe you should stay here. There's nothing you can do in there. That's not something you want to be involved in."

Nate was right, I didn't want any part of it, but I had to know what was happening. I still had to make sure my people were safe. And Jim was a friend. If there was something I could to help him I needed to try.

"Just do what I said, please," I told Nate.

Turning away from twenty sets of frightened eyes, I strode about ten paces back toward the exit where there was a little more elbow room. It seemed as though people were coming to their senses and instead of crowding the exits they'd moved away to make room. I tugged my cell phone from my back pocket and dialed the number for campus police. A recorded message played, informing me that circuits were overloaded and to try my call again. That was surprising. It would take a great many calls for the campus police switchboard to become overloaded. Something more serious was happening somewhere else on campus. Jim couldn't possibly be the only attraction.

I returned my cell phone to my pocket and glanced around. People were running in all directions in the quad while others were clumped together in groups, waiting for someone to instruct them. Almost everyone had a cell phone held up to their ear. Some were recording the frenzy and would no doubt be posting their movies on YouTube.

Suddenly a surge of shouts and screams tore through the air from the south end of the quad. Craning my neck to try to get a better view, I watched as a crowd of people nearest the Fine Arts Center quickly dispersed. Folks were bolting away from the center and the library, and were headed in my direction. They were moving fast, propelled by sick fear. I felt my stomach coiling up again and warning bells were sounding in my head. People were drawn to the macabre; they would stand around at the scene of a horrible accident, or look on as suicidal man or woman plunged to their deaths. If people were running instead of enthralled by the events, it had to be from something immediately threatening.

As the first wave of runners blurred past me, I overheard Nate shouting. At first his words were unintelligible but because he kept repeating I finally understood his message. He was yelling for folks not to go inside. His shouting was pointless. Something had spooked them into an all-out sprint. Fear controlled them now and simple verbal commands would be ineffective.

My eyes darted everywhere at once, trying to hone in on the source of the commotion. It was hard to focus on anyone for too long. Bodies were just colorful blurs of movement in all directions across the quad. I closed my eyes for a moment and rubbed them with my fingers. I brushed sweat away from my forehead with my shirt sleeve. When I opened my eyes again, my vision was drawn toward one of the crowd, a young man in his twenties with shoulder length blond hair. I spotted him because of the odd way he was running. He seemed to be favoring a leg. He looked like Quasimodo running all hunched over and uncoordinated. He wore black jeans and a blue T-shirt. His shirt was covered with blood.

"Son-of-a-bitch," I said.

Although I watched Jim attempt to attack someone, this was the first sign of someone injured. The sight of the wounded man drove home the seriousness of the situation. It also confirmed that something else was happening on campus. The incident with Jim was not an isolated event.

My eyes were glued to the blond man with the bloody shirt. Given the amount of blood on him and the way he ran, I expected him to keel over, succumbing to his wounds. But as I watched, he reached out and without warning, pulled a woman to the ground, the dead weight of his body falling against her, too much for her knees to bear. I cringed at the sound their bodies made when they hit. Without realizing it, I started to move forward but halted and then did a double-take. For a moment, I thought I saw him take a bite out of the back of her neck but I couldn't be sure.

Mary's screamed my name and that finally broke my fixation on the blond man. I turned my head in her direction, frightened of what I would see. Mary was pointing frantically toward the direction of the Fine Arts Center. Turning again in the other direction I saw what the fuss was about; a second guy running in a crazy, mindless fashion. His brown suit jacket hung down behind him, having fallen off his left shoulder. Maroon blood spread across his lips and chin, was smeared down his right cheek. He was pretty hefty, certainly heavier than I, and moving at full-steam, coming directly toward us. He showed no sign of stopping.

When it was clear that the chubby runner was out of control and would not deviate from his course of collision, I shouted, "Everybody move! Get back inside. Go! Go!"

I plunged forward pushing those who were too stunned to move of their own accord. Too many stunned onlookers were frozen where they stood. A quick glance over my shoulder revealed the man in the brown suit was almost on us. I had no clue why we were suddenly his target. I couldn't understand my sudden fear of what appeared to be a wounded man, probably just looking for someone to help him.

"Come on, move damn it!" I shouted again, my voice harsh and dangerous.

With my own fear rising to the surface, I roughly ushered the stricken folks back toward the building we'd exited just moments ago. The tone of my voice finally got them moving but in their haste to comply, many of them started to scatter in various directions, unsure where to go, where to move. Nowhere seemed welcoming; everywhere someone was running or screaming. I needed them all to stay together, damn it.

"Nate, keep them together for Christ sake," I yelled, making a circular motion with my arms to get my message through.

Nate shouted something I couldn't hear—the whole damn quad sounded like a Metallica concert—but his wide eyes and gesturing hands warned me what was about to go down, and I was the target. Turning back toward the direction of the library I immediately saw the man in the brown suit, still hauling ass in our direction. He was several yards away and for whatever reason he'd set his sights on me. Suddenly, I was a matador and he an angry bull. Our eyes locked and we were now engaged in battle.

Mary stood beside me, gripping my arm tightly as the bloody man took aim. He slammed through a couple of young kids who'd run right in front of him, and the two kids bumped off him like bowling pins and hit the ground, unaware of what had just happened. The bull merely stumbled a bit off course, barely breaking stride and then continued at us again, full steam ahead. I pried Mary's death-grip from my arm and pushed at her, trying to get her out of harm's way.

"Go!" I yelled.

Mary didn't move. She seemed to be in shock, frozen with fear, unable to get her legs moving beneath her petite body. The crazy bastard was now just several yards away and closing fast. Acting out of instinct, I shoved Mary away again, this time with enough force that she fell on her butt. I had very little time to brace myself for the hit; I turned my body sideways, crouched slightly, tucked my arms in and pushed my shoulder forward, just like I remember being taught in high school football.

My eyes squinted and my body tightened, anticipating the impact. The bull was just a yard away now. I could smell his sweat from this distance. His dull eyes fixed on me and his lips retracted revealing thick yellowing teeth. I knew he outweighed me, but from this distance he appeared enormous, at least three hundred pounds. At thirty-seven, I wasn't sure I could take a hit from a gorilla anymore. Before I could test my body's resilience against the crazed, bloody man the sound of a gunshot rang out.

The bull staggered slightly, veering to the right just a foot away from making bodily contact with me. He hit the small railing that separates the walkway from the courtyard and flipped over it head first. He hit the ground hard with his face—I heard a sickening slapping sound—but was up quickly, like he had springs embedded in his legs. Instead of turning back toward me, some unintelligible sound issued from deep within his diaphragm. Without giving me a second glance he ran in the direction of the computer lab and a group of people who had stopped to watch what was going on. For whatever reason, I was no longer his target.

I stood in my football stance a moment longer watching the man in the brown suit run, the jacket still hanging askew off his right shoulder. His sweaty white shirt was stained by a blossom of blood spreading from the back of his left shoulder where the shot had taken him. After the spill over the railing, landing on his face, and taking a gunshot to the shoulder, I would have expected any man to have stayed down. The man had sustained serious trauma, yet he continued his sloppy run toward the panicked, screaming, and running students. How the hell does that happen? He had to be on some sort of heavy narcotic.

"Holy shit," I whispered, my breath shuddering out of my lungs. Again I used my sleeve to wipe sweat from my brow.

Turning to Mary, I saw Nate crouched beside her. She was still shaken up, but with Nate's help she stood, and together they walked over to me. Mary held out her hands, and I saw that they were scraped and raw, and her left elbow was bleeding.

Mary continued to look at me but remained quiet. Nate asked, "Was that a gunshot?"

My mouth was dry. I tried to work up some saliva, but I felt like I had wads of cotton in my mouth. I nodded my head. I looked around in an effort to determine who had fired the shot, but I didn't spot anyone with a firearm. Things were so crazy and moving so quickly the shooter could have already disappeared into the crowd or given chase to the man in the brown suit. Although I was grateful being spared from the bull, I hoped the gunman was a trained law enforcement officer and not some student packing a gun. This whole situation might take an even greater turn for the worst if that was the case.

"Did you see who shot?" I asked Nate.

He shook his head. There was just too much going on. The fact that gunshots were fired changed the whole situation. The Virginia Tech and Northern Illinois University shootings came to mind. Two deadly massacres on university campuses. Getting off campus was now my number one priority.

The uproar from the crowd remained loud enough to drown out our voices. We had to shout to be heard above the din. People were screaming like they were on an amusement park ride. I saw people crying hysterically, while others just ran around making panicked noises. It was like a scene out of a bad movie, only it was real, and it was happening right now. I couldn't blame them, though. For the first time in a long time, I was scared, too.

"Get them inside," I shouted at Nate again.

Together we ushered our people back into the building, at least those that hadn't separated from our pack. Nate still held Mary's arm as he escorted her through the thick metal doors. I put a hand on each person's shoulder as they passed me or patted their back, trying to let them know everything was going to be all right. But inside the building did not offer any sense of safety. We were greeted by more screaming and crying people who were sprinting and shoving, not caring about anything other than getting out, getting away from danger.

Without having to tell him where to go, Nate led Mary north through the corridor and the rest of our staff followed. Our path led us pass the original source of disruption. Curiosity getting the better of me, I risked a quick glance and was just in time to see Jim's teeth locked currently onto some poor girl's cheek. He was tearing vigorously at her flesh, whipping his head from side to side, trying to pull loose the chunk of meat.

A tall black man stepped out of the crowd and came to the girl's aid. He reached in with long arms and grabbed Jim in a chokehold. Miraculously, another guy emerged from the throng of panicked people to help. He dropped low and gripped Jim's legs. Together the two men took Jim down to the ground. As Jim hit the ground one of the campus police officers joined the fray, piling on top, forcing Jim down onto the cold tile. The three men struggled heroically while Jim thrashed at them, kicking and clawing for purchase. The officer reached for his cuffs and after much straining was finally able to cuff the VP. The poor girl lay just a few feet away from Jim, screaming her head off. The flesh on her right cheek hung like the flap of an old baseball that had been hit too hard and popped its seams.

"Holy shit!" I exclaimed. Did Jim actually bite that girl? What the hell was happening here?

This all happened in a matter of seconds, but seemed a lot longer. Shocked and in awe, I turned my head away from the bloody scene, looking frantically around, trying to keep my staff in view. I waved my arms to my staff, trying to get them to move toward me. A quick count revealed I'd lost a few already. I walked beside those who were still with us, keeping up a brisk pace. We exited the building and I stopped just outside the threshold.

"Everyone listen! When we exit the building I want you all to go home! Just take whatever you have with you now and go! You can get the rest of your stuff tomorrow. The office is locked so don't worry about your belongings."

For a moment they all stood looking at me, as if they did not comprehend what I'd just said. Other students continued to exit the building jostling and shoving us, just wanting to get the hell away from this place.

"Did you hear me? Stop standing there and go!" I yelled and waved my hands again. I stomped my feet for emphasis. "Go! Get out of here! Go home now!"

My display got them moving although I probably scared them even more than they had been. I didn't care at this point, as long as they left here safely so I could leave. We all moved in the direction of the level one parking lot which was closest to our building. My car was parked out there.

I started when another gunshot exploded somewhere behind us. The muffled sound could have come from within the structure, or it could have just sounded funny because of the echo between buildings. I couldn't help but think of Jim. Did the officer shoot him? Everyone ducked in response to the report but I was elated to see they kept moving, dodging or pushing through the throng of people all flooding down the path. Just as I stepped onto the sidewalk a car blew past us, barely missing Nate, who'd already dropped down onto the blacktop. I recognized one of my missing people behind the wheel.

Out of nowhere a lady from our computer science department ran up to me hysterically. I thought her name was Sue. She grabbed my arm halting me.

"What in God's name is happening?" she shouted and sprayed me with warm saliva.

"I don't know," I said, shrugging her hand off of my arm and wiping her saliva off me with my hands.

"Is it terrorists?" she asked. "Who's shooting?"

"I don't know who was shooting. Just go home," I said and got moving again. "Just get the hell off campus!"

Now that we'd reached the parking lot our group broke up, everyone going off in our own direction toward our vehicles. Before they got too far I yelled, "Don't come in tomorrow unless I call or text you! Stay home unless you hear from me!"

Breathless, I reached my Santa Fe and unlocked the doors with the keyless entry remote. I reached for my messenger bag to toss it onto the passenger seat, but my bag was gone. I'd lost it somewhere in all of the action. Screw it, I wasn't going back. I dropped into the driver's seat and started the car. I looked at myself in the rearview mirror and didn't like the way my eyes looked. These were the eyes of a frightened man, not a fearless leader. Ignoring my haunted reflection, I shifted my gaze. I was blocked in my spot by a large red pickup truck. Throngs of pedestrians who were now exiting the main building where classes were held wove dangerously in and out of the line of cars. I heard a thump and felt the Santa Fe shudder. Two guys ran quickly between the parked cars, their bodies slamming into my car.

Word was spreading and people were panicked and wanted out. In their haste they were merely succeeding in prolonging their exodus. Seeing all those cars and people reminded me of trying to get home in 2001 after hearing about the 9/11 attacks. It took an hour just to get out of the parking lot and then another hour to get off the main residential street and to the expressway. I didn't have time for that. Whatever was going on was serious and I wasn't going to stick around and become a fixture in this parking lot.

I slammed the transmission into drive and firmly pressed the accelerator down. The SUV surged forward, crashing through the shrubs that surrounded the parking lot, jumping the curb and then dropping down another. I jarred in my seat as the SUV dropped five inches. I slammed my shoulder against the door and felt my ear hit against the cold glass, but then I was out of the lot and onto the street. I shot out into traffic heading eastbound on Bryn Mawr, just narrowly avoiding being hit by a Corvette. Swearing under my breath, relying strictly on my instincts at this point, I pulled the wheel to the right and swerved back onto the sidewalk, probably causing major damage to my tires in the process.

The lady in the Corvette gave me the finger and laid on her horn as I drove down half the block on the sidewalk. I swerved again halfway down the block to avoid a group of people who broke through the shrubs and ran out in front of me. I think I even clipped a portly gentleman, but I couldn't be sure. I took the first chance I got to get back on the street when I saw a slight opening. A parked car pulled away from the curb leaving me a hole and I exploited my good luck. I pulled hard to the left and cut in quickly behind him, again avoiding being hit by another car that followed too closely behind.

At the next northbound side street I stopped traffic and attempted to make a left turn. Horns blared behind me and angry voices drifted on the cool air. I had to force my front end into oncoming traffic because no one wanted to let me in. I burned rubber when I shot across traffic, fishtailing onto the side street. To my surprise, the side street was clear. Taking advantage of my luck again, I accelerated to fifty miles per hour, quickly putting distance between me and the campus.

Risking taking one hand off the wheel, I thumbed on the radio and switched it to AM where I could always find news. I really didn't expect anything to be on the news so quickly, but in this day and age everyone had a cell phone and camera and news spread quickly on the internet and other social media sites. There was not yet any news about what happened on campus, but quite unexpectedly, there were reports coming in from other parts of Illinois, portions of Indiana and Missouri, and as far away as New York, Pennsylvania, California and Texas, that people were being attacked and bitten by groups of crazed people. So it wasn't just here at the university or even just in Illinois that these bizarre attacks were occurring.

What the hell is this about? I wondered. Why would groups of people coordinate and physically attack people and bite them? For Christ sake, didn't they know that blood carried disease? The only explanation had to be that these people were experiencing some sort of mental breakdown. However, it seemed extremely odd that so many people were experiencing the same sort of mental breakdown across portions of the United States. Perhaps if this was an isolated instance that theory may have seemed reasonable.

The radio announcements continued to pour in. I left the one-way side street and turned left onto Peterson Boulevard. No sooner had I turned when I was immediately slowed by heavier traffic, most of which was from the mass exit from the university. I no longer felt the need to just get myself away from danger, but I now was concerned for my wife and children. This was no longer something scary that was happening at work; this was something scary happening all over the damn place. I needed to get to the kids, get them out of school and get them out of the city. I needed to get us home and into my wife's welcoming embrace.

Braking because of the traffic, I pulled out my cell phone and dialed my wife's number. I needed her to start getting our bug out bags and the rest of our gear together in case things progressed and we had to leave our home. Ever since Hurricane Katrina, I had nagged my wife about making preparations in case of a natural disaster or if we were invaded by whatever fanatical religious group decided to declare war on the United States. Although she balked at the idea in the beginning, telling me that I was being paranoid, she eventually relented. I bet now she would glad she'd relented to my paranoia.

On my first attempt calling my wife I was greeted with a weird beeping tone that resounded monotonously in my ear. I immediately dialed again with the same result. My third attempt prompted an "all circuits are busy" message. After the fourth attempt I was dropped right into her voicemail without any ringing. Angry with my service provider, I left a message with our danger code phrase, Alas Babylon, so that she would know to start getting prepared.

Traffic continued to be at a standstill. Frustrated with the gridlock, feeling like time was slipping away from me quickly, although it had only been less than fifteen minutes since the fire alarm started its relentless buzzing, I opened my door and stepped out to see what the heck was going on. The line of cars on the westbound side, the direction I was travelling, continued all the way down to Pulaski, about a mile and a half down. From my vantage point, it looked as though there might have been an accident ahead that had the intersection blocked. None of the cars on the eastbound side were moving either, which meant something was going on behind there, as well.

I picked up my cell phone and again dialed my wife, but circuits were still busy. I quickly pounded out a text message but almost immediately it was returned as undeliverable. With disgust, I tossed the cell phone onto the passenger seat.

Although I didn't know it at the time, almost all of the cell phone towers in the area had gone down simultaneously at 9:03 AM, and nationwide just minutes later. All across the country people were frantically dialing loved ones or calling for emergency services, while others were using their smart phones to access the web, Twitter, Facebook, My Space and blogs, looking for and sharing information. Apparently, cell towers were stressed so far beyond their limits in such a short span of time that they were unable to handle the unprecedented strain. In less than a half hour after the first reported events, we were left without our precious communication devices.

When I looked toward Pulaski Avenue again, having finally given up on calling my wife, I noticed the first wave of people running down the street. I stood flabbergasted a moment, digesting the fact that they were actually abandoning their vehicles. The frightened people were moving between and around cars, up the sidewalks, and some even struggled up and across the roof of parked vehicles.

As the first of the fleeing drivers passed I yelled, "What's going on up there? Why are you running?"

A woman passed by at full run, breathing heavily. She didn't even look at me. Another group of people passed me, running wildly through the street and moving east. I was quickly becoming accustomed to folks fleeing. None stopped to answer my query. I didn't think they would be frantically running from a vehicle accident, so something else must be going on down the road.

In the distance I heard the first screams. After a few more seconds ticked away I spotted several men and a woman, like those that had attacked people on campus just minutes ago. Their clothes were bloody and they had wild but dull looks on their faces. They ran together in a pack like wild dogs. To my horror, one of the men snared a balding fellow who was trying to skirt around a pick-up truck. The crazed man pulled the bald guy down quick and hard, his teeth darting down and coming up with a mouthful of baldy's flesh. Baldy screamed once, loudly, and then his scream was cut short when the crazy guy took a bite out of his throat.

"Oh my God." I reeled back a step and pressed my body against the Santa Fe. I ran my hands through my hair, trying to comprehend what I was seeing. I knew I needed to act now, act quickly, but I didn't know what to do. My mind seemed to be hibernating. I think I might have been suffering from minor shock.

A second crazy from the group tackled a teenage girl just yards away from baldy, taking her down like a lineman would sack a quarterback. Their bodies slammed loudly into an abandoned car, rebounded almost comically, and hit the pavement with a sickening sound. The bastard started biting her back, his head dipping quickly and tearing through clothing to get at flesh. The girl screamed as though she was being killed, and she was, damn it. Her screams were enough to break through my brief shock and to get me moving finally.

Running to the rear of the Santa Fe, I opened the back hatch. With fumbling fingers I pulled open the hidden compartment in the floor panel under the rubber mat where the jack and tools to change flat tires was stored when I originally purchased the vehicle. Shortly after buying the SUV, I'd removed all of the tools and instead, stored my Romanian SKS carbine there. With a slight tremble in my hands, I pulled my truck gun out of its hiding place, feeling awkward fielding a gun in the middle of a Chicago street.

Focusing my attention on my task, I reached into a green canvas bag that lay beside the rifle and grabbed a 10-round stripper clip. Carefully, I loaded the SKS, roughly thumbing the rounds into the magazine. I pulled back on the bolt carrier handle and chambered a round. The stripper clip pinged onto the street beside my right foot.

Screams and unintelligible, panicked voices were all around me now. It was difficult to remain calm. I could feel fear gnawing at my belly. Ignoring the sounds around me, I reached back into the canvas bag and pulled out the other nine stripper clips and started to distribute them into my pants pockets. Carrying the SKS in my left hand, I quickly returned to the front of the SUV.

Scanning the area, I immediately spotted the third crazed man and his target, a young Latino man, on the south side of the busy street. The crazy man gorged on one of the kid's arms. The terrified kid tried ineffectively to beat him off with the other. The fourth crazy, a woman in her forties dressed in khaki pants and a pale blue button down shirt, was just two cars away on my left, beating a bloody fist against the driver's side window of a red Honda Civic. Behind the wheel of the Honda, a young lady in her early twenties looked on in terror as the crazy woman left bloody palm prints against the glass. In the back seat of the small car, a young girl, about four years old—only a year younger than my son—huddled in the back seat with tears streaking down her horrified face.

The glass broke under the intense shock of the crazed woman's battering fists and showered the young woman with gummy chunks of safety glass. Once the glass barrier that separated her from her prey was no more, the crazy middle-aged woman reached inside and grabbed hold of the other woman's arm. As unintelligible utterances issued from her bloody lips, she tried to pull the young mother out of the vehicle.

Instinctively I raised the SKS to my shoulder and got a bead down the iron sights. I was comfortable using the stock sights on the SKS; I had taken it to the range and fired more than three thousand rounds through the carbine in the last several months. My hands trembled only slightly as I lined up my sights between the crazy woman's shoulder blades. I took a deep breath, controlling my breathing and my hands. I closed my left eye and held my breath.

Just as the crazed woman dipped her head to take a chunk of the woman's arm, I fired the SKS, hitting my mark just a half inch below my point of aim. Her body slammed forward against the Honda from the impact of the 7.62 x 39mm round, but to my surprise, she did not go down. Amazingly, she turned away from the vehicle, looking a bit stunned but otherwise unaffected. I watched blood spreading across her chest and the exit wound center mass. She set her eyes on me and started toward me, slowly at first, and then at a run.

Steadying myself by leaning up against the fender of the Santa Fe, I lined up my next shot and fired, this time hitting her in the abdomen. Again she did not go down. Undeterred by the bullet which tore her stomach open, she continued her charge. I fired again, this time scoring a thigh shot, but the woman merely stumbled, hardly breaking her stride.

"What the hell?" I shouted.

I shot yet again, the bullet tearing out her throat and the back of her neck. Another stagger and the crazy woman, just yards away now, still kept coming. I fired a fifth time as she closed the gap but still she stayed her course. Now only ten feet away from me, the next bullet tore out her left eye and blew out the back of her skull. Finally she went down. Her body crumpled to the ground just a few feet away from me, and skidded to a halt just a foot away from where I stood.

"Holy shit!" I let out a trembling breath.

I stood in amazement. All told, it took six shots to put the woman down. Mentally unstable, crazed and out of her mind, the first shot should have mortally wounded her. The second should have just been a nail in the coffin. But six shots? My God, how could she have kept coming after her throat was blown open?

I took a deep breath trying to regain my composure. I was shaking inside and my mouth was dry as hell. After a brief moment, and ignoring the pleas for help from the young mother in the red Honda, I turned toward the next crazy who'd attacked the teenage girl only moments ago. I felt terrible for ignoring the frightened mother in the Honda, but right now I had to deal with the other crazies first. The mother would have to wait.

The crazy guy still had the girl pinned down in the street. He straddled her from behind and in the minute or so it took to deal with the unstoppable woman, he'd gone from biting her back to munching on her right wrist. Even from this distance I could see white bone beneath the sheets of red blood that poured down.

The girl was screaming at the top of her lungs. Trying to block out her screams before they frayed my nerves completely, I lined up my shot, and with little hesitation, blew the right side of the crazy man's temple wide open. He collapsed immediately to the right and did not move. Unlike the woman, he actually stayed down with just one shot.

Ignoring everything else now, I started to move forward, only peripherally taking note of all the people running panicked around me. I had tunnel vision; I locked my sights on the next psycho. He was up and moving now, having ditched the unlucky bald guy—maybe dead or maybe alive, but certainly messed up. The crazy had moved on to new prey and was chasing down a young black man. The kid was obviously terrified; his eyes were as big as saucers and his mouth worked up and down, as though he was screaming. I couldn't hear anything. I blocked out everything that would distract me for the moment.

The young man ran as fast as he could with his pants sagging down, impeding the length of his stride. In a pretty nice move, though, he jumped over the hood of a parked car, Dukes of Hazard style, and then with another quick hop he leaped up onto the chain link fence of the nature center on the south side of the street and started to climb. He almost made it, too, but before he could get completely over the fence the crazy man grabbed his foot and started to pull. The kid held on tightly and screamed, trying to kick the bastard off, but the pursuer held firmly.

I stopped beside a cream-colored Cadillac and got down on my right knee. Snuggling the SKS comfortably against my shoulder I fired another shot and splattered the crazy's brain all over the back of the kid's sagging pants. The psycho immediately loosened his grip on the kid's foot and dropped to the ground, and a second later the hysterical kid fell to the ground on the opposite side of the fence, hopped up like he had springs in his legs, and ran like mad. He never looked back.

Still in my shooter's stance, I pivoted on my knee and scanned for the last crazy. I didn't see him. I stood and started moving again, westbound. I took no more than two steps before a man grabbed my arm from behind and screamed for me to look in the other direction. I turned and saw the crazed bastard. He was wearing charcoal gray dress pants and a lavender dress shirt. The back of his pants was stained with blood, as though he'd been sitting in a pool while he munched on some poor soul. In midst of all the chaos he had moved past me and was now dining on an elderly lady. He dipped his head and took a chunk out of her forehead, just above her left orbital socket.

The SKS barked again and the crazy keeled over, the front of his head blown wide open.

Now that I'd dealt with all threats, I was suddenly again aware of the rest of the people all around me. Some were hiding behind their cars, peeking over fenders or from behind wheels while others pressed against their floorboards, not daring to venture out. Others still continued to run pell-mell through the streets, not sure what was going on but the instinct to get away strongly driving them along.

After a quick scan, I detected no more crazies. I took the opportune moment to open the SKS magazine and dump the remaining rounds into my hand. Without thinking about it, I dropped the loose rounds into my pants pocket and loaded another ten rounds from a fresh stripper clip.

I returned to my Santa Fe. Standing beside the open driver's door I realized the car would be useless in this gridlock. Cars were scattered all over the boulevard and left little room to drive and maneuver. Most drivers had ditched their vehicles and were nowhere to be found. Even though I'd dealt with the threat, I didn't think they'd be back any time soon. If I wanted to get my kids, I'd have to hoof it.

At the hatch of my car again, I grabbed my 'go bag', a medium sized canvas bag with a shoulder strap. I opened it up and took a quick inventory: a poncho, LaRue tactical battle knife, small first aid kit, magnesium fire starter, two pints of bottled water, two MRE's, multi-tool, foldable jacket, pair of gloves, and some water purifying tablets. In one of the outside pockets I found the Zero Tolerance 300 folding knife and a Surefire flashlight. There were also more odds and ends in the bag but I confirmed all that I really needed already.

I pulled out the packable jacket, unzipped it from its self-containing sleeve, and opened it up. In my haste to get out of the office when the alarm sounded, I'd forgotten my vest. Although not the best garment to protect me from the cool November air, the jacket had pockets. After I shrugged into the jacket, I did some load distribution, moving the stripper clips into its pockets, stuck the Zero Tolerance into my front right pant pocket, and clipped the Surefire into my left pant pocket.

Satisfied with my distribution of gear, I moved back to the driver's door and reached into the car to grab the keys from the ignition. Although I wouldn't be driving, I needed them to get into my house and unlock my gun safe. I noticed a half full bottle of water from this morning's drive into the city, and stuck that into my go bag. I grabbed up my cell phone, too, while I was at it.

I took one last look around at the chaos on the street and then started walking. The kids' elementary school was nearly nine miles away. I needed another egress plan, one that included improvised transportation, to get my kids and make our way out of the city and back to my wife.

It was going to be a long day.

CHAPTER 2:
SCHOOL'S OUT FOREVER

A trip that would have normally taken me forty to forty-five minutes by car during the early morning rush took me about six hours by foot. It was dusk when I reached St. John's Catholic school.

Although I was walking, I could have made the trek an hour sooner, except I kept running into distractions along the way. Twice I had to stop to take out a couple of crazies that were wreaking havoc on my route. I hadn't done it to be a hero, or because I felt sorry for the people who were the targets of those crazies, but because those things were in my way. My mind was set on getting my children and getting out of the city, back to my wife.

Hiking down Peterson Avenue, I came across a viaduct that was crammed full of cars involved in a pretty bad pile-up. On the south side of the street, the eastbound movement halted when an oversized pickup truck smashed into a taxi and then flipped. More vehicles immediately smashed behind them, causing a massive tangle of steel and plastic. On the north side, the westbound traffic was blocked by a CTA bus that had fishtailed and wedged itself perpendicularly into the opening of the viaduct. By the time I came along, most of those lucky enough to survive the collisions had taken refuge in the bus, while a small group of crazies clamored around, smashing their limbs and bodies against it, trying to get at those inside.

Crossing this path was the quickest way to my children. There was no way to skirt them on the south side of the street. The moment I tried to navigate around or over the wrecked vehicles those crazy bastards would be on me. Moving north or south to find alternative routes would delay me further, and was not an option. I needed to get to my kids now. With that thought in my mind, I leaned against an abandoned car, raised the SKS and steadied it by planting my elbow for support. Taking aim, I shot each one through the head.

After dispatching a crazed group who was terrorizing the bus driver and his load of passengers, I immediately got pinned down by some cops who were probably responding to the pile-up. They returned fire on me with their pistols. The twang and thud of the nine millimeter rounds slamming or ricocheting off the vehicles alerted me to their arrival. Luckily, I had good cover from the abandoned vehicles.

I really didn't want to get into a firefight with a couple of LEO's. I did not want to kill a couple of guys doing their jobs, protecting and serving. But at the same time I had no intention of surrendering to them and spending the rest of the day in a cell while things got straightened out. I wasn't going to be stopped by anyone or anything until I knew my kids were safe and out of this crazy city.

With little patience for a stand-off, I was able to convince them that I had them out-gunned. I did this by displaying my marksmanship when I head-shot another crazy who'd come at them from their flank while they were worrying over me. When I had their complete attention, when the fear of death finally crept into their minds and they could think of nothing else, I strongly suggested it was best for them to stay alive and move on and check on their families. After seeing my shooting abilities and listening to their radios which were constantly sparking to life with dispatch calls for officers that needed assistance, they were finally persuaded to leave me alone and move on. I was glad I did not have to kill them, but, God forgive me, I would have. I don't think they really knew how close I was to ending them.

Now, six hours later, I came upon St. John's church from the north, having had to skirt around the southern route to avoid further conflict with the largest group of crazies I'd seen yet. An eerie feeling crept over me as I cautiously approached the sacred place; goose flesh broke out over my arms and the nape of my neck felt like there were spiders crawling on my flesh. Something did not seem right. The streets in the small Niles suburb were far too quiet, too empty, by comparison to the gridlock I experienced on the Chicago streets.

For a moment I was extremely relieved. I thought that maybe whatever the hell was going on in the city hadn't happened here, at least not yet. My relief was short-lived.

The church parking lot was empty save for three vehicles. The church itself was dark, an ominous foreshadowing; there were always lights on, even when it was closed. A quick tug on the side entrance confirmed that the doors were locked. I knocked on the solid wood door and cupped my hands against the glass and looked inside. In the dim light that filtered in through the skylight I could see the church was barren. I saw no movement among the pews, the nave or narthex.

My heart pumped faster now, and I tried to swallow the fear that formed a lump in my throat. I unslung the SKS from my shoulder and trotted toward the school. In my approach I saw only three or four other vehicles in the school lot. This was a bad sign. I stopped in my tracks when I saw what looked like a body lying prone near the north entrance to the school. Instinctively I crouch-walked, moving closer, trying to present as low a profile as possible without slowing my approach too much.

I continued to scan the parking lot, but I only saw the one body. No one else moved around the school grounds. Upon closer inspection, the body turned out to be one of the principal's office assistants, Nancy I think was her name. A little on the plump side, Nancy was cute, bubbly and pleasing to the eye, though you wouldn't know it looking at her now. Her neck was ravaged, most of the flesh on her left shoulder was gone and her back had also been torn and gouged. I did not care to turn her body over. I'd seen enough.

Still crouching, I made my way to the north doors of the school's main building and pulled. Of course, the doors were locked. Although a locked door at the church was unusual, locked doors at the school were not. The administration at this school took safety very seriously.

Feeling like an idiot, but with no alternative plan, I rang the buzzer, which was the usual procedure to enter the building. After an intense minute of silence, feeling extremely exposed in the openness of the main entrance and huge parking lot, I used the butt of the SKS to smash in one of the glass doors. It took a few blows before the glass spider-webbed and then a few swipes with the butt of the carbine to remove the excess glass from the frame. My actions made far too much noise.

With the SKS at my shoulder, I spun in a semi-circle to see if there would be any response to my vandalism. At this point, even the police would have been welcomed. Instead, a tall silhouette that I recognized as Father Thomas approached quickly from the rectory. I hadn't considered checking the rectory and I cursed myself. I should have been more careful, more watchful, and more considerate in my planning. If anything happened to me my kids would not make it alone.

My finger tensed on the trigger and then eased off only after I could see Father Tom's face clearly in the light. He wasn't one of the crazies.

"Mr. Danzig, what are you doing?" he asked. His eyes dropped down, took in the broken glass, widened at the sight of my SKS and locked on my own eyes.

"What happened here, Father?" I asked. "Where the hell is everybody? What happened to Nancy?"

I wish I'd had the foresight to pack a transistor radio in my go bag. I was starved for information. Since leaving my Santa Fe on the road, I had no idea what else may have transpired in the many hours that I'd been walking. I felt lost and confused and even more anxious to get my kids and go home.

"There was chaos," Father Tom said cryptically and then he nervously looked away. He put his right hand in his pocket and took it out immediately, then starting rubbing both hands together. "It happened just shortly after pick-up time, thank the Lord," Father Tom continued. "But the police did not respond to our initial call or our subsequent calls for assistance. I even pulled the fire alarms, but no help arrived."

He looked up again and we locked eyes. "You're the first person I've seen since we evacuated. All those children whose parents were here to take them were evacuated. Some were not as lucky."

"Where are my kids, Father?" I asked, standing now. My fear was at the point where it was about to overwhelm me and take over. In the hours I spent on the road I kept telling myself that my children would be fine, that my kids were all right. Even when I saw the empty parking lot, the dark locked church and poor dead Nancy, I still told myself everything would be fine. Now his words flooded me with fear and I came suddenly to the realization that things truly were messed up, that everything was not going to be fine.

"Mr. Danzig, please come with me to the rectory." Father Tom reached out with one long, thin hand. "Give me your weapon and let me counsel you."

"I just want to take my children and go home, Father," I said and stepped in through the new doorway I'd made.

I was probably close to shock at that point, although I didn't know it. My mind was a complete blank. I had no idea what I intended to do, where I intended to go; I just needed to move and find my children. The priest halted me with one hand on my shoulder. When he lifted his left hand and I saw the rosary; he hadn't been rubbing his hands together, but instead he'd been praying on his rosary.

"Mr. Danzig, I pray for them. And if you insist on going in there, I will pray for you, too."

"Fuck off, Father." I turned on him quickly, grabbing his wrist and wrenching it around and behind his back. My fear quickly turned to blind rage by his insinuation that my children were dead and needed his prayers. "My children are fine, you fucking coward. And if they're not and you didn't do anything about it, you had better say a prayer for yourself because I'm coming back for you."

I could no longer control myself. I kicked him in the seat of his pants and sent him sprawling through the broken door frame. "Go hide in your rectory, Father, and wait for my judgment you fucking coward," I yelled.

Now emboldened by my rage and the need to see my children alive, to hold them in my arms and tell them to not be frightened, that everything would be okay, I stormed boldly into the bowels of the school. Although only the emergency lights lit the halls, I did not take out my flashlight. I did not have time for that.

I stalked down the hall toward my daughter's second grade classroom, which was nearest the school's north entrance. I was at the door in seconds and I furiously pulled it open and stepped into the room with the SKS raised, expecting to see a horde of crazies and carnage. Instead, the room was silent and untouched. Each of the small chairs was turned up on top of each the desks, which meant that the day here had been normal, at least up until five minutes before dismissal when the kids cleaned up. I checked in the coat room and was confronted with more emptiness. Not wanting to waste time, I stormed back into the hall and ran quickly south with my shoes slapping loudly against the vinyl tile floor.

At the first cross-section of the hallway, I turned east and then south again at the next main hall. The kindergarten room was midway down. Winded, I burst into the kindergarten classroom, again with the SKS at the ready. Although not as tidy as the second grade class, it was obvious that nothing out of the ordinary transpired here. Some of the toys were out of place and some of the school supplies lay out on a couple of the miniature desks, but there was no sign of foul play.

"What the fuck?"

The last obvious place for me to check was extended day care, where children were sent if their parents were running late or if they did not have child care providers between when school let out and when they got out of work. Beyond that, I'd have to check every classroom, one at a time, which I was determined to do, but I felt like I was losing too much time.

Continuing southward and moving away from the kindergarten classroom, I made my way quickly toward the extended day care. I approached the room at a run, when my foot suddenly skidded in something slippery and I slammed painfully onto the cold tile, landing on my left side, jarring my left elbow and knocking the wind right out of me.

I didn't feel any immediate pain, but I suspected I'd suffer later, when the initial shock wore off and adrenaline no longer flooded my system. Rolling onto my stomach and pushing up onto my knees, I looked back at what I'd slipped in. In the dark hall of the school the liquid was almost black.

Black and slippery. Black and slippery.

Jesus Christ, it's blood and a lot of it.

Standing once again, feeling my heart pound in my chest and my pulse racing, I traced the origin of the puddle. The blood trail led to the day care's west entrance. I put my hand on the knob and tried to open the door, which moved a few inches and then stopped. Something was blocking the door. Using my shoulder and shifting my body weight, I leaned against the door and pushed it open. Even in the darkness I could see an arm and the back of a woman's head. The lower half of her body was still partially blocking the door.

Shoving harder this time, I managed to get the door fully open. I moved in quickly, trying not to trip over the body or step in the pool of blood that surrounded the dead woman. She was either Ms. Lewis, the day care instructor, or Ms. Ivy, her assistant.

I immediately went to one knee when I came more fully into the room and aimed the SKS. No movement in the room. As my eyes adjusted further to the darkness, I noticed the room was in disarray. Two of the small tables were overturned and the chairs were scattered all about the room. The television set was toppled and the screen was cracked in a long zigzag pattern. There were more blood patches around the room and each looked like pooled oil in the darkness. My eyes took all this in, and in less than a second, dismissed it all quickly when my gaze locked on the three small forms that lay on the floor near the windows.

I ran quickly and dropped down to my knees next to the three children. The SKS clattered to the floor beside me, shattering the silence of the night. My poor Katie lay before me with her neck torn open and much of the flesh from her upper right shoulder bitten to shreds. My little Mark lay beside her. His thin legs were bitten all over. I could see the exposed bone of his left thigh. My babies were holding each other's hands.

I screamed, then. I screamed loudly until my voice failed. I held my children in my arms and cried until my head hurt. I held each of them close to me, smoothing their hair and whispering to them in the cool, dark room. My sobs wracked my body like jolts of electricity, each bringing forth an anguished, unfamiliar noise. I don't know how long I held my children before I became aware of the wet noise that issued from somewhere deeper in the room. I could not remember if I'd heard the wet sound when I'd first entered the room and had just been distracted by the devastating sight of my mangled children.

Slowly laying my children's bodies back onto the cold tile, wincing as Mark's head lolled to one side —I grabbed the SKS and turned to survey the room. The sound came from the front. In my mental image of the room the sound would be coming from near the teacher's desk. The sound grew louder as I approached; it sounded like someone chewing with an open mouth.

I moved silently across the room, reaching into my left hip pocket to pull out my flashlight. When I was just a few feet away from where I remembered the desk standing, I pushed the button and activated the LED. I yelped when I saw Ms. Lewis and the horror she held within her hands. Her face was covered by her blond, blood streaked hair. She was chewing on the left leg of a young boy. His little body moved limply on her lap as her teeth tore into his flesh.

Rage took over and blocked out any sane thoughts. I didn't take time to wonder why the thing hadn't heard my screams and attacked. I didn't even wonder why, now, with my flashlight pinning it like a spotlight, it only remained focused on its meal. Instead, blinded by my rage, I dropped my flashlight and took the SKS in two hands. With all the might I could muster, I brought the butt of the gun down hard on the back of the monster's head as she bent to take another bite of the child's flesh, and took great satisfaction from the bone crunching sound produced when metal and wood struck her skull.

I lost all control of myself, then. I lifted the SKS and smashed it against the creature's head over and over. I smashed at her skull until my shoulders ached and I could no longer breathe. To anyone on the outside listening I sounded like an animal grunting and growling with the force of each blow. When I could no longer lift the SKS above my head, I slid down to my knees and let the carbine fall from my weak hands. In the canted beam of light that still emerged from the fallen flashlight, I caught a glimpse of Ms. Lewis. There wasn't much left of her head; I had caved it in and smashed her brain to the consistency of jelly.

I vomited, turning my head to the side in just enough time to avoid getting it all over my knees. I gulped great breaths of air into my tortured lungs, and stayed there on the tile until I thought I'd be able to stand again.

After a long while, I went to the rectory.

CHAPTER 3:
LAST RITES

The rectory was an attractive yellow brick two-story building situated on the extreme west of the school property, midway between the church and the school. I'd been there a couple of times in the past to request copies of baptismal records and to drop off our donation envelope. I did not know the place well, but I knew enough for my intentions.

The attached garage was at the rear of the building with driveway access from one of the secondary roads that passed the front of the church and led to the main parking lot. The rectory was surrounded by chest-high shrubs that screened off the lower level windows and the side entrance to the garage. Although the rectory was far from being an eye-sore, the architects did their best to mask the rear of the building since it was in direct view from the front of the church. I slipped through a small barren spot between two of the shrubs on the east side of the rectory.

From where I stood it appeared that all of the lights were still out. If Father Thomas was in there, he gave no indication through use of electricity. Perhaps he'd taken my advice and was praying for forgiveness or deliverance in the dark. I would deal with him soon enough, but right now, I had to honor the dead.

The garage door was locked; the electric opener kept the heavy door held firmly in the closed position. I approached the garage's only side window, cupped my hands against the glass and peered inside. The darkness was deep and almost impenetrable but I was sure that what I needed was in there. I'd watched Ray, the grounds caretaker, carrying his equipment to and from the garage many times when I'd picked up my kids from scouts or other after-school activities.

Again I used the butt of my trusty SKS to smash the upper pane of the garage's sole window. Carefully I reached in to unlock the lower sash and then slid the window up. I unslung my go bag and dropped it into the dark garage and then climbed over the sill, setting both feet on the cold concrete. I crouched just inside for a moment, letting my night vision adjust a bit and at the same time listening for any kind of movement.

After a minute of silence I pulled out my flashlight and turned it on. The LED illuminated the entire space with crisp white light. In front of me, in the center of the garage, two vehicles stood coved by heavy tarps that were turning gray with age. To my immediate left, against the east wall was a work table that was neatly cleared. Tools hung on the wall from a pegboard in front of the work table.

Ray was well organized. I was envious; my garage was a mess by comparison. To my right was the side access door which was dead bolted. I spotted the light switch and the garage door opener switch on the right side of the access door where one would expect to find such things. I walked over and turned on the overhead light so I could save my flashlight for when I might really need it. I didn't open the larger garage door but I did thumb the dead bolt open in case I needed to make a hasty retreat.

Moving around the two tarp-covered vehicles, I made my way toward a set of wall-to-wall shelving units. As tidy and organized as anyone I'd ever met, Ray had all of his equipment stored neatly in large plastic bins which were all labeled. There were bins with extension cords, holiday decorations, flags, lights, ribbons, banners, and all sorts of other things. There was a large two-tiered tool box on the far southwest wall. Beside the toolbox was a double-door cabinet where I found what I needed. I took a spade shovel and pick axe from the pegs where they hung neatly inside of the shelving unit. Carrying them both under my left arm, I slung the SKS over my right shoulder and exited the garage via the side door, leaving it stand open.

I cut back through the opening between two shrubs, crossed the north-south service road and made my way to the center of the grounds. After some deliberation, I chose a spot in the grassy area near a small circular garden, where four gray stone benches sat arranged in a semi-circle. Even in mid-November the roses were still in full bloom. Red and white and beautiful they filled the garden. In the center of the roses stood a statue of Saint Nicholas, the catholic saint of children. On either side of him stood a boy and girl, his hands resting on their shoulders. In this place, I planned to lay my children to rest.

It took more than an hour to dig the first hole. It was rough going in the beginning. I have to admit I'm a bit out of shape. I became winded quickly and kept pausing to survey the area because I had a constant feeling I was being watched. I didn't want to be taken off-guard and killed before giving my children a final resting place. After the first grave, the second went quicker as my body adjusted to the labor. I continued to dig graves for the other children I had found in the day care room. I assumed something must have happened to their parents and I could not bear the thought of leaving their small bodies in that room among the remains of Ms. Lewis.

I made one trip back to the garage after digging the third hole. I was feeling dehydrated and I'd left the water in my go bag. I was gone for just a few minutes and when I returned, refreshed but still wary of the work ahead of me, I spotted movement at the north entrance. Setting my go bag down, slowly I reached down and picked up the SKS. I paused only a moment to confirm a round was chambered before I moved in closer for a better look. I found one of the crazies feasting on Nancy's right thigh. These things seemed to have a fondness for necks and thighs. I shot the wretched thing through the head and left him to rot where he lay.

There were no other interruptions and within another hour and a half I finished. When all was said and done I had five crudely dug graves. My hands felt raw and blistered and burned all over. I had a pair of gloves in my damn go bag but I hadn't even thought to put them on. I cursed myself. I had to stop doing stupid things like that or I wasn't going to make it back home. Stupid things, especially stupid little things, could prove to be my undoing.

As hard as the digging had been, the next part was harder. I had to return to the day care. I had to bury the children.

I carried only the SKS with me, slung over my shoulder, because I would need both hands for the delicate work. I put two stripper clips of ammo in my back left pocket and my flashlight in the hip pocket. This time I remembered to put on my gloves. Although I could be stupid at times, I took comfort in the fact that I did actually learn from some of my mistakes.

I moved through the school as quietly as possible. I had not had time to search the place room by room, so I had to be cautious because there could be other crazies around. At this point, I did not want to draw any attention to myself. I was tired and my mind wasn't as sharp as it had been earlier in the day, and my stomach was screaming for food. The last thing I wanted was a close-quarters conflict in the dark.

When I entered the room, I went to the right, toward where Ms. Lewis' dead body lay. When I bashed her skull in, I'd been too angry and disgusted to look and see who she'd been dining on. My flashlight revealed a chubby blond haired boy. His name was Ryan. He'd been in my daughter's class. Ryan was a funny kid and he'd always been good to Katie. Ryan's throat was bitten out and his left shoulder torn to pieces. Again I thought about how many of the crazies I'd seen bite the neck. Perhaps it was just a natural place to strike. Perhaps their animal instincts just took over and demanded they go for the throat.

I put my flashlight away and removed Ms. Lewis remains from Ryan's body. I cleaned him as best I could, using pieces of Ms. Lewis' torn shirt that weren't stained by blood or brain matter. Gingerly, I lifted him into my arms, getting one arm under the crook of his knees and the other behind his back, just like I carried my kids when they fell asleep in the car and I had to carry them into the house. I walked with him out to the garden and placed him into the fourth grave. I'd only dug it four feet deep, but I figured it would be deep enough. There weren't many wild animals in the area that would dig down that far.

After setting the boy into his final resting place, I spent a few moments buttoning his shirt and trying to smooth his hair. I used a bit of my water to clean his face a bit more. I crossed his arms over his chest and left him.

I returned to the room and this time used the flashlight to find Red's body. Red was also in my daughter's class. I didn't remember his real name, just that they called him Red because of the shock of orange hair on his small head. His body lay just a few feet away from my daughter. I didn't take inventory of his wounds; instead I bent and lifted him gently and then carried him to the third grave.

After I lay Red in the ground and cleaned him the best I could, I had to sit for a minute. My arms were shaking and I'd broken out into a sweat. A slight breeze blew through the courtyard and chilled me. The foldable jacket I wore was windproof, but it didn't really do anything to fight the cold from seeping into my bones. I wish I'd grabbed my vest. I wished a lot of things at the moment, but I didn't have time for wishes.

I drank some more water to quiet my stomach. I'd have to eat soon. When I put the bottle back into my bag, I noticed movement in the rectory. I caught the movement in the upper floor out of my peripheral. I stared intently at the windows for a long moment. I thought I saw a figure there, looking out at me, but there wasn't enough light to make out the features. It could only be Father Thomas.

"I'll see you soon," I shouted. If it was him, I wanted to let him know that I intended to keep the promise I'd made.

Now it was time to get my boy. Mark was a little on the small side for his age and his lifeless body felt so small and vulnerable in my arms. I carried him vertically, with his head against one of my shoulders and my arm around his butt. I held his head against me and kissed his hair as I made the long walk through the dark hallways. When I got outside I sat on one of the benches overlooking the roses and held my little boy for a while. I found myself rocking him like I did when he woke from a nightmare and had trouble getting back to sleep.

With regret so deep it hurt me physically I laid my boy into the second hole I'd dug. I knelt in the hole with him and crossed his arms over his chest. I smoothed his hair with trembling hands, but even now, I couldn't get his stubborn cowlick settled. I leaned over and kissed him once on each of his cheeks.

"Sleep well, son."

I struggled to pull myself from the hole. I was racked with sudden tremors and I couldn't stop myself from bursting out into tears. I sobbed loudly; those strange, guttural sounds came from deep within me. I crawled on my knees to one of the benches and used it to pull myself into a standing position. I took deep breaths trying to regain some semblance of my composure.

It took a few minutes before my breathing was normal. I wiped burning tears from my eyes and swiped at the snot running down my nose and the corners of my mouth. I noticed how silent the night was, except for the occasional puff of wind that soughed through the nearby trees and brought tin melodies from the wind chime at the center of the gazebo.

The SKS was riding up on me and choking me a bit. I was suddenly aware that my right arm was bleeding at the elbow. Something had torn through the light material of my jacket and gouged the skin beneath. I'd need to check on that and dress it before it got infected.

I realized I was stalling, putting off the last trip into the bowels of the school.

Trying to be brave for my daughter, I stood taller, readjusted the SKS to a more comfortable position and strode boldly through the shattered hole I'd made in the glass door.

For the last time I entered the extended day care.

I knelt beside Katie, slid my hand under her neck, and lifted her head slightly. Her eyes were open and she seemed to stare past me. The expression on her face was one of pure horror and I prayed to God that I'd never have to know what transpired in this room. I couldn't bear knowing how frightened my little girl had been. I couldn't stand to know how my children screamed when teeth tore into their flesh. I couldn't think about those things, because I'd lose my mind.

My poor Katie. She was my first child and I spoiled her something rotten. She was a daddy's girl to the core and everyone knew it. I didn't care. I was so proud of her. She was the greatest daughter a father could ask for. She was an excellent student, a kind friend, and a great sibling. She always took care of her brother and watched out for him. She taught him everything she knew and she did it with the patience of a saint.

With my left hand I lifted her left hand. When I first found them, she'd been holding hands with her brother. In death, they'd sought each other out. They'd locked hands and no matter what happened, they did not let go. Although I died inside seeing their two small hands folded together, I took some comfort in knowing they were not alone. They had been there for each other, just as I'd always told them they should be.

I lifted my little girl into my arms. She'd gotten so big this last year—she was growing like a weed. But I held her ferociously against my body while I walked her out of that place.

I sat with her on the same bench overlooking the roses. At the end of each day I usually asked her how her day was, what happened at school, what she learned, what books she'd read. I asked her those questions now as I held her, and I heard her soft voice clearly in my head, answering me as she always did.

After a while I laid her in the first grave. Her eyes were still open. I took off my gloves and using my thumbs, I closed her eyes, holding them for a moment. I kissed her on both cheeks and crossed her arms over her chest.

"Daddy loves you, cutie."

My voice trembled but I was determined not to break down again. I was on the border of being overwhelmed by emotions, but I still had business to attend.

Weary in mind and body, and drained in soul, I unslung the SKS and made my way back to the rectory. This time I went to the main entrance. Instead of a normal door like you'd see at the entrance of any home, this door was glass, just like the doors to the main entrance. I did not have to break it, though. Father Thomas had left it unlocked.

I stepped into the place. It was warm in there; that was the first thing I noticed. There was a hum from somewhere to my right. It reminded me of the old clocks in grammar school that they made a humming noise that drove you nuts when you were sitting silently in detention. I noticed a church- like smell, too, like incense.

I'd never been beyond the lobby, so I wasn't sure how to navigate through the place. But I didn't need to. Father Tom seemed to materialize from the darkness beyond the doorway that led deeper into the rectory. He carried his rosary still, and he also held a small leather-bound bible between his hands.

"I am very sorry for your loss, Mr. Danzig," he said.

"Come outside," I replied, and turned. I had no doubt that he'd follow me.

I walked to the fresh graves and stood at the foot of my daughter's. When I looked up Father Tom stood opposite me, looking down at Katie.

"May God have mercy on your soul, child"

"I want you to give them last rites, Father."

He looked at me. "Last rites are for the dying," he said, "not for the dead."

"Do it," I said. "Just do as I ask, Father. Don't deny me this."

His eyes did not waver from mine. We stared at each other for a long minute. Finally, Father Tom knelt before the grave and prayed.

"O my God, I am heartily sorry for having offended Thee, and I detest all my sins, because I dread the loss of heaven, and the pains of hell; but most of all because they offended Thee, my God, Who are all good and deserving of all my love. I firmly resolve, with the help of Thy grace to confess my sins, to do penance and to amend my life. Amen."

"Amen," I said and crossed myself. "Katie, Mark, I love you with all my heart. You were the best kids a dad could ask for. I'm going to be with you soon. Take care of each other. Go with God."

I reached down and lifted lose soil into my fist and let it fall softly onto my daughter's chest. I did the same for Mark, Red and Ryan.

I picked up the shovel and with trembling hands started the hard work of burying the innocent. I ground my teeth and pushed through the pain. I shoveled and shoveled until my shoulders ached and my back screamed.

By the third grave my knees started to falter, yet from my knees I continued to fill the graves. When I could no longer lift the shovel, Father Tom put a heavy hand on my shoulder. He took the shovel and finished what I could not.

I sat on the bench and watched as his long slender frame bent to the task. I don't think he even broke a sweat. I sat on the cold stone, drinking greedily, finishing pints of water. After what seemed like a long time I actually began to close my eyes. I caught myself dozing and snapped my head from side to side.

Suddenly, Father Tom sat next to me. "It is done."

"Thank you," I replied.

We sat on the bench for a few minutes in silence. He clutched his bible and his rosary on his lap. I sat exhausted. I couldn't take my eyes off the four mounds of fresh earth.

After another long moment Father Tom said, "There's one more."

"Yes." I looked at him. "It was for you."

He was stunned into silence.

I stood up and shouldered the SKS.

"It's still yours if you want it. But I'm not going to be the one to decide your fate. I leave that to you and God."

I collected my go bag and stopped one more time at the four graves. "I'm so sorry," I said to my children.

It was almost midnight when I pulled the tarp off the John Deere riding mower, the nicer of the two that sat silently in the center of the garage. As luck would have it, the key was in the ignition. When I started it, and saw that the gas tank was full, I secured the SKS and my go bag to the back rack of the mower with heavy rubber bungees. I pushed the button that opened the garage door. It clattered and clanked and hummed as it rose.

As I rode out of the driveway and turned east onto the access road, I saw Father Tom had not moved from the bench. His eyes remained fixed on the empty grave.

CHAPTER 4: PIT STOP

The John Deere made for good riding. The night was chilly and I certainly wasn't dressed for it but the steady hum of the engine and the smooth ride of the well-built mower was hypnotic.

The problem was, with a top speed of about 15 miles per hour, it was slow going. A few times I considered ditching the mower and trying to find another vehicle but most of the roads were clogged, especially the main roads, and required a smaller vehicle to navigate around. Plus it had gas and I just didn't want to stop anywhere. I really wanted to get home and the John Deere beat walking.

It was an exhausting day and an even more exhausting night. I never quite realized how out of shape I was until this evening. My back, neck and shoulders burned and ached. My biceps felt like jelly and my hands continuously shook even just holding the steering wheel.

A few times I caught myself dozing off but luckily I never actually fell asleep. I was zoned out, my mind and body operating the machine on auto pilot. After about an hour of driving, I finally decided to pull over and find something in my bag to eat. I'd only reached Arlington Heights, still less than the halfway point. I chose an empty Dunkin'

Donuts parking lot to rummage through my go bag. I pulled in behind the building and selected a parking space with the best vantage point to see anything that might come at me. I situated myself within easy access of both entrance and exit in case I needed to make a speedy get-away, not that it would be too speedy on the John Deere.

After a moment of idling nothing came to get me so I turned the mower off. My butt immediately felt numb and my torso felt weird now that the constant vibration had ceased. There were no other vehicles in the lot. There was dim illumination from inside the structure. This was obviously not a family friendly 24-hour job like most of the DD establishments were these days. Either that or the employees had pulled up stakes early and got the hell out to be with their families while whatever the hell was going on continued to go on.

The village of Arlington Heights was quiet and that started to weird me out a bit. In the past sixteen hours I had seen more crazies than people. It seemed like everyone knew something I didn't and they were smart enough to stay indoors.

I found that really hard to believe. There were bound to be others, like me, away from home when this shit-storm came down and were trying to get back home. I couldn't believe that they would all just hunker down for the night and wait while their loved ones were at home or school or God knew where else.

I decided for the moment that the quiet was a good thing, but then I wasn't so sure. Quiet meant no people but it also meant no crazies. Come to think of it, I expected to see more crazies in the street during my trip. I mean, in my travel from work to the kids' school I'd encountered at least seven or eight. More if I counted those I spotted from a distance and chose to go around.

Where the hell were they?

I suppose there could have been only a certain number of these crazies that had been infected by whatever drove them crazy and they'd either all been killed or captured by civilians or LEO's.

But if that was the case, where were all the people? Wouldn't they be out on the streets? Surely they'd be coming to get their cars or check on their business, right? There'd at least be people from the local government agencies picking up the bodies of both the people and the crazies, wouldn't there? Surely there would be.

This was all just too damn crazy. I needed to stop thinking about this shit right now. I needed to get some food into my body and then get the hell home. I'd figure out the rest of the shit later.

Turning slightly in the seat, I unhooked the ends of the bungee cords and grabbed my go bag. It seemed heavy as hell in my weakened state. I dropped it onto the fuel hump in front of me, opened it up and started to rummage through it.

I was completely out of water; I'd drank the last of it outside of the rectory and hadn't been smart enough to replace it with water from the hose that was neatly rolled up in the rectory garage. As far as food, I had two MRE's, but without water, those were pretty useless. I might find some crackers or something inside them, but not enough to sustain me.

I'd have to raid the Dunkin' Donuts. I felt bad about it but I'd leave enough money to cover whatever I took. If I had enough I'd leave extra cash to cover the lock or window or door I'd have to break to get inside.

Reaching behind me again, I snagged up the SKS. I opened the bottom of the fixed magazine and dumped out all of the rounds onto my lap. I pulled back the bolt and also removed the loaded round. I took a quick count; eight rounds. I replaced all eight and then grabbed two of the loose rounds from earlier that I stored in my pocket and added two more to make the magazine full. I disengaged the bolt and then pulled it back and released it to load a round. The safety was already disengaged. My finger was my safety for the time being.

I dismounted the mower and stood on shaky legs. They, too, felt as numb as my ass. Pins and needles burst all over, especially in the back of my thighs. I had to just stand a moment while my blood got recirculated and my leg muscles became re-accustomed to holding my body weight.

When I felt ready enough to move I took my bag, slung the strap over my head and put one arm through. I carried it on my left side so that I could easily dip in for more ammo if that became necessary. I didn't think I'd need to, but I wasn't taking any chances. Also, I'd be able to drop food and drinks into it once I got inside.

I approached the rear door. It was orange-pink in the dim light and was made of steel. Most of the lock housing was covered by a steel plate and only the key hole showed through. I had no tool that I could use to punch it out and I didn't want to take a chance on shooting it out; I didn't want the sound of the gunshot attracting any attention. Also, it was such a small target I feared I might miss and have the bullet ricochet.

I moved around to the right, passed the drive through window—which proved to be locked when I pushed it a little with my left hand—and the main door. It was locked, too, but it was made of glass and I could easily get through that, same as I did at the school. But again, that would cause a lot of noise and make a big mess.

I went back to the drive through window and studied that for a minute. It was pneumatic, so it operated through electricity and air. It was secured with a small metal bar that swung down on a hinge and latched between two handles. There was a very small gap between the two doors where the rubber weather strip did not quite seal. If I could get the edge of my knife in there, I could probably pry it open.

I set the SKS against the side of the brick building and searched around for my LaRue tactical knife. I found it near the bottom. I removed the knife from the sheath but before I even tried it I could see the blade was going to be too thick to fit between the two doors. I tried it anyway and proved myself right. I put the knife away and went to plan B, my Gerber multi-tool.

Although the multi-tool was much thinner and would definitely fit, I was worried that it might not be able to handle the pressure that might be needed to lift the metal bar. I would find out soon enough, though.

I opened the saw blade as it was the thickest of the edged tools and would probably take the greatest licking. I locked it into place with the slide lock and dipped it in between the two windows. It fit great. Even better, the small pronged tip at the end caught perfectly under the metal bar and I was able lift it immediately with little force.

"Yippee ki-ya mother fucker!" I said to myself, proud of my achievement. I folded the multi-tool and put it back into its black sheath. Once again, that little bad boy proved its weight in gold.

My celebration was short-lived though when I pulled the two windows apart and the damn alarm system activated. The piercing bleet-bleet-bleet pause bleet-bleet-bleet sound of the burglar alarm scared the shit out of me and I jumped back a couple of steps and fell flat on my ass. I got up quickly and grabbed my SKS. I froze in the crouched position for a moment, stunned by the turn of events and not quite sure what to do.

I stood now and looked around. No one had yet responded to the alarm, but it had only been a few seconds since it started. I pushed the two windows shut, hoping that the alarm would cease, but no such luck.

"Do I go in, or leave?" I asked myself aloud.

I turned back to the window. It would take some time to maneuver my slightly rotund body into that window. I'd have to drop the bag and the SKS in first which I really did not want to do. But I really needed food and drink.

"Damn it, go in or leave?"

I heard the shriek—that's the best way I can describe the noise—to my right, coming from the street. A second shriek arose from the same direction just a second later.

Instinctively I dropped to my left knee and turned in that direction. I spotted two of the crazies approaching quickly from the gas station across the street. I had no idea they were there; I hadn't seen them at all when I drove past the place just minutes ago.

They didn't see me at first. They were just running blindly toward the sound, probably hoping to find some people that they could munch on. It wasn't until they came up the curb that one of them saw me.

He was a pretty big guy, about six-one and a couple of hundred pounds. His cheeks were dark with dried blood and he had blood all down the front of his Old Navy T-shirt. He didn't miss a beat and he stepped up onto the curb and switched directions toward me. He was actually pretty graceful for a man of his size.

I fired quickly without actually lining up a shot. His left pectoral burst as the shot struck him, spraying blood into the air. His forward motion stopped and he fell to the ground, landing on his left side.

The woman he was with hadn't noticed me yet, but the shot alerted her to my presence. This crazy was a blond girl in her early twenties. She was actually quite pretty. She wore tight jeans that showed off her sexy figure quite nicely and her tight T-shirt accentuated her other assets.

I shot her center mass, a quick double-tap that sent her flying off her feet and backward onto the pavement. The big guy was starting to get to his feet so I fired quickly again, scoring a shoulder hit that knocked him back to the ground.

I turned and ran for the John Deere. I got about halfway to the mower when I saw another crazy coming toward me from the other exit.

Where the fuck were they coming from? Just moments ago the streets were deserted.

I shot from the hip as I ran, missed the first shot and winged him with the next. He stumbled a bit to his right and it gave me enough time to get onto the mower. I turned the key and thanked the Lord when it started right up.

The John Deere was too slow to make a great escape like they do in the movies. There would be no tires screeching as I peeled rubber out of the lot, probably taking one of the crazies out with the rear end of the John Deere as it slid gracefully out of the lot.

Instead, I would have to kill them quickly before more crazies showed up and I became overwhelmed.

Now seated, I turned toward the last crazy to join the party because he was the most immediate threat. He was moving too fast for me to attempt a headshot so I shot him in the chest. He went down, as expected. While he tried to get up, I shot him in the head. He didn't get back up.

I turned back to the original pair. The girl was lagging behind, moving very slowly. The double-tap to the chest had really taken the wind out of her sails. But the man had closed the distance nicely, and was just several feet away from me. Way too close for comfort.

I pulled the trigger twice in quick succession, scoring hits, but the bastard lunged at me. Instinctively I fell backward and to my left off the mower. I felt the thing's hand touch my foot as I went down but he wasn't able to get a grip on it.

Frantically, I squirmed backward on the pavement to get some distance between me and the crazy. I made it to my knees but he was already on his feet. Apparently, he was so focused on me he didn't notice that there was a John Deere between us because he lunged forward again and fell face first over the mower and onto the ground. I heard the wonderful sound of bone thudding against the pavement and was rewarded with the sight of blood flowing freely on the ground from busted lips and an obviously broken nose.

When the dude looked up at me with those dullard eyes, probably wondering what the hell just hit him, I put a bullet almost perfectly between those stupid eyes and he fell silent.

Still kneeling, I turned toward the former hottie. She was still about twenty or so feet away, grunting and wheezing and walking toward me holding both hands to her breasts. I aimed and fired, hitting her in the neck, and she staggered a bit to the right. I adjusted my aim and fired again but there was no report. The bolt was out of battery. I was empty.

"Son of a bitch!"

I rested the front of the SKS on my knee, digging into my bag for a stripper clip. My fingers touched everything but any of the loaded clips. I reached into one of the outside pockets, already having forgotten where I put the extras. This was taking far too long.

The chick had closed the gap to fifteen feet. I took my eyes off her and put the SKS on the ground. Using both hands now, I pulled open the bag and looked inside. I started moving things around, my eyes frantically trying to see into the darkened compartments. I looked up again, checking on the girl. She was now only ten feet away.

The fucking alarm continued to bleet-bleet-bleet, the mower idled in front of me and the bitch kept grunting and trying to form words that her brain no longer knew.

And my goddamn hands were shaking again.

Damn it!

I pulled the MREs out and tossed them onto the ground, moved the LaRue out of the way, and finally spied a clip. I grabbed at it desperately and pulled it out, slipped it into the slot on the end of the bolt and pushed down hard with the ball of my thumb. The first several rounds went down nicely but then stopped. I pushed again, harder still, and a couple more went in.

The grunting sounded so close now. When I looked up Blondie was just a few feet away from me. There was no time left to load the damn SKS.

I jumped to my feet and charged her, screaming at the top of my lungs, remembering the last major bayonet charge I'd seen in a documentary about the Korean War. Although I hadn't unfolded the SKS's bayonet, I hit her hard with the barrel of the gun and pushed her backward, knocking her off her feet.

Before she could get back up I kicked her in the side of the head and watched as blood burst from her ear. I kicked again, and again and again, but the woman would not die. She moaned now, a godawful sound, and squirmed on the ground. She could not get to her feet, so I used this to my advantage and forced the last rounds down into the SKS. I threw the damn stripper clip away in disgust.

I paused a second, considering leaving her on the ground squirming and just driving the hell away while I had the chance. I considered that for only a second, because, although she could not get up right now, she might recover in a few minutes or a few hours, and then she might happen upon some other unsuspecting person. I didn't want that on my conscience, so I put her out of her misery and made my way back to the John Deere. I surveyed the area again, hoping that there were no more crazies within ear shot. The alarm would not stop and it was bound to attract more unwanted guests sooner or later.

I quickly gathered the items I'd pulled out of my bag and strapped it to the back of the mower, laid the SKS across my lap so that I'd have it handy, and then accelerated.

I pulled out onto Dempster and headed west, toward the highway, planning to check it out and see how it was. If I could get by on the shoulders or the embankments it would save me a lot of time. If I couldn't, I'd get back onto the streets and continue my journey home.

After a few blocks—after which I couldn't hear that damned alarm anymore, thank goodness—I found the entrance ramp to the highway. It was packed all the way down the ramp and there was no room for me to slip by on the mower. I'd have to stay on the streets and plod along at 15 miles per hour.

Maybe this was a better idea anyway. Much of the next leg of the journey would lead me through forest preserve and wooded areas once I passed through Schaumburg and the shopping mall.

Less people might mean less crazies. Or it might not. I just didn't know enough about anything right now to make assumptions. I didn't know who the crazies were or why they were the way they were, but they were obviously people, and my assumption seemed sound enough. Besides, I really had no other choice.

I passed the mall without incident. I had expected it to be full, teeming with crazies. Yes, I had seen way too many movies, but I did not consider that fact to be of any benefit to me.

My behavior so far, although I couldn't say this was fact, seemed to be silly mistakes performed only by actors in movies. Things that seemed right at the time, had been done with little thought and less planning, and could have been disastrous.

The mall was full of cars, which might mean people, but I saw no one walking around the lot or the perimeter of the mall. I slowed to about five miles an hour, driving along the sidewalk. I saw no movement inside the glass doorways of three of the major stores, nor at any of the two main entrances on this side of the mall.

That did not mean that people weren't in there hiding out. There might even be help in there. Certainly there would be food and water. I stopped the John Deere but did not shift to park. I held the brake and idled on the sidewalk considering my next move. Was I really planning on trying to get into the mall? It was a big place. There could be people in there, yes, but there could also be others in there that I did not want to encounter.

My stomach almost decided for me but the memory of the Dunkin' Donuts fiasco was still too fresh. Although I knew I couldn't go much longer before hunger and fatigue just took over, I was not willing to try my luck here. There were just too many unknowns in this equation and my math skills sucked.

Besides, home was just sixteen or seventeen more miles away. Just an hour or two more and I'd see my wife. She probably even had dinner ready, sitting in a Tupperware container in the fridge. She probably had the heat turned up and the thick quilt on the bed, too. I could almost feel the warmth now.

But you'll have to tell her about the kids, I thought.

That shut my mind up real quick.

I throttled up and got moving again. I'd go as far as I could go and just fight the hunger and the fatigue. I'd have to just do my best to keep my eyes open and focused on the road, being observant of my surroundings. And with any luck, those sixteen or seventeen miles would just breeze by.

I did manage to drive another nine miles before my mind and body just shut down on me. I remembered cruising along Route 20 heading west, just passing the exit to Route 59 and thinking I had not too much further to go, and the next minute I was up the curb on the wrong side of the road and smashing into a light post in the parking lot of a diner.

I flew out of the seat of the John Deere and rolled a bit on the blacktop before dinging my head on the pavement. Once I stopped rolling I looked up, but the world seemed to be spinning now.

Through my blurred vision I could see the John Deere up against the pole, which was slightly bent at an angle now but not really in danger of collapsing. My eyelids drooped and I fought to open them back up.

I managed to sit up but I wasn't even going to attempt to stand. I stayed where I was, watching the John Deere swirl and blur. I noticed the SKS about twenty feet away on my right, just ahead of the mower. I started to crawl for it.

I made it several feet on my hands and knees when I saw the front door of the diner open and a man came running out, waving his hands back and forth above his head, as if he were signaling a helicopter or something.

I didn't hear any rotors or the loud engine of a chopper. He was yelling something, too, but damned if I knew what the hell he was saying. At first I thought he was coming to my aid but he veered toward the mower. He studied it a second and then reached down and turned off the ignition.

He looked around, his eyes as big as saucers. He looked scared as hell. I tried to tell him not to worry, I'd be all right, but only a small croak came out of my throat.

The man coming toward me looked to be about sixty, with a head full of white hair and a thick white mustache. He reminded me of Mark Twain, only he was much taller than I'd imagined Mark Twain would be, and he was dressed like a fry-cook.He wore gray slacks and a white apron and had one of those white paper hats on his head. His shoes were really polished, too. I got a good look at them from my vantage point.

"That was too much noise," Mark Twain said as he reached down and helped me to my feet. "We have to get inside, now."

"My gun," I managed to say.

I limped forward with my arm around his shoulder, leaning most of my weight on his body. He was pretty strong for an old man.

"Yes, yes, but keep moving," he said.

We stopped and I stood shakily on my own while he stooped down and grabbed my SKS.

"I'll go back for your bag if they don't come," he told me when he returned to my side.

"Who's coming?" I asked, completely out of it now.

Mark Twain ignored the question and kept moving, only stopping long enough to open the door and put his body in front to hold it. I staggered inside, managed to make it to one of the booths near the door, and sat down hard. I heard the lock snap into place and some other sound that might have been a secondary lock.

That was the last thing I remembered for a long time.

CHAPTER 5:
EAT AT KAPPY'S

Mark Twain turned out to be John Kaplan, owner of Kappy's Restaurant, in which I currently sat eating a most wonderful breakfast.

John, or Kappy to his friends, sat across from me in one of the cozy booths. He was repacking the first aid kit he'd used on me just a few minutes ago to clean some of the minor cuts and bruises I'd suffered sometime during the night.

"You made it through pretty unscathed," John said as he stuffed a white roll of tape into the kit.

"Considering..."

I took a bite of a sausage link. It tasted absolutely delicious. I'd told John as much as I dared about my journey last night. Although I did tell him about going to the school to pick up my kids, I left out the part about them being torn to pieces by their aftercare teacher.

John finished packing the kit and zipped it closed. He pushed it to the side and picked up his coffee.

He took a sip of coffee. "My day wasn't quite as... adventurous. I came in early to get the bread started. I noticed something was wrong when the busboy didn't show up by six. I called his cell a few times and couldn't get through. None of the waitresses showed up at seven and that was when I knew something was really wrong. At eight when I went to unlock the door I saw Julio, the busboy, dead beside his car. And I saw... them... for the first time."

I ate some of the eggs and hash browns. After washing it down with some coffee, I asked, "What do you know about them, Kappy?"

"About those things?"

"Yes. I call them crazies."

"Well, that's as good as anything I've heard them called."

He lifted a coffee carafe and freshened my cup. Kappy was going to get a good tip.

"So, what do you know about them? What does the TV say?"

He got up from the booth and moved to the front door. He checked the lock again, for about the fourth time since I woke up. He looked out at what was left of Julio and without turning to me he said, "The TV calls them 'infected' but it doesn't say what they're infected with. There's all kinds of speculation, of course, but most people think it has something to do with the H1N1 vaccinations. The government says otherwise, but they wouldn't tell us the truth anyway, probably thinking that the truth may cause panic."

I started on my pancakes and fresh coffee. "What else?"

Kappy finally turned away from the front doors. "No one knows when the first infected actually sprang up. Earliest accounts say sometime over the weekend. There were reports coming in from most of the large cities, so they can't really say where first. Probably New York but could be California."

"How does the infection spread?" I asked.

"Bodily fluids. Blood and saliva. When they bite they transfer the disease."

"So do they die and then... resurrect?" I felt stupid asking this question. I'd obviously watched too many movies.

"No, the infected ones aren't dead."

"I saw people who'd been bitten and died. Will they reanimate?"

John shook his head. "As far as I know, they won't. If the infected kill a person before the infection can take hold of the nervous system, the person stays dead."

I took comfort in the knowledge that my children would not become one of those creatures and claw their way out of their final resting place.

He returned to the table but didn't sit. He asked, "You want something else? More eggs?"

"No, I'm fine. Thank you so much, Kappy. You really saved my skin out there."

"You gave me a good scare. I saw your headlights coming right toward the front of the place and I thought you were going to crash right through my front door and wake the bastards up."

"So they actually sleep, huh?"

I couldn't help but ask questions. I was fascinated by this information. I'd had no radio and I was starved for information.

"Yes, they sleep. They actually sleep a lot of if you let them. I think it helps them rejuvenate or something. I guess that's lucky for us; allows people to move around somewhat during the night if they're careful enough not to make too much noise. When those 'crazies' wake up at first light, they're hungry, but most of them don't seem to have any real cognitive functions to do any real thinking to help themselves and seek nourishment. They sort of just operate by instinct or something."

Thinking of people as nourishment for the crazies was an odd thought. Letting that image go quickly, I asked, "What makes you say that?"

He looked at me a moment, downed the rest of his coffee and said, "Here, come with me a second."

We both wiggled out of the booth and I followed him over to the front door. The main entrance was pretty exposed. Kappy pulled down the thin film shades that blocked out most of the sun but were transparent enough to see outside.

I noticed my bag sitting on a chair that stood next to the doors. My SKS leaned up against the chair and I felt a sudden relief.

"You got my bag," I said and touched the canvas with the fingers of my left hand.

"Yep. Went back out last night after you'd passed out. It seemed important to you and when they didn't stir with all that racket you made I figured I'd chance it."

Although he didn't know it, Kappy had scored more points for his kind deed.

"Look there," he pointed, indicating the nearest light post just to the right of the front doors.

I looked and saw three of the crazies milling around. They had that stupid, dazed look on their faces. They just kind of walked around the pole, staring at the ground. Occasionally they bumped each other and the stupid look changed to awareness and then shifted back when they realized they were among their own kind.

"See the little guy there wearing the red wind breaker? He's been there since yesterday morning. I think he's actually the one that got Julio, but I can't say for sure.

"Anyway, see how it's like all in a daze? They don't have no sense to even move on to where they might find some food. It's like they're just waiting for dinner to come to them."

As we watched, the guy in the red windbreaker stopped his circular movement. After a moment of remaining still, he turned to his left and went to the mower. He looked at it for a moment, took a few steps toward it, then turned around and rejoined his kin.

"See what I mean? Dumb as rocks, but when they see live flesh walking around out there that look on their faces changes. They get real interested and then instinct takes over. They seem pretty smart then."

I didn't like looking at them. They looked human but they were alien to me. I'd seen them up close and personal. I'd seen them at dinner time and I'd seen the carnage they'd left behind.

For a moment I felt rage swell behind my temples. My eyes slid to the SKS. I could easily pick it up, unlock the door, step outside and lay waste to the three monsters. I could end them. I should end them.

As if he read my thoughts, Kappy put a hand on my forearm and squeezed a bit. "Let's leave them be right now. There's no one around. Maybe they'll starve themselves. Maybe I'll just have an experiment right outside my front door and see how long they last if they don't eat."

I considered ignoring Kappy and going with my own instincts. But I let that idea fall away and when Kappy turned away from the front doors I followed.

At the booth again, I slid in. I intended to finish my breakfast but I suddenly didn't have the stomach for it any longer. Instead I turned to the coffee. The caffeine was what I really needed right now.

"What time is it?" I asked. My watch was busted, probably when I was thrown from the John Deere.

"It's just past one," Kappy said. Again, as if he could read my mind, he added, "Only about four more hours until nightfall. If you're planning on leaving, you'd best do it then."

"Will they sleep then?"

Kappy considered this a moment. "No. Not that early."

"I really should go. I have to get to my wife. I don't even know if she's okay."

"A few more hours and it will be dark. Better to move in the dark."

"A lot could happen in a few hours," I said.

I shuddered. I had done a pretty good job of putting the horrible images of my children's torn bodies out of my mind but it was getting harder by the minute. I couldn't stand not knowing if my wife was alive or dead.

"Yes," he conceded.

Kappy and I stared at each other while we drank coffee. After a moment I looked away, using a coffee refresher as an excuse.

"What about you, Kappy? Is your wife okay?"

He shook his head.

"Cancer took her a few years back. This place is all I have left. I guess it was fate that brought me here just before this outbreak. I have enough food and water, and a roof over my head. I have nice generators for if and when the power dies. I think I'm pretty safe here, and it's a good place for people to stop, should they find themselves on a long journey and need a rest."

"There's no way I'm going to talk you into coming with me." It wasn't a question.

He shook his head again.

I gave him some peace for a while by keeping my mouth shut and enjoying the coffee. The television was on somewhere in the back but the volume was down low. And as much as I was starved for information, right now I didn't want to hear about these crazies.

Right now, I wanted to just enjoy the break I'd been given and take some time to get my thoughts organized.

Soft sunlight filtered in through the thin space between the blinds. Dust particles floated on the air. The place was warm and my belly was full. After a while I felt my eyes begin to sag. I shook my head, trying to desperately to stave off sleep.

"Why don't you grab a few winks?" Kappy asked. Before I could argue, he said, "I'll wake you up in a couple of hours, just before dark. I'll feed you a nice dinner and then pack you a doggy bag and you can be on your way. How does that sound?"

I paused for a moment, considering. As much as I wanted to get home, it wouldn't do much good if I fell asleep on the John Deere again. Next time I wrecked I might not be as lucky and come through unscathed. No, it would be best to take a rest and recharge my batteries.

"Sounds great," I said finally.

"What do you want for dinner?"

"Whatever you have is fine." Right now I didn't want to even think about food. I was in no mood.

"Come on, what do you want? This is a restaurant, and this is what I do for a living. Don't deny me cooking you a meal."

"Are you insisting?" I asked.

"I am. Don't deny an old cook his pleasure."

I sighed. "Okay, I guess some meatloaf with mashed potatoes would do just fine."

"Now you're talking, Matt. Go on and grab yourself some sleep. I'll wake you soon."

After packing up my packable jacket to form a pillow, I lay on my side in the booth and closed my eyes.

Although I didn't think I'd actually sleep, I was out in a matter of seconds. It seemed like I'd only been sleeping for a few minutes when Kappy shook my shoulder.

"Time to wake, buddy." His face loomed over me and he was grinning. "Did you enjoy your sleep? You were snoring like a chainsaw."

Sitting up, I cleared my throat, rubbed the remains of sleep from my eyes, and graced him with a smile.

"My wife says the same thing. Of course, I don't think I snore at all."

"Dinner will be up in a few. Come on and get washed up."

I followed Kappy down the aisle and into a small corridor. The men's and women's rooms were on the right but we bypassed those and continued through the door at the end of the short hall that led to Kappy's office. He showed me to a small bathroom that had a shower stall, commode and small sink.

"There's soap in the shower and all the towels are clean. Call me if you need anything."

When Kappy left, I stared at myself in the mirror for a moment. I had a pretty good cut on the right side of my forehead. Kappy patched that up nicely but I could see a thin line of blood underneath was beginning to seep through, and my left eye was starting to show the beginnings of a shiner. My eyes were red from lack of sleep but other than that I thought I looked pretty good, all things considered.

I let the hot water run in the sink for a bit and then washed my face and ran my wet fingers through my hair getting it in some order. I used my finger and some toothpaste to brush my teeth. Feeling quite refreshed, I returned to the table.

Kappy sat across from me again. Two plates with thick cuts of meatloaf and a billowy mound of mashed potatoes covered in brown gravy sat before us. Between us sat a large bowl of rolls and cuts of French bread. Kappy had also brought two pitchers of soda: one Coke and one Diet Coke.

"Looks fantastic, Kappy."

Frankly, I really wasn't in a mood to eat. At breakfast I'd eaten out of necessity, but now, try as I might, I kept thinking about Katie and Mark. Right now they should be home watching Bakugan or Pokemon, not buried under four feet of cold ground.

"Dig in," Kappy said, unaware of my inner turmoil.

He buttered a piece of French bread and put it onto a small dish in front of him.

"Regular or diet?" he asked, indicating the two pitchers of soda in front of us.

"Diet, please"

As he poured, I poked at my meatloaf. I forced myself to take a bite. Although I was sure Kappy's meatloaf was heavenly, I didn't really taste it. I chewed and swallowed, running on automatic.

While I nibbled at my dinner, Kappy told me about his wife. Before the cancer, the two of them had enjoyed sailing. Kappy had a schooner he kept docked on Lake Michigan, but he hadn't sailed it since his wife passed.

He showed me a picture of his wife, a beautiful older woman with dark brown hair and blue eyes. It was a professional photo and both Kappy and his wife smiled brightly for the camera. Kappy wore a charcoal gray suit and light blue tie. In the picture he looked like a serious Wall Street type rather than a fry cook.

While eating his desert of cheesecake and coffee, Kappy asked, "So, what's your plan?"

"My house is about ten miles from here." I'd given up on the meatloaf and focused on moving the food around my plate. "If I can get the John Deere running again, I should be home in less than an hour. Once I get there, I'll probably fortify my place and wait it out."

Kappy nodded. "You have enough supplies?"

I thought about this for a second.

"Yes. Last year I finally talked my wife into stockpiling food and water. What convinced her was hurricane Katrina. Before that, she thought it was ridiculous, and assumed that I was stockpiling supplies, waiting to be invaded by North Korea. But I convinced her that being prepared for a natural disaster was a good idea and she agreed. I think we'll be okay."

"Sounds like you'll be fine."

I pushed my fork through my mound of mashed potatoes and smiled.

"Sure I can't talk you into coming with me? I could use a good cook."

Kappy smiled. "I'm sure your wife has that angle covered. I appreciate the offer but like I said, this is where I belong."

After dinner, Kappy packed a doggy bag as promised, which actually turned out to be four meatloaf dinners to go, complete with dinner rolls and a six pack of Diet Coke.

"I don't know if that will fit on the back of the John Deere," I said, setting the large brown bag onto the table.

Kappy held out a set of keys. "Take my Jeep. She's four-wheel drive and will get you around or through most anything."

For a moment I was speechless. "No, Kappy, I can't take this, it's way too much."

"It's just a car," Kappy said. "Go on, take them."

I shook my head, "Kappy, I—"

"Take them, Matt. Get home to your wife and family. Please."

I reached out and accepted the keys. "Kappy I don't know what to say."

"Don't say anything. I'm glad I could help. I've done a lot of things in this world for which I need atonement."

"Come with me, Kappy," I said again, now getting all choked up.

"Get out of here now." I could see he was getting emotional, too.

I reached for the bag of food, but Kappy said, "I got this. Grab your bag and your rifle."

I went to the door and grabbed my gear. I put the shoulder strap over my head and slung the SKS over my left shoulder. A quick look out the front revealed two more crazies had joined the red windbreaker's clan.

"Kappy, I really should take care of the problem you have out here. They might keep congregating out there."

Kappy appeared beside me and looked out. I could see he was a bit unnerved by the newcomers.

I thought he'd make up some excuse for me to leave them alone, but he surprised me when he said, "If you could get them without getting yourself hurt, I guess that would be for the best."

I unslung my bag and set it back down on the chair, dug inside, pulled two stripper clips of ammo out of the bag and put them into my left hip pocket.

After pulling on my packable jacket and Nomex gloves, I turned to Kappy and asked, "Is there access to the roof?"

He nodded his head and led me back to his office. He pointed to an overhead trap door inside the small closet, reached up and pulled the door open, then unfolded the ladder.

"Give me your rifle. I'll hand it up after you get up there."

I handed over my SKS and climbed the ladder. When I emerged onto the roof, the cool wind struck me, flapping my jacket and mussing my hair. I reached down and grabbed the SKS.

"I'll be back in a minute."

After taking a moment to get my bearing, I moved toward the north side of the roof. When I reached the edge, I crouched down on one knee and peered over the side. I had a perfect line of sight to my targets.

This was going to be like shooting fish in a barrel, and I was going to enjoy it. I lifted my trusty SKS and settled it onto the narrow wall. It made a good rest and I felt I could shoot accurately.

I looked down through the iron sights and found one of the new-comers. She was a middle aged woman dressed in a pink sweat suit. The front of her sweater was stained maroon and her lips were stained with blood. She'd been busy.

I pulled the trigger and watched her ear explode into the right side of her skull. She went down gracefully, onto her side.

I targeted the young man in the North Face puff coat next, putting a well-placed shot into his forehead. He turned off like a light and dropped like a sack of apples.

The black man wearing the black suit was next. The first shot took out his left jaw and the second pushed his left eye into his brain.

The guy that looked like Bon Jovi was next. He wore a leather biker's jacket and too much hair spray. The shot tore the back of his skull open, ruining his hairdo.

I saved the dude in the red windbreaker for last. I watched as he moved stupidly around his fallen comrades, blundering and tripping over their strewn limbs.

Taking a bead on him, I yelled, "Hey motherfucker!"

Red windbreaker stopped suddenly and looked up at the sound of my voice. When he locked eyes with me, the stupid look was gone in an instant, like a shade being pulled down, and his eyes were full of rage. He opened his mouth and screamed.

Before he could even begin his charge, I shot him in the mouth, shattering his teeth and blowing a hole through the back of his neck. He stumbled backward and went down to one knee. He looked up again, trying to scream, but no sound emerged from his ruined mouth.

I shot again and he fell to his side; blood flowed freely from the large hole in the side of his head.

I waited a moment longer before standing up and returning to the ladder. When I looked down, Kappy was staring back at me. He reached up and took the SKS that I handed down to him. After closing up the ladder and the trap door, I followed Kappy back out to the front, where I shouldered my go bag.

Kappy was staring at me. "What's wrong, Kappy?"

He was quiet a second and then said, "When I was in Korea, I came across a squad patrol. I had really good cover and my men had high ground. So I ordered them to open fire and boy did they ever. And as my guys were firing, I heard one fellow from my squad, a really quiet private named Lawry. He was screaming at the top of his lungs, shouting profanities at the Koreans. When I ordered them to cease fire, I pulled Lawry aside. I asked him what all the hollering was about. He said he was just doing his duty. And he was. But he was also enjoying it."

I was quiet, waiting for Kappy to make his point.

"What you did up there was your duty. But I think you were enjoying it, too."

I didn't speak.

"I know you have some anger in you," he went on. "You told me you went to the school to get your kids…but they're not with you now."

Again, I remained silent. Tears began to well in my eyes.

"Whatever happened, I'm sure your anger is righteous. But don't let it eat away at you and change you. I don't want to see you turn into Private Lawry."

"Point taken, Kappy." I wiped tears from my eyes and swallowed the lump in my throat.

He looked at me for a long moment and then he picked up the doggy bag. "Let's get you to the Jeep and home to your wife."

A few minutes later I was behind the wheel of Kappy's Jeep Wrangler. I waved to him as I pulled away, happy to be on the road again and one step closer to home. I watched Kappy in the rear view mirror until the restaurant faded from view.

CHAPTER 6: HOMECOMING

In the first twenty minutes after leaving Kappy's I encountered substantial blockages on Route 20 where the next three exits emptied into downtown Elgin.

In most cases, the vehicles had simply been abandoned in their lane, while others were driven off to the shoulder or into the ditch below before being abandoned.

The spacing between blockages was sporadic; you could not just easily weave from one lane to the next. At a few points I had to drive down the ditch and up the sloping wall to get around a few of the blockages, and I thanked Kappy for the use of his Wrangler. Without the four-wheel drive, I would never been able to navigate around the worst of the blockages.

I approached mile marker eight, just three miles from home, and the road suddenly opened up. The cars, which I assumed had been on the road, had for some reason been pushed aside, off to the shoulder and into the ditch.

Some had been pushed with total disregard and were flipped onto their sides, and in a few cases onto their hoods. There were at least fifty cars that had been plowed through. It would have taken several people with tow trucks or other large vehicles to have cleared the road.

Why had it been done? Why just in this stretch of Route 20? I had a bad feeling about this new situation and I slowed the Wrangler to about five miles an hour, slow enough for me to scan the area.

Although it was dark, this section of Route 20 was relatively well lit with spaced street lamps. The vehicles that flanked both sides of the road seemed suddenly ominous and my focus sharpened as I passed each one.

I expected at any moment for a horde of the crazies to appear from within the abandoned vehicles and rush me. I reached over to the passenger seat and pulled the SKS a bit closer. I also cursed myself for not checking and reloading after taking care of the loitering crazies outside of Kappy's place.

From memory, I think I fired five times or maybe six. That meant I had either four or five rounds left in the magazine.

Stupid.

And again I had to wonder how I'd survived this long.

Several minutes passed while I continued to cruise at five miles an hour, carefully watching the road. I was now approaching the Randall corridor entrance, the last entrance onto Route 20 for a long stretch. Beyond this main entrance onto Route 20 were only small, one-lane blacktop roads that led into several of the recently developed subdivisions of single family homes and townhomes. I lived in one of those subdivisions.

I neared the Randall overpass, and noticed two large SUV's parked in the road in front of me. Their front ends almost met, covering the two lanes entirely. This roadblock surprised the hell out of me and I quickly stopped the Wrangler.

Although no one appeared to sit in either of the vehicles, nor did I spot anyone milling around, alarm bells were sounding in my head.

Something was definitely wrong. Although this roadblock could have been set up as a defense against approaching crazies, I didn't think that was the only reason.

Whoever had set it up had done some planning. It was a pretty perfect spot; if you were travelling west on Route 20, as I was, there was no exit or side streets that you could use to leave Route 20 in retreat.

The nearest exit was three miles back, and there was no place to turn around because the east and westbound lanes were separated by a substantial ditch that I doubted even the Wrangler could navigate.

I was pretty sure these folks, whoever they were, had another blockade set up further west to catch any vehicles that merged onto Route 20 from the Randall entrance. Or they may have just blocked the Randall Road entrance altogether.

With the Wrangler idling and my brain still trying to take in the situation, my hands did their work. Lifting the SKS, I opened the magazine catch and dropped the remaining ammo onto my lap; several of the loose rounds fell down onto the seat and the floor but I'd worry about those later.

I reached into my left pants pocket and pulled out one of the stripper clips, inserted it into the slot on the bolt, and pushed ten rounds down into the magazine. This time I had no trouble getting the rounds down. I released the bolt and the SKS was loaded and ready.

I reached down and pulled the door latch, and right then a man with a blue baseball cap appeared from behind the SUV on the left and aimed what looked like an M1 Carbine in my direction. I quickly pushed the door open and heard him yell for me to put my hands in the air.

Ignoring him, I stepped out of the Wrangler, leaving the door open for what little cover it offered. Once my feet hit the ground, I immediately ran to my left, around to the back of the vehicle.

Two shots rang out. Already winded, I ducked around to the cover of the rear of the Wrangler. The bastard is actually firing at me. I was incredulous. He had to know I wasn't one of the crazies; I was driving a vehicle and carrying a rifle, for shit sake.

The man in the blue cap shouted for me to come out with my hands up. Instead, I risked a peek through the back windshield. I saw the guy with the blue cap still holding his position behind the SUV on the left. However, a second guy now appeared around the corner of his right. He wore a light brown coat and was carrying an AR-15. He was crouched behind the bumper of his SUV and aiming in my direction.

Shit. This was turning into a scary situation.

The ditch on my left was just a few feet away. I could probably scramble there and dive in before they could get a bead on me, but once in, I'd be a sitting duck. From their elevated position they'd be able to rain down fire on me while I tried to climb the slope to get onto the eastbound side. That was pure suicide. To my right the ditch was way more manageable, but the ditch rose into a steep slope, about twenty feet up to Randall Road. There was no way I'd make it up the slope fast enough to avoid being shot down.

"What do you want?" I shouted.

I slowly peeked through the rear window of the Wrangler again, hoping they were not rushing me. Both men were still holding their positions, which was good. I could keep my eye on them while my slow mind tried to figure a way out.

"Put down your gun and step out!" one of them shouted.

"No!" I shouted. "I'm not one of them."

There was a moment of silence and then one of them called back, "Yes, we know. Just come out here. We don't want to hurt you."

I risked another look through the back windshield and confirmed they were both still holding their ground. I was suddenly aware of my knees aching. I wasn't used to staying in a squatting position for this long. I shifted my position slightly and kneeled on my right knee.

Patting my pocket to confirm I had at least one more stripper clip of ammo, which I did, I cursed myself for not grabbing my bag. I had no idea what I was going to do at this point but if forced to ditch the Wrangler I'd be without the remainder of my gear. Another stupid decision. How many more before they caught up with me?

"Don't make this hard," one of the guys said. He almost sounded sympathetic.

"Give me a minute to think about it."

If they knew I wasn't one of the crazies, what reason did they have for wanting me to come forward? With no escape options, I might have to comply. If they intended to kill me, they would have just opened fire when I stopped the vehicle, right?

So if they didn't want to kill me, what? Supplies? If they took my SKS and whatever gear I had with me but let me pass, I could easily resupply at home. I'd hate to lose the SKS but I had better weapons. What was in my bag could also be easily replaced.

"You've got thirty seconds to come out!"

"Or what?" I shouted. I was feeling salty now. That old fighting spirit was back and I liked it.

Again, another pause that seemed to go on forever. Then one of them said, "We all don't want to find out. Just come on out. Let us clear you and you can be on your way."

Son of a bitch, my knees were killing me. I shifted again, this time on to my left knee. Another look through the windshield revealed the men had not moved from their original positions, but now a third man revealed himself when he raised his head up between the nose of both SUV's. From where I stood it looked like he had a pump shotgun.

The third man pretty much sealed the deal for me. I really had no way out. The road beyond me was cleared of vehicles which left no cover for me in that direction. The ditch on my left I'd already ruled out. Even using the dumped vehicles for purchase to climb out, I'd be shot as I climbed.

In a firefight between me and these three men, I'd be outgunned, outmanned, outflanked and out of luck. And I had no idea how many more people they had with them, lying in wait. They could be flanking me right now, closing me into a kill box.

"I live just up the road!" I shouted. "Over at the Randall Oaks sub-division. I'm not one of those things and I just want to get home to my family."

"That's fine." I think it was Blue Hat doing the talking. "We know people that live there, too. We're just looking out for our community and neighbors. If you live there, we'll let you pass."

I decided there were probably more than three men with him. "What assurances do I have that you won't just kill me and take my stuff?" I asked.

I checked again through the windshield but still saw no movement on their end. Maybe they were just as scared as I was. Maybe they truly did not want trouble and it was like they said, just looking out for the community.

Too many damn maybes.

"You don't have any assurances. You just have to trust us."

"Would you, if you were in my position?"

Another pause and then, "I guess not, but what choice do you have? You have nowhere to go, and if we wanted you dead, we would have already killed you."

I sat quiet, clutching the SKS tightly.

"We all want to get home alive, so help us out."

Having gotten by so far in spite of my mistakes I figured I'd press my luck one more time. What he'd said was right; I either complied or I'd be dead. I'd have to take my chances and trust these men.

Holding the SKS in my left hand, I raised it above my head and stood slowly. "Okay, I'm coming out!"

"Easy!" Blue Hat shouted. "Let's all go easy. Step out from behind the vehicle!"

I took a step to my left, still holding the SKS above my head. I closed my eyes, expecting to be shot now that I was out from cover, but no shots were fired.

"Good! Now put the gun down at your feet. Slowly, please!"

I followed his orders.

"Now walk forward twenty paces!"

Again, I did as directed.

"Okay, stop there," Blue Hat said.

I stood in the middle of the road with my hands up, no more than twenty feet from the roadblock. Keeping the M1 Carbine aimed at me, Blue Hat stepped around from behind the SUV and approached slowly.

"Keep your eyes on him, Phil!" he shouted over his shoulder.

"I got him," Phil said. Phil was the guy on the right flank with the brown Carhartt jacket. He had a pretty good tangle of windblown brown hair, and his eyes were sharp and aware.

Blue Hat stopped a few feet away from me. His eyes were blue and crisp under the glow of the street lamp. He was tall, about six-two, and young. He was probably in his very early twenties. Bristles of dark black hair poked out around his ball cap.

"Hello, fella. You have some ID?"

"I do," I said, but didn't reach for it.

Blue Hat looked a bit frightened and I didn't want any accidents. If my luck held, I'd be home in minutes.

"Go on and get it slowly."

"Okay." With my left hand I reached slowly into my back pocket and pulled out my wallet. I held it out for him to see and then opened it slowly. I thumbed out my driver's license and held it out.

Blue Hat paused a moment and then reached out quickly and snagged the ID from me. He backed up a few paces, still aiming the carbine around about at my chest, and took his eyes off me to quickly read the address.

He looked back at me. "You alone, Matt?"

"Yes," I said. My voice was scratchy and I needed water. Too much yelling had rubbed my throat raw.

There was a pause as he studied me. I was starting to feel a bit of hope about this situation but I didn't want to jinx it.

"Where's he from?" Phil asked. He still watched me with sharp eyes and hadn't yet dismissed me as a threat.

"He's from just where he said he was from," Blue Hat told him.

He lowered the carbine and slung it up on to his shoulder. "Welcome home."

I let out my breath in a rush. I was suddenly aware that I was perspiring. The cold November air chilled me as it blew across my sweaty brow.

"Sorry about the drama," said Blue Hat. "We just had to be sure. We heard things are starting to get bad in the city. Even down in South Elgin things are getting a bit out of control. We're just trying to be proactive."

"Yeah, good idea," I said, still shaken.

"I'm Frank, by the way," Blue Hat said. He stuck out his right hand for me to shake.

"You know my name." I took his hand.

"That's Phil over there, and that short fella there is Mike," Frank said.

"Pleased to meet you," I responded and raised a hand.

"Whereabouts did you come from?" Mike asked.

"I was in Chicago night before last. I holed up for the night at Kappy's up the road and now I'm trying to get home to see my wife."

"You came from the city?" Phil asked. "How was it out there?"

"Not good."

I just wanted to get my gear and get moving but I knew they were just as anxious for information as I was. And since I'd been in the city, the mystical place that always seemed to be the source of action for us suburbanites, they expected I had all the answers.

"I ran into a number of the crazies and had to put them down."

"Crazies?" Mike asked. "You mean the zombies?"

The other guys laughed.

Frank said, "Crazies is as good a word as any. Zombies are dead that come back to life. These people ain't dead yet near as I can tell."

"That's my experience anyway," I said. "I don't know too much about them. I haven't had any news since I've been on the road."

"So you've been out there since yesterday?" Frank asked.

"Yeah. Whatever the hell is happening started just after I got to work yesterday morning. All hell broke loose. I tried to get my kids from school…but I… I didn't quite make it in time."

"Shit, man," Frank said and put a hand on my shoulder. "Sorry I asked."

"You couldn't have known. Listen, Frank, I'd really like to get home to my wife."

"Yeah, no doubt, man," Frank said and clapped my shoulder. Over his own shoulder he yelled, "Phil, make a hole!"

"Thank you."

I reached out my hand and we shook again.

Frank said, "Listen, I'm over at number 12 Encounter Court. When you have some time, I'd really like if you could drop by. We should talk about you volunteering for Community Watch. We're trying to get organized. If this shit doesn't sort itself out, we could really use a hand."

"Hey, you got it."

I waved at Phil and Mike, then nodded at Frank, and made my way back toward the Wrangler. I picked up my SKS, jumped into the Wrangler and drove forward. Phil had backed up the SUV on the right and made a hole for me. As I drove through, Frank motioned for me to roll down the window.

He said, "I radioed ahead at the next check point at let them know you're coming. Bob Brown is the leader there, and he says he knows you."

"Yeah, I know Bob." Bob Brown lived a couple of houses over from me. He and his wife had been by my home a few times for dinner. Bob was a good man. He was a patrolman and that made him the logical choice.

"Well, good luck," Frank said. "I hope to see you soon."

"Take care," I said, and drove on.

The next roadblock was about a mile and a half up the road, just west of the sole entrance to the Randall Oaks subdivision. It was good to see that my area was so well covered. Security was now one less thing I had to concern myself with at the moment.

I saw Bob out in front and gave him a quick salute, stopped the Wrangler beside him and rolled down the window.

"Good to see you, Matt," he said, reaching in to shake my hand.

"Yeah, good to see you, Bob," I said.

As one of Bob's crew moved a large pick-up truck to make a hole for me he leaned into the window. His eyes were watery and I could smell the heavy scent of his cologne.

"I'm sorry about the kids. If you need me or Peg for anything, anything, you know where to find me."

Frank had obviously passed the word along.

"Thanks, Bob. I'll do that. Give Peg my regards."

"Done," he said and patted the door. "We'll talk soon."

I put the Wrangler into gear and made my way past the roadblock. I turned right, drove through the open gates and onto Randall Oaks Drive. I followed the road as it wound back into our subdivision.

A minute later I saw my house, set up on a slight incline, with a beautiful view of Harper's Knoll. A figure was sitting on my front porch. I suspected the figure was my wife waiting for me. I wanted to see her so badly, but at the same time I feared breaking her heart when I told her our children were dead.

I drove the Wrangler around the side and parked it behind my garage. I got out, taking the SKS and my bag and walked around to the front. Instead of my wife, my brother, Brian, met me halfway down the walk. He was wearing dark blue jeans and his black fleece sweater. His choppy long hair covered his brown eyes which always seemed to give him a haunted look.

He had his STG 556 slung over his shoulder and a cigarette jutted out of the corner of his mouth.

"Dude," he said as I drew closer.

He tossed his cigarette onto the ground and tried to lift me. Although I was his little brother, I'd outgrown him in both height and weight. He released me from his grip and stood back a step.

"Where the fuck have you been? I've been worried as hell."

"Long story." I set my bag down and slung the SKS over my shoulder. "I'm glad you're here, man."

Although he lived in my basement family room, he spent most nights with one college girl or another. He'd finally taken to Facebook and MySpace and was building up a steady stream of "friends".

"I wouldn't miss the apocalypse, man." He pulled out a pack of Marlboros. He offered me one and I took it; he lit us both up. "Where's Katie and little dude?"

I made eye contact with him for a brief second and then looked away. He'd always been close with my kids, especially since he'd lost his job and started living in my downstairs family room. He was good with them, too. Whatever faults my brother had, he was always on his best behavior around the kids, and he was so patient with them, although he was quick to lose his temper with anyone else.

"Where's Alyssa?" I asked. "I have to talk to her. Now."

My brother looked at me for a moment. "Answer me, Matt," he demanded. "Tell me what happened."

I sat down on the walk way, dropping the cigarette and the SKS into the grass. I covered my eyes with my hands and cried.

It was a long journey and I really did not have time to properly grieve my children. I'd done everything I could to block out the memory of their mangled bodies. Now I was overwhelmed and I couldn't control myself.

"Aw fuck," my brother said and dropped down beside me. He had no idea what happened, but he knew it had to be bad.

He put a hand on my shoulder as I sobbed and shook and let all of my emotions out. I have no idea how long I sat there and cried but it felt like forever. I felt completely drained. My eyes stung and I had snot running down my nose. Again. I wiped it away with my sleeve.

When I looked up at him, his eyes were moist.

"They're gone," I finally managed.

"Not Mark." He shook his head. "Come on man, him? He was just a little guy, man."

"He's gone." Another sob escaped me. "And my Katie's gone, too. They're fucking gone!"

"Motherfucker!" he shouted.

He jumped up from his crouched position beside me and kicked the shrubs to his left, kicked again and again as he screamed, a guttural sound that frightened me. He continued to kick at the shrub until all of its branches were broken and twisted and fallen.

When his immediate anger smoldered, he finally turned to me. "What happened, man? How did they die?"

"Not now," I said and tried to get up. I made it to my knees and then fell back down on my butt.

"Just stay down, man," Brian said.

He turned away from me again. In a motion too quick for my peripheral vision to follow clearly, Brian swooped up one of the metal porch chairs. With a long grunt, he slammed the chair against the side of the house. A chunk of brick dislodged itself and fell to the garden and with another pirate-like yell he sent the chair sailing across the lawn where it tumbled a few times and landed on its side.

Another minute passed. I sat where I was, too tired to move. My head ached all over and my eyes felt like they were being pushed out of my skull.

Brian faced me again. This time, when he spoke there was no harshness in his voice.

"Look, we'll talk about that later man. You need to get inside and get some rest. But I have to tell you something before we go inside."

Crouching, be picked up his discarded cigarette and took a long drag. He exhaled a cloud of smoke that sounded like a long sigh.

"I need to see Alyssa," I said. "I have to tell her."

My brother stared at me a long moment again. He swallowed hard. "Alyssa's inside, but she's not well. After you left for work yesterday, she went to do some shopping and she was at Meijer's when those things…well, one of them scratched her."

"What are you saying?" I asked. "So the thing scratched her, it can't be that bad."

He shook his head. "She's not well. I think…I think she might be infected."

"No." I reached up and grabbed my brother's jacket and pulled myself up. "She's fine. If it's just a scratch she'll be fine."

"She's not, man. I know this is hard for you, you've been through a great trauma, but she's really not fine. You have to prepare yourself."

I looked into my brother's eyes and I knew he told the truth.

CHAPTER 7:
MERCY

I stood behind the bedroom door with my ear against the cool wood. Long silence greeted me from the other side. My hand lay upon the doorknob but I did not immediately open the door. I was afraid. My mouth was dry and my hands moist with sweat.

Fear clenched in my belly like a coiled snake waiting to strike. I did not fear attack, but rather seeing my wife in an advanced state of metamorphosis, and in her eyes, that damned blank idiot stare.

It's what I feared most, seeing the change in her eyes when she realized there was fresh meat in the room.

"It's not locked," my brother said from behind me.

"I know."

I wished at that moment that he'd waited outside. I wanted to be alone in my sorrow.

The doorknob turned slowly in my moist hand. A slight creak issued as the door swung on the hinges.

I'll have to oil that, I thought stupidly. Then, What does a creaky hinge matter now? There will be no one left in this house for a creaky hinge to wake.

Alyssa sat at the edge of the bed with her head cocked slightly to the right, toward the window. The blinds were closed tight and the curtains drawn. Pale light filtered into the room and cast shadows along the carpet.

My breath caught in my throat; she looked so beautiful sitting there, so normal. I started into the room and my brother halted me with a heavy hand on my shoulder.

"Easy dude. Looks can be deceiving."

Shaking Brian's hand from my shoulder I approached slowly until I was no more than a foot away from her. She did not stir or cast a glance in my direction. I knelt down beside her and placed my hand on her knee.

"I'm home, baby"

My voice cracked. I needed to be strong, but this was hard, so very hard. She did not respond. I shifted my position so that I was in front of her and took both of her hands into mine.

"Honey, look at me."

For a moment I thought she wouldn't respond but then her head turned slowly and her eyes locked on mine.

"You…I…" she trailed off.

"What happened to you, honey? Can you tell me?"

Her eyes flickered to the right for a moment, as though she were thinking and then returned to my own eyes.

"You came back," she said.

"Yes, baby, yes, I came back."

I put her hands against my cheeks and kissed her wrists. She smiled briefly and then her gaze slid away from me again. Her face went slack and she turned back toward the window.

"Honey, look at me," I said.

I shook her hands trying to get her attention.

Turning her head again, she said, "Mmmmat."

"Yes?" I asked. I thought she was trying to say my name.

Her eyes widened and she looked at me with fear on her countenance. With much difficulty, she tried again, very slowly.

"My…words…"

"It's okay, baby, don't worry about that."

The fear in my belly sprung now, uncoiled, and heartburn crept up into my throat, burning something fierce.

My wife looked away again but this time she reached out one hand toward the window and then let it fall to the bed at her side. My brother was beside me again, his hand lying on my shoulder like a weight.

"Look at her left arm," he said.

I looked and saw the angry red scratches down the inner forearm, each about four inches long, the edges turning white from infection. Red lightning lines of infection zigzagged up to her elbow and down to her wrist.

Brian looked down at me with sympathy in his eyes.

"Come outside. We have to talk."

"Guh lab oy," my wife said suddenly, startling me. Before I could respond, she spoke again, "Mas noh." She swallowed hard and tried once more. "My...home."

"Yes, this is your home, honey," I said because I couldn't think of anything else to say.

She turned to me again but this time there was no recognition in her eyes. She stared at me blankly, as though this was the first time she had laid eyes on me.

Her mouth tightened and her eyebrows knitted together in a frown. "Who nah suh?"

"No, baby, please." I took her hands again, pulling them to my face and covering my eyes.

My tears fell now, wetting her hands. Her skin felt so suddenly hot with fever that my cheeks felt windblown from the heat of her hands.

"Nah ket la," she said and pulled her hands away, holding them up in front of her to inspect them.

"Let's go now," Brian said and pulled me up to my feet.

"What's wrong with her?" I asked stupidly, but I couldn't help myself.

I turned to my brother and grabbed the front of his shirt. "What the fuck is wrong with her?"

"She's going to go soon," he said, grabbing me in a bear-hug. He started to walk us slowly toward the door.

"Let me go, Bri!" I shouted. "Let me be with her, please."

I fought for a moment, shaking and trying to push him off of me, but I had no leverage and his grip was tight. In moments we were outside of the room. He let me go and turned to shut the door.

Immediately I was at his back, trying to push past him to get back in. Brian turned suddenly and pushed me against the wall with one forearm against my chest.

"Dude, you don't need to see this, now fucking chill. You have to get your head straight."

"That's my wife in there," I said as if this was news to him. My body slacked, though, and I felt all the energy run out of my body. I looked at my brother and pleaded, "Just let me say goodbye. Please."

He was quiet for a few seconds and then, "Be quick about. No bullshit."

I nodded my head.

His forearm relaxed and then I was unpinned. I fixed my shirt and took a deep breath and entered the bedroom. In this room we had created life, two beautiful, exceptional children who no longer inhabited this Earth. In this room, my wife and I had made love, shared our concerns over taxes, and the housing market. In this room, we planned our future and regaled each other with stories of the past.

Now, in this room, we would say our goodbyes and my life would change forever.

I sat beside her on the bed. She did not move at first but when I put my arm around her shoulder, she flinched and then became still. I turned her face toward me and her eyes looked at mine. Her brow was no longer furrowed and she looked peaceful.

"Oh, baby, I'm so sorry. I'm sorry that I wasn't here for you. I'm sorry that I could not save our children. I let you all down and I beg for your forgiveness. I don't know if I can go on without you."

My wife continued to stare at me but she remained oblivious, uncomprehending. I moved slowly toward her wanting to kiss her and stopped cold when my brother shouted, "No!"

I turned to him, confused.

"Infection passes through saliva."

I was dumbfounded, in shock. This was so unfair. I couldn't even kiss my wife or I'd be infected and become one of the crazies.

In a moment of weakness, I almost kissed her anyway. What did I have left to live for? My children were dead and my wife was good as gone. Why not go together? All I had to do was kiss her and let the infection take me. We could both lie in bed together until what was left of our brains rotted and then someone would come and put us out of our misery. What else did I have to look forward to?

As if Brian could sense what I was thinking, he moved boldly into the room and grabbed my arm.

"Come on, man, don't do anything stupid."

I did not struggle this time, but instead allowed myself to be escorted out.

I paused at the threshold and said, "I love you with all my heart."

As Brian closed the door, I thought I saw the last spark of what had been my wife go out, and what remained was nothing but a rotted, infected brain.

Brian and I sat at the kitchen table smoking cigarettes. I hadn't had a smoke in nearly nine years and I was a bit lightheaded.

I took the bottle of Jack Daniels and poured two inches into my tumbler.

"There's nothing we can do for her," Brian said. He pushed a strand of long brown hair out of his eyes and puffed on his Marlboro. "I'm sorry, dude."

I couldn't get the image of my wife out of my head. When I went into the bedroom and she looked at me with little to no recognition, my heart just broke.

"What did the news say?" I asked. "So these crazies just scratch people or spit on them and all of a sudden those people become crazies too?"

I drank some of the bourbon and pushed it aside. My stomach was sour and the heartburn was back.

"No, it's not that sudden. Takes a few hours before it sets in then it snowballs."

"What's going to happen to her?"

"She's already past the first stage, forgetting stuff....you already saw that. I don't think she even knew who you were, man. After that they basically lose their minds. And after that, well, then they get hungry and try to eat you."

I slumped in my chair and let my cigarette drop into the ashtray.

"Dude, that sounded messed up, I know. But that's the way it is. I think she's already moved into phase two. Did you hear what she was saying when you went in there?"

"She wasn't saying anything." I picked up the cigarette again.

"Well, nothing that you understood. She was just talking gibberish. It was more like just making sounds."

"Have some fucking compassion!" I yelled and surprised us both. I stood up from my chair abruptly, knocking it over. "That's my fucking wife in there."

Brian nodded his head sympathetically. "And she's my sister-in-law. But I'm just trying to detach myself from that fact and see the truth here. This is happening to us and we have to deal with it. It hurts like hell that one of the only people in this damn family who thinks I'm not a class-A fucking loser is in that room losing her mind. It fucking kills me that my niece and nephew, the best damn kids I ever met, aren't here anymore. But it is what it is and I have to deal with it. And you have to deal with it, too."

I picked up my chair and set it right. "Yeah, I'm aware that I have to deal with this. I just need some time. I'll be fine."

"Will you?" He puffed his Marlboro again. "You're pretty fucked up right now, not that I blame you. But I don't think you'll be fine, at least not for a long time."

Sitting in the chair again, I picked up my smoke.

"I know something that will help ease my mind. Once my wife is gone, I'm going to go out there and make sure every last one of those things die. I'll never know which one got to her, so I'm just going to kill them all."

Brian put down his cigarette now. He was quiet for a few seconds and then said, "Dude, I like the idea of revenge as much as the next guy but don't make it your life. If you go out there with that attitude, you're going to do something stupid and get yourself killed."

"So? I'll take as many of them with me as I can."

"You're not yourself right now. That's shock talking."

"No, that's me talking. I've never felt more sane or sure of my purpose in life than I do right now. I'm going to lead a holocaust. I'm going to lay waste to every last one of those things and leave dead husks in my wake."

My brother sighed.

I suppose he realized that at the moment there was no use trying to talk logically with me. The fact was, I was out of my mind and I knew it, but there was nothing I could do about it.

We both jumped when we heard the bedroom door bang.

"Holy shit!" Brian bolted out of his chair faster than I'd seen him move in a long time.

Before I realized it I was also out of my chair. I stood for a moment, unsure what to do. Another series of loud bangs issued from down the hall and were followed by the sound of wood giving way.

"Shit," Brian said. He came to me and grabbed both of my arms. "You have to end this now. Don't let her suffer like that."

I said nothing. My tongue was stuck to the roof of my mouth.

"Matt, you have to do it now. She'll get worse. You have to end it. Don't do it for yourself, do it for her. I know that's a shitty deal but you have to do it now!"

A chunk of wood flew from the door and landed in the small hallway. More loud sounds issued from the bedroom as my wife's pounding grew more intense.

"I can't," I whispered. I looked up at my brother; his face was intense and his eyes were serious. "I can't do it," I said more clearly.

His grip on my arms grew tighter for a moment. His fingertips dug painfully into the flesh of my bicep and triceps and then suddenly he let go.

"I'll do it," he said. "I owe you that much. I owe her."

He turned away from me and walked down the short hallway. As he walked he pulled his Glock 17 from the waistband of his pants. His hand hung at his side, the muzzle of the gun pointed toward the floor.

Another piece of the door, a much larger portion, arched lazily through the air, bounced off Brian's shoulder and landed silently on the carpet. A gap opened up in the door now and through it I could see one of my wife's eyes. It was the eye of one who was insane.

Brian turned toward me now and said, "Wait downstairs. Please."

Without pause I turned toward the stairs and ran down into the family room as fast as my legs could carry me. I threw my body onto the sofa and pulled several pillows over my face. Harsh sobs wracked my body as I tried to block out the noise upstairs. When the single shot rang out, I cried so hard that I couldn't breathe.

That night, we buried her in the rose garden on the west side of our house. It was her favorite place, where the sun seemed to sit for long hours throughout the day. From this very spot you could look down the hill at Harper's Knoll and most of the homes in our community. It was a spectacular view, and I knew that she would appreciate her final resting place

CHAPTER 8: RANDALL OAKS

Several days after my wife was laid to rest, I was summoned by Frank to attend a Community Watch meeting being held at the community center across the way in the neighboring community of Providence.

Bob Brown brought the invitation. For the last few days he'd been organizing our residents and setting up defenses. He looked exhausted to say the least.

Bob and my brother sat at the dining room table while I poured some coffee. When I sat down, Bob said, "I'm really sorry to hear about Alyssa. We really miss her. My wife is hurting pretty bad, as I know you must be."

"Thanks, Bob."

"What's going on at the gates?" Brian asked, quickly changing the subject. I was very grateful.

Bob sipped his coffee and then nodded his head. "I'm glad you asked. We haven't seen much action at the gates, at least not yet, but out at the roadblocks they've had a number of those things they've put down. Frank has extra men out there 24/7 now, and he thinks he's going to need more really soon."

"Jesus," I said.

When I checked for news this morning, I found that all of the broadcast channels were down. The few stations that were operating were looping re-runs of shows like Two and a Half Men or NCIS.

I'd tried my cell phone again and found that it was completely dead, not even a dial tone or any messages. Even the land lines were down. The radio was still broadcasting on a few frequencies and the news was more of the same. There were now outbreaks as far away as Hong Kong.

This was getting really serious and I had a feeling it would just keep getting worse.

"Have we got any guys at the roadblocks?" Brian asked.

Bob shook his head. "Not yet but Frank is asking for support. His community is closest to the road but if the crazies break through...I don't know if we're prepared for that. We need to give him any assistance we can without leaving ourselves wide open."

"What's our overall situation here?" Brian asked.

Bob hesitated a moment. He looked at me and then back at my brother.

"Well, we're not very organized, I'm afraid. I've got five guys right now that are manning the gates in twelve hour shifts. I've got two others that alternate patrolling the fence around the perimeter but that isn't going to cut it."

Brian shook his head. "If you need us out there, we're there. And I'm sure we can get the rest of the guys in the community to help out. I'm sure they all want to make sure this place is safe for their families."

"Thank you," Bob said.

He took another drink of his coffee and cleared his throat. "They want to help but the thing is, I don't know if most of these guys are ready for this. I mean, most of them are office workers, managers, teachers, day traders. I doubt any of them know the first thing about guns. I'm afraid to put them out there because they're liable to do more damage than the crazies."

"You have to train them, Bob," Brian said matter-of-factly. "And I bet most of these guys have shotguns for hunting season."

"They do need training, but I don't think I'm the guy for the job. To tell you the truth, I don't want to be in charge. I'm not cut out for leading. I'm in way over my head here and I'm worried someone is going to get hurt and it'll be my fault."

"Easy, Bob," I said. "Tell us what you need from us. We'll help you."

"Look, I've talked this over with the guys who are out there at the gates and we all agreed it would be best if you took over things here, Matt. It will be best for all of us."

"Whoa, hang on," I said. "Bob, I appreciate the vote of confidence but I'm definitely not the right guy for this."

"I'm not the right guy for this, either," Bob said, "but I got stuck with it. And I'm telling you I can't handle this. You've got experience, both of you. I need your help here. Please, I can't do this, Matt."

I was about to protest but Brian stopped me. "What do you think it is we can do that you can't, Bob?"

"First of all you can train these people the right way. I know you were both in the Army. You were a drill sergeant, Bri. These people need someone who can teach them and give them the tools they need to survive."

Bob turned to me now and grabbed my arm. He said, "And you were an officer. They need a leader like you that they can look up to and trust. I'm not that guy. You are."

"Bob, I don't think that's true. If they picked you to be leader at the gate they must have some confidence in you."

"I was the only one with a gun who wasn't too shocked to take action. They think because I'm a patrol officer that I'm prepared for this, but this is totally different. It's not that they have confidence in me, I was just the wrong person in the right place at the wrong time. Listen, Matt, seriously, I really can't do this. Don't make me take this responsibility. I didn't ask for it and I don't want it."

Brian and I both exchanged looks and I could see we were both embarrassed for Bob, but I had to admit it took a lot of guts for him to come in here and admit he was in far over his head.

"If Matt takes this responsibility, Bob, it will have to have conditions," Brian said.

"Yes, anything."

"What he says goes. No debate. This isn't going to be a democracy."

"I understand."

"And everyone is going to have to do their share. Everyone. No exceptions."

Bob was nodding his head. "Agreed."

Brian looked at me. "What do you say, brother? Are you up to saving the world?"

I smiled at that. The world? No. This little community that I called home? Definitely, yes.

The fire of vengeance I felt burning through my veins last night passed with the burial of my wife. Putting her into the cold ground had sobered me and brought me back to reality.

I did have something to live for; I needed to honor the memories of my lost family. And also, I would avenge them, yes, but I'd do it smartly.

"If it's the will of the community I'll do it," I said. "Get them together and put it to a vote, Bob."

"We need to do this before tonight's meeting," he said anxiously. I could tell he was enormously relieved.

"That doesn't give us much time," Brian said. "We need to work out some details, create some sort of hierarchy, draw up regulations and TOE for the militia. We need a plan."

Bob finished the rest of his coffee and slid the cup into the middle of the table. "I'll start rounding everyone up and tell them what's going on and put the vote out. In the meantime, you guys come up with your plan. Whatever it is, we're in."

"Just like that?" I asked. "You'll just fall in?"

"Yes." Bob leaned forward in his chair. "Look, I'm not just turning over command to you because I don't want it. I know what you guys are capable of and I trust my life, hell, my family's life, to you. I know you'll do whatever is necessary and what is best for us as a community. That's good enough for me and it will be good enough for them."

I nodded my head. "Thank you, Bob."

"Get out there and do your part, Bob," Brian said. "Meet us back here as soon as you're done. You need to be involved in some of this planning, too. We're going to need you."

"I'll be back soon." Bob grabbed his coat and was out the door.

When he was gone I picked up my coffee cup and looked at my brother for a sign of how he really felt.

He shrugged his shoulders and asked, "What do you think?"

"I think this is crazy."

"Yep." He smiled.

"So where do we start?" I asked.

"Work on the hierarchy," Brian said.

"Okay, let me think on it." I paused long enough to light a fresh cigarette. "Here, write this down. I'm first in command. You're second and Bob's third. We're done."

Brian looked up at me and pushed his fallen locks out of his eyes. "And you graduated college? Twice?"

I grinned. "At least I can spell 'college', can you?

"A-s-s-h-o-l-e."

We both had a good laugh at that. I went into my office and grabbed a notebook, then sat beside my brother again.

"Aside from being second in command, I need you to be in charge of the militia. Form them up, train them, get them prepared. We can work on the regulations and the TOE as we go along. I'll help you with that. You still think you're up for this?"

He considered this briefly and said, "Yeah. I can handle this."

"Good. Just tell me what you need to get started."

"I just need everyone to have the will. But once we get trained, we'll need to open up our armory. Contrary to what Bob said, I'm willing to bet maybe half of these people have guns. And those that do probably have a handgun that they keep in a safe in case they hear something go bump in the night. That won't be good enough, though. We'll need real guns. And ammunition."

I sighed. That was the difficult part.

Between us two, we probably had enough firearms to outfit most of the members of our community. Ammunition, however, was another matter entirely. I'd used most of mine up for target practice in the spring.

"We'll figure something out."

Brian nodded his head. "Quickly, I hope. Let's not wait too long."

While we waited for Bob to return with news about how the vote went, we made our way down to the family room to inventory our weapons and ammunition.

The family room was actually where my brother slept on the pull-out couch. My office was down a small hallway from the family room, and outside of my office was an 8x10 room that was billed as a play-room when we purchased the house, but it was currently dedicated to my armory. Brian kept his stash there as well. And as long as it was out of sight and locked away, and the kids could not get into the room, my wife didn't care what we stored in there.

God, I missed my wife. Every moment I was alone I couldn't get her and my children out of my mind. If I was not careful, I'd fall into a deep despair that I feared I might not find my way back from.

The door to the armory stood open. I entered this familiar space and sat behind my work table to start a list while Brian went through and called out what we had.

"I'll start with the shotguns," he said. "We have two 870's with six round magazine tubes. Here's an Ithaca 37 riot gun that will hold four shells and your Mossberg 500 will hold five."

"Got it. How are we on shells?"

Brian knelt down beside one of the lower shelves and pulled a large .30 caliber ammo can marked 'Shotgun' with black permanent marker and pulled it off the shelf. Setting it on the floor he opened the lid and started pulling out boxes.

"There're two boxes of birdshot, twenty-five shells per box, so that's fifty. And there's ten boxes of 00 buckshot, five shells per box, so that's another fifty. And you have, oh, about four hundred of those Estate high velocity shells you thought you were going to use on waterfowl."

"So I never got around to it. I've been busy. Some of us have jobs."

Brian gave me a dirty look. "I have a job. I'm just laid off right now, dickhead."

"So that's five hundred shells for the shotgun," I said, trying not to laugh. "That's not too bad. What about the C&R's?"

"Are we really going to hand those out?"

"Yeah, we'll probably need them. You have a problem with my curios and relics?"

Brian shook his head. "We better test some of them. I don't trust them. I don't know what the fascination is with these old things anyway."

"You wouldn't. Now just inventory and don't think about it too much."

I reached under the work table and opened the small refrigerator. I pulled out a Diet Coke. "You want a soda?"

"Nah, not yet. Write this down. We have five Mosins that are all in good order. One K98K? Dude, that's pathetic."

"How many do you have?" I asked.

"None, but I don't have my C&R. What kind of collector are you?"

"Focus, please," I said and swigged the soda. "How many Swiss K-31's?"

"Five of those, too."

"So that makes 12 C&R if we count the SKS. Check the ammo."

"You've got over seven hundred rounds of surplus for the Mosins. Good but could be better. You only have about two hundred rounds for the K98K and six hundred rounds for the K-31's.

"We can probably find more ammo for the Mosins and the K98K but it's going to be hard to find for the Swiss."

"I think I know a place."

"I hope you do," Brian said and put the ammo cans back on the shelf. "What next?"

"AK's. There's three of those. The WASR works well enough for what we need it for. The Yugo folder just had a G2 trigger group replacement so there won't be any more trigger slap there. She's good to go. The Bulgarian hasn't been fired but I have no doubts it will function. What about ammo?"

"I'll check." Brian reached up to the top of the four-shelf fixture and pulled down one ammo can. "You've got about one thousand rounds here. What do you think?"

"I think we need more. I have no idea how many crazies we're going to have to kill. And we don't know how many people we're going to have to send away if things get too crazy. At least two or three thousand more rounds would be nice."

"Now the .223's?"

"Yes. Tell me what we've got."

I downed the rest of my Diet Coke and dipped back into the refrigerator for a bag of Red Vines and started munching.

Brian put the ammo can back and moved to the other side of the room. "We have four AR-15's, one M16, two Mini 14's, and we have two MSAR STG's, that's including mine."

"Only four AR's?"

"Uh, let me check." He counted again with the same result. He opened another cabinet and found what he was looking for.

"There're two more but they need some work. One needs a barrel torque, an easy fix, but the other one had some problems with the trigger pack. Do you have a replacement?"

"I think so. Check the bin in that locker."

"I don't see one right now, but we'll look more. So we have nine .223's and maybe one more if we can fix it. Now let's see about ammo."

Brian closed the door on the open locker and then went back to the other side of the room.

"Ammo, ammo, okay, we have…a pathetic two thousand rounds of .223. That's, like, enough for 7 magazines per. It's a start but we really need to bulk that up."

"So noted," I said. "What about the 10/22's?"

"Seriously?"

"Yeah, seriously. We need to arm them with what we have. They'll be good for women and teens. And besides, let me shoot your ass with five or ten rounds of .22 and see what happens."

"Whatever, dude. Don't be a baby I'm just fucking with you."

"Shut up and give me a count."

After flipping me the finger, Brian moved on down the line.

"You have three 10/22's including one that you dressed up in a Krinker-Plinker kit. The good news is you have like five thousand rounds of ammunition. We're good there."

"What are we forgetting?"

"Handguns?"

"No, long guns. We're missing something."

"Oh, yeah, M1 Carbine," he said.

He went back to the ammo shelf and took a quick inventory. "You have five hundred rounds."

I wrote it down in my book. "Okay, now handguns. Forget the C&R this time."

He went to another cabinet and opened the door. "Let's see, you have two 1911's, one Sig in 9mm, you have a Ruger P95DC in 9mm, two Glock 17's—why?—a S&W three-inch in .38. Dude, this is really pathetic. Seven hand cannons?"

"Please, no comments from the guy who has one pistol. We'll keep handguns for anyone on patrol who needs the backup."

He shrugged his shoulders. "Add one more Glock 17," he said and lifted his shirt to show me his pistol.

"Got it. Ammo, please."

"Wait for it…wait for it…wait for it…five hundred rounds of 9mm, five hundred rounds of .45ACP and a whopping one hundred rounds of .38 +P."

"Yeah, definitely one for the 'needs more' list. That's it then?"

"Magazines?" he asked.

"Nah. I have so many magazines I don't even want to count. Anything else?"

"That's it for now. We can have the guys load magazines as part of their training."

"Done deal," I said.

I finished off the bag of Red Vines while waiting for Bob. He showed up fifteen minutes later with news that the vote was unanimous. I was now the commander of the Randall Oaks Community and its soon to be formed militia.

In a couple of hours we'd join Frank and his Community Watch group in an effort to coordinate our defense and supplies. There was a lot of work to be done and we had very little time to do it.

CHAPTER 9: PROVIDENCE

After a late lunch of peanut butter and jam sandwiches, Brian and I met with Bob Brown in my office. Bob was excited and nervous all at the same time. I could see that he was immensely relieved to have turned over command of our community, and he was his usual animated self again.

"From this point forward, anyone going outside the community must be armed," I said. "And I want no less than teams of two, but I'd prefer teams of four."

"Sounds good," Brian said.

Bob nodded in agreement. He moved around anxiously in his chair like a child who needed to pee.

"Bob, do you have any firearms besides your shotgun and pistol?" I asked.

Bob shook his head. "No. We had AR-15's in our patrol cars, but I never got my own for personal use."

I nodded to Brian and said, "Let him pick something."

After a few minutes Brian and Bob emerged from the armory. Bob was carrying the Mini-14 in one hand and four loaded magazines in the other. He was smiling like a kid that just came out of the candy store but Brian was shaking his head.

"Is there a problem with Bob's selection?" I asked.

Brian rolled his eyes. "There's better in the armory but he's set on that thing."

Getting up from my chair I grabbed my SKS. I raised an eyebrow and asked, "Problem with my selection?"

"Dude, are you fucking kidding me? Grab an AR or an STG. Don't embarrass me with that damn thing."

I laughed at his frustration.

"It's gotten me this far. I took out more than ten of those crazies with this beauty. How many heads do you have on your STG?"

Brian blustered. "That's not the point."

I chuckled. "And if Bob's comfortable with the Mini, that's his business."

"I used to shoot the ranch rifle a lot when I visited my uncle in Arizona. I'm partial to the platform," Bob said.

Brushing past Brian, I grabbed my go bag and set it on the table, adding another 10 stripper clips to what I already had in the bag.

"I'd like to take one more guy with us when we go to the meeting. Do you have anyone in mind, Bob?"

"I have a few ideas. Kevin from across the way—"

"Uh-uh, he's a freaking moron," Brian interjected. "I don't want him with me."

I gave Brian a stern look. "You're going to be responsible for training that moron, so take it easy. Whatever feelings you have about anyone in this community, you need to put that shit aside. These people are going to be our responsibility as well as our lifeline. We're going to have to depend on them, and you're going to have to work with all of them so get over it."

I paused a moment and then added, "Kevin is a moron, though. Do you have anyone else in mind?"

Bob thought about it for a second. "There's John Morris, the mechanic from up the block. And also Charlie Pruett. He's a good guy. He's been helping cover the gates the last couple of days. He's pretty sharp."

"Bri, what do you think of Charlie?"

Brian shrugged. "He's cool. Maybe he has some cigarettes. I'm dying for a smoke."

"I guess he's our fourth," I said.

Picking up his backpack and loading it with full mags, Brian said, "Before we go we need to walk the perimeter and see what security is like. We need to see where our weak points are and plug them up. I know there hasn't been much action here yet, but we need to be preemptive. Do you have shift rosters, Bob?"

"I do. For the last two days I've had teams of three guarding the gate around the clock on eight hour shifts."

Bob unzipped his coat and reached inside, pulling out a piece of paper. He held it out to Brian, but my brother didn't take it.

"Hang on to it, Bob. Brian's responsible for training and militia operations but I want you to be in charge of community security. You're in charge of militia police."

Bob was quiet.

Brian jabbed him in the arm. "You can handle that, right, Bob?"

"Yes, I guess I can," he said. He put the duty roster back into his pocket. "I'd like to make some changes to the rosters then. Add some more men and have shorter shifts. I'm also going to want some patrol groups to wander the grounds and report back."

"Sounds good, Bob," Brian said. He looked at me and said, "We're all going to need a base of operation. I think we should take over a few of the inventory homes that haven't sold. One can operate as a police station for Bob. I'll take one as our CP for mission planning and operations, and I think we'll need a third one for supplies. And we're going to need someone to act as supply officer."

I was nodding my head as Brian talked.

"Excellent ideas, bro." I glanced at my watch. "We still have couple of hours before we need to be over at Providence. Let's go house shopping."

★ ★ ★

It took about an hour for the three of us to walk the grounds and find three unoccupied homes that would fit our needs for police station, command post and supply depot. There was no debate about the choices.

The three model homes were already furnished. We'd remove any furnishings that were not appropriate for the purpose of particular rooms. Furnishings were a bonus, however.

We chose these particular homes because they were centrally located within the community which we all agreed was a plus. The largest of the three homes was chosen as the supply depot. It was a raised ranch model that had a large semi-finished basement, which was perfect for our needs. The smaller of the remaining two homes was designated the command post, with the large family room perfect for planning operations. And the last home would be Bob's station. It too, boasted a large basement, but this one was finished with four separate rooms, which were currently set up as bedroom, office, family room and workshop. These rooms could easily be converted into holding cells.

As we made our way toward the main and only gate on the south end of the community, we discussed the need for additional security teams on the north end, which butted up against a large wooded lot.

Being furthest from the hub of the community, we felt it a liability. If anyone were to make it over our wall, they'd go unnoticed until they were well into the community. Bob felt the playground and its small field house would make an excellent second sentry post.

"Whoever draws duty will have cover from the elements as well as some protection against small arms if attacked," Bob said. He was still excited and his hands moved all over as he talked. "One of the first things we need to get when we go for supplies are radios and lots of batteries. Communication is key for security."

"First thing tomorrow we need to form up and start training. It's time to stop talking and start doing," Brian said. "There's no way we can make supply runs until I can train a group to work as a team. They need to learn to shoot among friendlies, to move as a team, learn offensive and defensive formations... damn we have a lot of ground to cover."

I slapped Brian on the shoulder. "You'll get it done. I have faith in you, brother."

We neared the main gate and I halted our group.

Tomorrow things are going to change. Bri is absolutely right. Time to stop talking and start doing. I'm anxious to get things moving, too. And I know we have so much to do I find myself wondering where the hell to even start. But the answer is obviously with the basics.

"Tomorrow morning we muster the community and we start selection. We'll each interview these people and see what types of skills each person brings to the table, and gauge their ability to learn more important survival skills. This is how we'll begin to pick our soldiers and our peacekeepers and our support staff. Remember, everyone here can do a job, and every job, no matter how small, will be important in the coming months if this situation is as bad as people seem to think it will be."

"We're with you," Bob said. "I have no doubt we made the right decision in putting you in charge."

"What the hell are they doing over there?" Brian asked suddenly.

I turned to him, saw that he was looking in the direction of the gate, and shifted my gaze. The front gate was open and three men stood just outside of the threshold, staring off into the empty cornfield immediately across Route 20.

"Don't know," Bob said and started toward the men.

I could see in his face that he already felt this was his responsibility, and I was glad to see he was ready to step up and handle the situation.

Brian and I followed our friend. As we closed the distance I got a better look at the men at the gate. The first guy was tall, about six-five, with a shock of windblown blond hair. I recognized him but didn't know him. I often saw him walking his black lab early in the morning before I left for work. He wore a quilted flannel jacket and black jeans. I saw he held a pistol in his right hand, which was currently aimed at the ground.

To Blondie's left was a shorter, stocky man in his mid-thirties wearing a desert camo field jacket. His name was Randle, and he lived in the house closest to the gate. There was always a large pick-up truck with ladders in his driveway; I think he worked in construction. He held a shotgun at port and seemed very interested in whatever was going on over there.

The last guy was Charlie Pruett. He had light brown hair and bright blue eyes, was about average height, and he was wearing a dark green fleece and a khaki colored baseball cap. He had no weapon that I could see.

Bob reached the men first. "What's going on... " he trailed off. A moment later I stood beside him and saw what they were all gawking at.

Across the road, a solitary farmhouse stood, long-ago abandoned. Jutting into the sky beside the dilapidated barn stood a grain tower that definitely had seen better days. The original owner sold the land to housing developers early on at great profit, but in the last three years the housing market had taken a dive and the developer had yet to build on it. What had been a cornfield when the farm was still operational was now just empty level land.

About one hundred yards away, in the middle of the dead field, one of the infected hunched over a body and was having dinner.

"What the fuck... ?" said Brian.

Randle turned toward him, a bit surprised by our appearance. "I ain't never seen nothing like that before."

"No one's seen nothing like that before," the tall blond said without taking his eyes off the gore.

"They've seen stuff up the road," Charlie Pruett said. "We haven't seen anything like that here. Well, until now."

I unslung my bag and put it down beside me, moved to the right of the group about three yards, and got down on one knee into my favorite shooting position.

"How the hell did he get there?" Bob asked.

"Who's he munching on?" the blond asked.

"Why don't you go find out, David?" Randle asked.

"We should probably do something," Charlie Pruett said. He turned to David and said, "Give me that gun."

I fired the SKS then, shattering the late afternoon silence and scaring the shit out of the five men.

"Holy shit!" Bob said as he watched the crazy fall back from his lunch.

Brian turned to me. "Damn, dude, you blew his freaking head off!"

"Not quite."

I stood, brushed off my knee, and picked up my bag. All five of the guys were looking at me with surprise.

"What are you gawking at?" I asked with a bit too much bitterness in my voice. "That's what we do when we see those fucking things. Shoot them. That's why you have guns. And if you want to survive, if you want your family to survive, then use them!

"Next time I see anyone standing around with their thumb up their ass while one of those things is in our backyard I'm going to kick some ass."

The five men were quiet for a moment and one by one each of them dropped their stare and found something else to look at.

Before I could say anything else, Charlie Pruett started toward the gate and said, "Let's get back inside and close the gate. If we have to come out again, someone needs to stay inside and keep the gate closed."

Randle and David followed quickly.

"Charlie," I called out, halting him just as he neared the gate. "May I have a word with you, please?"

"Sure," he said. He turned to David and told him, "Close it up." A moment later he stood in front of me. "What's up?"

"How long have you been at the gate, Charlie?" I asked.

"This is my second day. I did two shifts yesterday because we came up short on the roster. Today I've been out here since morning. Why?"

"How'd you like to take a walk with us? We'd like you to come to the Community Watch meeting at Providence."

Charlie paused a second and looked back at the gate, then he looked at me. "Who's going to cover the gate?"

Bob cleared his throat and took a step forward. "David, go get John Morris up here to fill in for Charlie."

"Sure thing, Bob," David said and trotted off.

"Taken care of, Charlie," Bob said. "Now come on and walk with us."

After another brief pause Charlie shrugged. "Alright."

Now we were four. We stretched out across the two-lane blacktop road and started our walk east toward Providence. By car, the ride would take about five minutes, but on foot it would probably take a half hour. I did not want to risk driving a vehicle. Although we were not concerned at this point about gas shortages, I had no idea what would happen over the next several weeks and we needed to be frugal where we could. Also, we needed to be able to work and move as a squad on patrol. Fighting from vehicles is difficult and we could not always count on the advantage of a motor vehicle. There were many places vehicles would be unable to traverse. We needed to get used to the physical demands of foot patrols and the advantage of advancing silently among the enemy. Besides, I could gain a whole other perspective from the ground that I could not get from a vehicle.

As we passed the cornfield on our right, I was the only one who didn't glance over at the two bodies. The dead things no longer interested me.

Once we passed the field Brian said, "Charlie, what did you mean when you said they've seen stuff up the road?"

Looking down at his boots as he walked, Charlie replied, "For the last two days they've sent a group of guys up here every four hours to give us reports about what's going on at the roadblock at Providence. Sounds like they've been in contact with those... what did you call them? Crazies? If you believe what they say, seems like they've seen a lot of action."

I glanced over at Bob, who read my mind. "This is the first I'm hearing of this," he said. "I need to know these things when you hear them, Charlie."

Charlie looked up at Bob and said, "Yeah, I know. I hadn't had a chance to tell you yet. Sorry."

"Did they provide any details about this 'action' at the roadblocks?" Brian asked.

Charlie shrugged and looked back at his boots. "One of the guys, fellow named Phil, said the roadblock was charged on two separate occasions by groups of five or six of those crazies. He said there were also a number of attacks by individual crazies throughout the night. I think I even heard one of the other guys say there were some attacks inside Providence."

"Inside the community, like on the streets?" Bob asked.

Charlie nodded his head. "The other guy said one of the crew from the roadblocks must have been exposed during one of the attacks. I guess he went home at the end of his shift and... I don't know, changed or something. I think he killed a couple of people before they took him out."

"Christ," Bob said.

We reached the midpoint of our walk as we passed the Nicor sub-station on our left. On our right we continued to pass Providence homes. Unlike our gated community that was surrounded by walls, Providence was open to the road, perched on a small hill of land. Protecting these outer homes would be challenging for Providence and I did not envy their situation.

"Bob, do you coordinate with Community Watch on these update patrols?" Brian asked.

"Sort of. When we were first organizing the roadblocks, Frank suggested that we share information and volunteered to send runners up to us."

"Good idea," I said. When I met Frank at the roadblock he'd made a good first impression with me. This bit of news solidified my impression.

We walked the next ten minutes with little talk between us. I could see that the others in my group felt a bit odd carrying weapons and gear. They almost seemed uncomfortable.

In Illinois, the only state without some sort of carry law, it was taboo to be out on the street with a firearm. And here we were with rifles and gear humping our way down Route 20 in the early evening. It was almost surreal.

Just as I was falling into rhythm and beginning to zone out, I heard a gunshot. It sounded a bit distant but close enough that we all scattered from the road, taking cover in the slight dip on the south side of the embankment. A few seconds later another shot rang out.

"Where did it come from?" Bob asked. He held the Mini 14 at the ready, his eyes wide and alert.

"Couldn't tell," Brian said.

He instinctively took a position to Bob's left and directed his attention to our six and scanned the area.

When the third shot rang out I said, "Came from the roadblock at Providence."

Leaving the safety of the ditch, I adjusted my bag to a more comfortable position and started trotting in our original direction of movement. I didn't have to turn to see if my group followed; I could hear their footsteps in time with my own.

As we jogged down Route 20 another couple of gunshots rang out and as we drew closer I heard what I thought was laughter.

Within a minute we crested an incline and the roadblock came into view. I could see four men standing behind the two vehicles. One on the extreme right fired a shot to the east, the direction I'd come from Kappy's. The other three fellows roared with laughter.

"What the hell?" Brian asked as I came to a halt. He knew immediately something was out of place here.

"Are they laughing?" Charlie asked.

"Sure as hell are." Bob was a bit out of breath.

"Let's go easy," I said and started walking slowly forward.

When I drew near, I could immediately see that things had changed at the roadblock since I entered yesterday. The Randall entrance that had been left open was now blocked by a smoking shell of what might have been a UPS or FedEx truck. Over on the eastbound side, where the two-lane split to four divided by the deep ditch, I saw a section had been taped off with yellow tape. From this distance I could see wafts of smoke drifting from the pit.

"Dude, what is that smell?" Brian asked.

"They're burning the bodies," I said, knowing I was exactly right about that.

If all hell had broken loose, like Charlie had described, there would be dead husks of crazies lying about. Anyone with any sense would know right away the best thing to do would be to burn the remains.

"Pretty disgusting," Charlie said, covering his nose.

We moved closer still, until we were no more than twenty feet from the men at the roadblock. The one on the right stood poised over the front end of the SUV with a Remington 700 aimed out at the road.

When I glanced in that direction I saw a crazy down in the street. I could see he was riddled with bullet holes. His legs were severely damaged by gunfire and he was unable to stand.

The guy with the 700 fired another round, hitting the crazy in the arm, right at the elbow. The arm severed and the crazy fell forward, his face smacking into the concrete.

"Fucking awesome!" he shouted, pleased with himself. He turned to see his friend's reaction and spotted us from his peripheral. His face changed from one of excitement to surprise. "Hey guys, turn around."

The men all faced us and my group came to a halt. I raised my hands in front of me in a calming gesture. "We're from Randall Oaks. We're here for the Community Watch meeting."

Two of the men exchanged glances and whispered something to each other. The one with the rifle turned back to me and said, "Yeah, come on over."

He and his friends turned to each other now and picked up their conversation as though we weren't even there.

"I don't like these guys," Bob said quietly.

"Feeling is mutual," Charlie said. "The one with the rifle that was shooting the crazy came up the other day with Phil. I didn't like his attitude. He thinks everything's a joke."

As if on cue, the group broke out into laughter again. When I stopped a few feet away from the Comedian, he glanced at me and said, "Put your guns on the ground right there and I'll have someone take you in."

Brian and I exchanged glances now. I could see he was about to raise some hell. Before he could, I said, "Excuse me, friend, but we're not going to leave our weapons here."

"Then you don't go in," the Comedian said. Now he turned fully toward me and looked me in the eyes. I could see he, too, was looking for some trouble.

Standing my ground I said, "Frank invited us here. He didn't mention no weapons were allowed. Is there a reason why you would disarm us?"

"Those are the rules," insisted Comedian. "And rules are rules. If you don't like rules talk to Frank Senior about it."

Brian took a step forward now but I put an arm out to stop his movement.

Comedian looked at him, smiled, then turned back to me. "What exactly is your problem?"

"I'd like to talk to Frank." I was trying to keep my cool. Although my temper had a longer fuse than my brother, sooner or later I'd blow.

"Sure. Leave your guns here, and you can go on in and talk to him as much as you want."

I stepped forward to close the distance between me and the Comedian. I was taller than him by a couple of inches and had about thirty pounds on him. Lowering my voice I said, "We're going to go in, as we were invited. And we're taking our arms with us. If you want to stop us, that's your call, but you're going to make one hell of a mess here."

"Back off," Comedian said and took a step back. His eyes changed now that he realized this wasn't a joke.

"Or what?" I asked. I took another step forward.

"What's going on here?" someone shouted from my right. A moment later another man stepped up beside me. I turned to look and saw it was Phil. I'd met him the other day with Frank at the roadblock.

The Comedian blustered immediately. "They don't want to leave their guns," he said.

"These guys are from the Randall Oaks crew. They don't need to leave their guns. And quit screwing around out here. Kill that thing over there and drop him in the pit."

Comedian flinched as if slapped and then turned to his crew. "Somebody kill that skag out there, come on already."

Phil turned back to me and shook his head in disgust. "Sorry about that. You guys come with me, I'll take you to our Community Center."

We followed Phil away from the roadblock and through the main entrance of the Providence community. As we passed through the arches, I had a feeling that our lives were going to change drastically.

CHAPTER 10:
COMMUNITY WATCH

Phil led us down Providence Drive, the main access road into the community. Unlike Randall Oaks, Providence was an enormous community of single family homes, intermingled with townhomes of varying sizes and shapes.

The community spanned eight square miles of land and was a virtual maze of streets and cul-de-sacs that could confuse even those that were somewhat familiar with the lay of the land. Also unlike Randall Oaks, the community was completely open on all sides; no fences or barriers surrounded this thriving community. The concrete pillars and arch we passed through at the main entrance merely gave the impression of security but was just for show.

"We're gathering at the community center just up the road," Phil said as we made our way up the slight incline. "Frank Senior is going to introduce the heads of the surrounding communities who we've aligned with and then he's going to give a state of the community address. After that I guess he'll open the floor and hear concerns."

"How many communities are you talking about?" Brian asked.

I could tell that he was as surprised as me that the other communities had aligned so quickly. I could almost hear him thinking we were sadly behind.

"Oh, I think there's about five as of this morning," Phil said. "We've got you all to the northwest, we have the Gardens to our immediate west, Oak Hills to our south, Crestwood is on our east and then some private homes that are built into that little cul-de-sac to the northeast. They're not really a community but they're a pretty tight and they stick together."

"You're right in the middle," Bob observed. "Nice place to be."

Phil glanced over at him but didn't say anything.

"We heard there's been a lot of action at the roadblocks," I said.

I hitched my bag up onto my shoulder trying to get more comfortable. I'd have to think of some other way to carry extra ammo and small gear when making these local trips.

"Yeah, been pretty constant the last couple of days. Most of them come in from the east, feeding in from Randall Road and down onto Route 20. I imagine most of them are coming from the shopping strips out there. Some might even be coming from our neighboring communities."

At this point, Phil turned to me and asked, "Anyone in your community infected?"

I shook my head and turned to Brian. He shook his head. Bob looked down at the ground and said nothing and that was probably for the best.

Charlie just shrugged because he had no idea that my wife had turned into a crazy and my brother had to shoot her. Charlie had no idea what was buried in my front rose garden.

"We've had a few here," Phil said. When he didn't elaborate I was about to ask how many when he said, "We're here."

He pointed to our left at a one-story structure, about four thousand square feet. The lawn in front of the building was crammed with people. Some had guns but many didn't.

Most of the people had formed into smaller groups, probably friends or neighbors. They talked animatedly and we could all feel the excitement in the air.

"That's a sight," Charlie said.

He jammed his hands into the pockets of his coat. I just realized Charlie hadn't brought a firearm with him. He must have given the shotgun back to David before we left.

"That's nothing," Phil said. "Inside is probably packed. Stick close to me and we'll make our way through. We have some space saved for you."

"VIP," Bob said and raised an eyebrow.

"Let's go," Phil said and started to move forward.

We hit the crowd almost immediately and had to shoulder our way through. Moving through the crowd with firearms and gear was tough going , but everyone was polite and no one became angry when we bumped accidentally.

Although the distance to the front entrance was short, it took us nearly ten minutes to navigate through the crowd and actually enter the structure.

The main doors opened onto a pretty large foyer that spread out to the left and right, about fifty feet across. At the center was a small counter with a computer and phone. On either side of the foyer were crops of chairs and tables with the usual plastic potted plants and trees.

The foyer was as crowded as the lawn out front but in here you could smell perspiration and the murmur of voices rose loudly, making it very difficult to hear what anyone was actually saying unless they were a foot or two in front of you.

"This way!" Phil shouted as we huddled together just inside the doorway.

To the left and right of the center desk were two sets of double doors which led into the main speaking room. Phil led us to the right and as we pushed our way through the doors, the room opened up auditorium style, with rows and rows of chairs from left to right facing a stage. There was a center aisle that separated the walls of chairs.

This room was by far the most packed and most chaotic. People were in the aisles and rows talking and chattering, others were pushing through various groups in an attempt to get a good seat or be near their group.

The din grew louder as voices bounced and echoed off the walls. This place would be a death trap should a fire break out.

I quickly took note of the emergency exits and pointed them out to my group. Brian and Bob nodded in unison. Charlie gave me a brief salute and jammed his hands back into his pockets.

"Amazing," I said.

Phil stopped and turned to me. "What did you say?"

"I said this is amazing," I repeated, louder this time.

Phil smiled and nodded his head. "More like crazy if you ask me."

We continued to wade our way through the crowd and eventually Phil halted us about seven rows from the front. He leaned over to a man at the aisle seat and spoke something into his ear. Whatever it was I couldn't hear, but the man nodded and stood from his seat. He started to scoot a few men further into the center of the row and left three empty seats at the very end of the aisle.

"Your guys can sit here," Phil said to Bob. "You come up with me."

Bob shook his head. "Matt's in charge now," he said, patting my shoulder.

"Okay," Phil said. "The rest of you sit here. Matt, you're with me."

The guys crowded into the empty seats with Brian at the row end, Charlie in the middle and Bob squeezing in next to the man who had occupied the row seat only moments ago.

I followed Phil again and he led me to the stage up front. Before we walked on, we stopped at a small table to the left of the stage where a couple of men sat. I recognized Frank immediately and he obviously recognized me.

"Hey, Matt, right?" he asked as he stood and shook my hand.

"Yeah that's right. How are you Frank?"

"Not too bad, considering."

Phil leaned in and said, "Matt's the head man at Randall Oaks. He's relieved Bob."

Frank raised an eyebrow. "Any reason?"

I shrugged. "Bob felt I had a bit more experience. I served in the Army a bit."

"Good deal," Frank said. "Good to have you here. Phil did you tell him how things are going to go?"

"I told him a little," Phil said. "I have to get back to the checkpoint and make sure things are kosher."

"Thanks, Phil," Frank said. He turned to me and said, "You'll sit up there with the other heads of community. My dad, Frank Senior, will introduce each of you, thank you for your alliance and then he'll give a state of the community address. I'll need your name, title and a brief description of how things are at your community."

"You have my name. We haven't really decided on titles. What are the rest of these guys calling themselves?"

Frank laughed. "Some are calling themselves general or commander of their community."

"Well, just say 'Randall Oaks Community Leader' and we'll leave it at that."

"Good enough," Frank said.

He picked up a pen and jotted that into his notebook.

"What's been happening in your community? Any infections? Attacks from the infected?"

I considered this for a moment. I was definitely not going to report that my wife was infected. As far as attacks, I didn't want to report none. After seeing what was going on at the roadblock, I didn't want them to feel that we had it too easy. I didn't want us to look untested and weak.

"No infections I'm happy to say. We did have an attack just a bit ago on the way up. One of those crazies was out in the field behind the abandoned barn to the south of our gates. He was dining on someone and we had to put him down."

Frank smiled. "I forgot you called them that. I like it; 'crazies'."

"Seems to fit," I shrugged, and shifted my bag again.

"Anything else to report?"

"Not at the moment. We're still getting organized. I'll have more to report in a few days."

"Okay. Why don't you get on up there? Take the fifth seat in."

"Okay." I shook Frank's hand again and made my way up onto the stage.

The first three seats were already occupied and I nodded to the men as I passed them. I sat in the fifth seat with another fellow on my left. I gave him a nod and looked out toward the audience trying to find Brian, Bob and Charlie, dizzied by the amount of people out there.

I counted rows and eventually found my group. They were talking animatedly amongst themselves and they blended perfectly with the rest of the people that surrounded them.

From my vantage point on stage, these people looked like frenzied ants moving in and out and around their mound. All the movement of bodies and limbs created an almost sea-like motion that made me a bit queasy.

"Ain't that a sight?" the gentleman on my left asked.

I turned to look at him. "It certainly is."

"I'm Jim Brewer from the Gardens," he said.

Jim was a burly man with a bushy beard and mustache. He wore a khaki colored Cabala's hat. His hair was long and stringy, his grip strong and firm.

"Nice to meet you. I'm Matt Danzig from Randall Oaks."

"Hell, we're practically neighbors," Jim said and smiled.

Only the small patch of abandoned farm separated our two communities. As a matter of fact, from our front gate, if you looked past the old farm you could see a few of the homes from the Gardens.

I nodded my agreement. "I feel like I'm at an AC/DC concert right now."

Jim laughed again and clapped one of his meaty hands on my shoulder. "That sounds right."

The murmur of voices was like the chirping of crickets in my ears. After a while the noise got into your eardrums and grated on your nerves.

Just when I thought I couldn't stand it anymore, an older man in his late fifties or early sixties entered stage left and made his way up to the microphone at the center of the stage.

He stood average height but was slightly overweight. He had a stocky frame; you could see he was strong for a man of his age. I guessed he had probably worked in construction most of his life.

He stepped up and tapped on the microphone. The sound barely carried across the din of the room. He cleared his throat into the microphone with the same result.

With a smile on his face he looked out at the crowd and waited patiently. After a moment the crowd became aware of him and everyone started to shush each other. Eventually the murmur died down and the room was suddenly quiet.

"Thank you," the man said. He waited a second and continued. "For those of you who don't know me, my name is Frank Castellano, Senior. Since I share my name with my son, you all can call me Senior."

A small cheering section front and center rose up and made some noise as well as some groups interspersed throughout the hall. Obviously Providence residents were here in number to support their leader.

Senior raised his hand and managed to look modest. As the noise level dropped he said, "We have a lot of things to discuss about our current situation, but before I do, I'd like to introduce you to some important folks who are helping keep our borders safe."

There was a small round of applause that went around the room. Senior raised the piece of paper he held in his hands.

"To our northwest we have Matt Danzig, leader of the Randall Oaks Community."

I stood up feeling quite self-conscious and raised a hand to the audience. A round of applause went up and I immediately looked over toward my small group. They were all standing and waving their arms.

I sat back down quickly and Jim clapped me on the shoulder.

Senior raised his hands again. "To our west we have Big Jim Brewer, Commander of the Gardens."

Big Jim stood and posed like Hulk Hogan. The crowd ate it up and it took more than Senior raising his hands for the crowd to get quiet this time. It seemed like a full minute of applause while Big Jim popped another pose.

Finally, Big Jim sat down. He winked at me and said, "Gotta give them a show."

Senior spent the next couple of minutes going through the list of men on the stage, pausing for applause in between. It was like a State of the Union address, full of long, forced rounds of applause. After the introductions, Senior got down to business.

"As most of you know, we've got a real problem. We're still not sure what happened out there and why these people have become the way they are. It's only been a few days since this all started here and there is little news.

"I know there are lots of rumors going around. I've heard many of them myself—zombies coming back from the dead, Nazi experiments that started in the forties finally completed and unleashed on the United States, voodoo. All of this is just B.S. and I don't want to hear talk like this. It just gets people riled up.

"We've heard other things, too, that maybe have a bit more merit. We've heard that maybe the H1N1 vaccinations were tainted. That may be true, but I'm not buying into rumors that some North Korean dictator or Castro had anything to do with that. Whatever happened at this time is a moot point.

"Those things, those infected, those... 'crazies' as my son's friend calls them, are out there and they are coming. It doesn't matter how they got the way they are. What does matter is that we are prepared to defend ourselves until someone who really knows what's going on figures out a way to fix the problem."

The silent room suddenly erupted with applause. I admit, I was caught up in it myself and clapped right along with the rest of them. The room was so packed now with people standing in the aisles and against the back wall and milling in the doorways that the sea of clapping hands made me dizzy again.

"Now, we don't know how long we're going to have to ride this thing out. For all we know, this could end tomorrow or it might never end, so we're going to need to start thinking long term.

"We're already organizing scavenge parties here at Providence and we're going to encourage you all to do the same. We need to get out there and start gathering supplies."

"It ain't safe out there!" someone in the audience shouted. A murmur rose up but quickly died down.

"That's obvious," Senior said and a few of us on stage chuckled. "It's not safe anywhere. Our roadblocks are probed daily, and we've even had some of those things wandering right here in the middle of the community.

"And we've had some of our own who were infected and didn't know about it until they turned. They've been hit pretty hard at Oak

Hills to our south, probably the biggest wave of the crazies we've seen yet.

"The point is, we can't sit around in the relative safety in our community only to die of starvation, dehydration or infection because we've run out of food, water and medicine. What's the difference? We might as well just walk out there now and let those bastards take us and save us the suffering."

Shouts of "No!" rose up around the room as well as some other profanities.

"Yeah, I'm not ready to let that happen. I want to live, and I see you all agree. We've got to protect ourselves from more than just the likes of those infected bags of flesh out there.

"We're going to have to work together to survive. We're going to have to find our weaknesses and strengthen them. We're going to have to dig down deep where it counts and we're going to have to rely on every last bit of energy we can muster. It's going to be hard, but I know you are all up to the challenge!"

The noise in the room became even louder than before. Everyone stood again and hands pounded against each other with great vigor. People were standing on their chairs and waving their arms or throwing fists into the air. I stood, too, clapping until my hands hurt.

Scanning the crowd, I caught movement against the crowd and watched as a man tried to push his way down the aisle on my right. He zigzagged and pushed his way through and he looked like a fish swimming against a strong current. As he struggled through and drew near, I recognized Phil. His face was flushed, he was sweating, and he appeared out of breath.

I stopped clapping and tracked his progress. The look on his face told me something was wrong.

After what seemed like an eternity, but was probably only a minute, Phil broke through and rushed to the table where Frank sat. He said something that made Frank stand up and at that moment I felt a weight drop in the pit of my stomach.

Frank said something back to Phil and pushed his shoulder. Phil immediately turned and started back the way he'd come, but Frank stopped him, pointed toward a door to his immediate right. Phil nodded and ran. Frank started up the stage steps.

"Okay everyone, okay," Senior was saying with his hands raised. He was trying to get the crowd to settle. "Let's get back to business—"

Frank touched his father's arm and turned him away from the microphone. He whispered something into Senior's ear that made the old man's face instantly turn to stone. Senior leaned into his son and said something in return. Frank nodded and turned and walked immediately toward me and Big Jim.

"What's wrong?" Big Jim asked. He obviously knew something was wrong just as I did.

Frank came to his knee in front of us and the other leaders that sat close to Big Jim and I leaned in to hear.

"We've got a problem. Some of the crazies have breached our security and are inside the community."

"How many?" Big Jim asked.

"Not sure," Frank said. He paused a moment and continued. "I'm told it could be a group as large as twenty."

Behind him Senior said, "Everyone please calm down, we have an emergency situation."

"That's not a good idea," Big Jim said, referring to Senior's remark. "People are going to panic."

"Yeah, I told him the same thing, but Senior does what he wants," Frank said.

"We've been breached," Senior said. "There are infected in the community. Don't panic. Please wait and listen. Do not go out there, everyone just stay calm and stay inside."

"I would suggest you all get out the side door there and try to get back to your homes. There may be other attacks and you may be needed," Frank said.

Big Jim and I both stood. I lifted my go bag and my SKS and I noticed that Big Jim had an AR-15 with him.

"Good luck," he said.

"You, too." I looked at Frank and said, "We'll bring back help if we're not under attack."

"We'd appreciate it. Now get moving."

"Everyone stay calm!" Senior shouted. "We've got men out there and they will handle this. Please stay inside."

I left the stage and was greeted by Brian, Bob and Charlie. They were waiting for me.

"What are we doing?" Brian asked.

"We're going back home," I stated.

Bob said, "They're saying to stay inside."

"Yeah I know. But we need to get back and see what's happening at home. We might be needed."

"Fucking right," Brian said.

"I'm with you, boss," Charlie said. He was often so quiet I almost forgot he was with us.

"Follow me," I said.

I led my group toward the side entrance that Frank had pointed out. People were already using that exit to vacate the hall. Most of the men who left via this exit were armed and I figured these were the men who Senior had referred to.

We funneled out into the evening. People were running in various directions but I heard no gunfire yet. That was a good sign. Perhaps the breach was further away and the crazies had not yet reached us. Providence was, after all, a huge complex.

As a group we turned left and started back toward the main entrance. We moved quickly, passing the front of the building, trekked over the grass and back onto the main street. When we stepped onto the pavement I heard the first screams to the west. We all froze for a moment and then turned toward the sound.

More screams rose into the evening in the same direction. About one hundred yards to the west, between a cluster of single family homes, a group of crazies made their way toward the crowd. They actually seemed to be moving together as a group, although a few had veered off to grab the nearest flesh.

"Holy shit!" Bob shouted. "They're organized!"

Before I could tell Bob to calm down, a gunshot rang out to my left. I turned to see Brian on one knee, firing at the approaching horde.

"What are we doing?" Bob shouted.

I turned to him and said, "Shoot them, Bob. Just be careful not to shoot the people."

"This is nuts!" Bob shouted, but raised the Mini 14 to his shoulder.

I turned to Charlie who stood slightly behind me and to my right. I pulled my S&W 64 with the three-inch barrel from my holster and handed it over to him.

"Use it if they get close enough or while we reload. And watch our six!"

Charlie took the revolver and the three speed loaders and nodded his head.

Turning back toward the threat, I raised the SKS and popped off a few ineffective shots. Too many people were running around, crossing in front of our line of fire.

"Move you fucking idiots!" Brian shouted, waving his hand. He carefully lined up a shot and when there was room between darting people, he shot one of the crazies in the chest, dropping him to the ground.

"Go for the head!" I shouted, "It's the only thing that kills them!"

The crazy he dropped with a chest shot sat up, and I blew a hole in his right temple to emphasize my point.

To my right I heard Bob fire a round. From off in the distance I heard faint pops which I assumed were gunfire, but it was at a distance. We seemed to be the only ones shooting.

Brian was reloading while I fired a few more rounds. I killed another crazy and put another one to the ground briefly.

Bob had wasted a whole thirty rounds of ammunition with no kills. At this rate, we would be out of ammo shortly.

I moved beside Brian and crouched down next to him. "We need to move. We're going to waste all of our ammo here and we might have our own problems at home."

Brian nodded. He fired a few more rounds at the horde, which was now no more than fifty yards in front of us. Shouts and screams and the sound of the dying was getting to me.

"Peel right! Peel right!" I shouted to Brian and tapped his shoulder. I moved quickly now to Bob who was loading another magazine.

"I can't hit anything!" he said. His eyes were wide and sweat trickled down his brow.

"We're moving, Bob. We're going to peel right. Fire and move. Watch Brian and watch me. Can you do this?"

"Yeah, I'm good," Bob said. He gave me two thumbs up.

I turned to Charlie. He was waiting patiently. "Charlie, you're on me. When I move, you move. Stay right on my ass, okay?"

"Yes, boss," he said.

Charlie and I ran about five yards to the right and then I took to a knee and raised the SKS. I fired several shots and watched as Brian rose and ran toward us. As he passed Bob, he tapped his shoulder. Bob held his ground and continued to fire until his third magazine was dry, and then he turned and ran.

I thumbed in a new stripper clip and fired five rounds rapidly. The next five I aimed carefully and killed two more of the horde. They were now about twenty-five yards away, but they switched direction slightly and were angling south.

"Now us, Charlie," I said.

We both stood and hoofed it, touching Brian's shoulder and then passing Bob. After ten yards I kneeled again and turned to see that Brian was already moving. When he reached us I stopped him and he took to a knee beside us.

"I think we're good now, they're moving south."

"Should we follow?" he asked.

"No," I said. "We need to get back home."

Bob came running up and stopped beside us. He was breathing heavily and perspiring quite a bit. "I got one. I fucking nailed one, finally."

"Good job," Brian said and clapped Bob on the back.

I reached into my bag and handed Bob a bottle of water. He took it and eagerly drank, downing half the bottle. When he recapped it and handed it back to me, I nodded toward Brian and Bob handed it off.

After everyone had a drink I tossed the empty bottle onto the pavement. I made sure everyone reloaded and then it was time to move. We walked cautiously down the main road toward the entrance and

Route 20. I led our column and Brian brought up the rear. Charlie stuck on me, as promised.

"That was intense," Bob said as the arch of the entrance came into sight.

"Did you check your undies, Bob?" Brian asked. "I think you shit your pants back there."

"I might have," Bob said and we all laughed.

"Keep your eyes open," I told them, "and keep moving."

After a few more minutes the roadblock came into view. It was quiet. Only three men were posted here. We approached them and I immediately regretted doing so. Comedian was still out here.

"What's going on in there?" he asked. He trotted up to us and stopped a few feet in front of me. "Did you see what's going on?"

I nodded my head. "We saw about twenty or so of the crazies in there moving southwest. We took out about six or seven of them."

"Nice job," Comedian said. I thought he was being sarcastic, but a look at his face told me otherwise.

"Nothing going on out here?" Brian asked. He stood to my right with his STG at the ready.

Comedian shook his head. "No. Haven't seen one in about an hour now."

We were all silent for a moment, not sure what to say.

"We have to get going to check on things at home," I said.

Bob stepped up and said, "I hope things turn out okay. If you need help here, send a runner and we'll be here in minutes."

Comedian nodded. "Thanks."

We turned and started to make our way back home. The night air was cool and sweet and felt good against our hot faces. The air tasted sweet as I pulled it into my lungs and expelled the pungent aroma of cordite.

"You guys did well," I said. "I'm proud of you."

They were all silent as we hoofed it the rest of the way home.

CHAPTER 11: MORNING AFTER

I awoke with sunlight pouring in through the bedroom window. I had forgotten to pull the shades, as usual. I sat at the edge of the empty bed and rubbed my eyes with the back of my hands. I'd never been a morning person and I guess I wasn't going to start being one today.

I stood and stretched, then pushed my bare feet into my slippers. After putting on my glasses, I turned to look at the empty bed again. I'd been married for eight years and it had been so long since I'd had to sleep alone.

Most nights the kids found their way into our king sized bed at some point during the night. Mark usually cuddled up on his mother's side and Katie on mine, her feet always seeming to find my kidneys or another sensitive part of my anatomy.

Before I could become consumed with emotion, I turned away from the bed and went to the bathroom to relieve myself and brush my teeth.

I tried really hard not to look at the place where the carpet had been cut out, exposing the bare plywood beneath. Brian had used his knife to remove the maroon-stained portion of the carpet the night before.

Wearing jogging pants and a white t-shirt, I went to the kitchen and put on a pot of coffee to brew, then poured myself a bowl of Raisin Bran and cut up a banana to put on top while I waited.

I stood and ate my cereal leaning against the kitchen sink, feeling so strange with the quiet that seemed to overwhelm the house. Up until a few days ago, each morning had been filled with sound; blaring televisions in two different rooms, showers running, kids arguing or fussing about getting dressed.

I placed the unfinished bowl of cereal into the sink and poured a cup of coffee, thankful that we had not lost power. I don't know what I'd do without coffee and I didn't want to find out.

Taking my coffee cup with me, I put on a fleece sweater and went out onto the deck off the dining room. As soon as I stepped outside, I was greeted with beautiful sounds of the morning and people hard at work.

I went to the far end of the deck which gave me a view of Harper's Knoll as well as the main common grounds just outside my front door. I was quite surprised to see Brian leading about sixty or seventy people in morning PT. They were currently in the middle of jumping jacks.

Looking further to the south I saw a group of men at the front gate post, although from this distance I could not tell who stood guard. To the southwest I saw another group of people whom I did recognize. Bob stood with Katherine, a retired supply sergeant, and Ravi, a twenty-something Jewish girl who attended nursing school and lived with some roommates in one of the townhomes on the northeast side of the community.

To the north, in front of the home that we designated the police station, I spotted two vehicles parked in the driveway. The garage door stood open and it appeared that two men were moving some furniture around, but I couldn't tell if they were bringing it in or taking it out.

When we returned from Providence last night, news of the run on the community spread quickly throughout our own. The tale of how I shot one of the crazies in the field across the way had already made its way around, and the new tale that included us wiping seven or eight crazies off the map made for an even greater tale.

I expected that this would peak the interest of some in the community, but I hadn't expected our actions to fuel a fire. I was shocked and surprised by the turnout this morning, just twelve hours later. I was also relieved.

After what happened last night, I realized how truly unprepared and vulnerable we actually were.

I sipped my coffee and had the sudden feeling that things were just passing me by. It was only six thirty in the morning, but I seemed to be the only person in this community that wasn't busy getting things prepped.

Feeling sorry for myself, I turned away from the hustle and bustle and looked down at the rose garden, my wife's final resting place.

"I miss you so much, baby."

I wish I had been able to bring my children back with me and lay them to rest with their mother. I missed them dearly.

I thought about the many times I asked them to leave me alone in my office, or the times that they wanted me to play and I said later, I have work to do. I thought about Mark asking if we could go fishing on the weekend and Katie wanting to fly the new kite her grandmother bought for her.

I always had so little time for them. And now they were gone.

I felt like the worst father in the world, and there was no taking that back.

I left the coffee cup sitting on the deck railing and went back into the house. I needed to get dressed and get busy. I had to keep myself busy before my thoughts overwhelmed me.

After a quick shower, I got dressed in jeans and a printed t-shirt, slipped on a soft shell jacket and a pair of boots and left the house. I had one of my 1911s in a paddle holster on my right hip with two spare magazines in holsters on my left. My SKS was slung over my right shoulder and my go bag was over my left, repacked and stocked with more ammo.

I exited through the front door and walked down the slope of grass, heading right for the group. Brian was still leading them in PT. They had moved on to up/downs, which brought back memories of football practice in high school.

My legs started to ache just watching. As I said, I was a bit out of shape these days.

When I drew closer, I saw Brian's backpack and STG lying about ten feet to his left. Good boy. I hoped Bob, wherever he was, was also packing.

I had to find Charlie and let him have his pick from the arsenal. I also had to check on supply and medical and make sure these designated homes were staffed. I'd need to make lists of supplies and put together a group I could lead on a supply run.

And I almost forgot that I had promised to review Bob's security and patrol procedures. I started this morning feeling like I had nothing to do, and now I found myself wondering where I'd find the time.

"Okay, three more, people. Don't quit on me now!" Brian shouted.

He saw me from the corner of his eye and he held up a finger in my direction.

"Okay, two more, push it, come on. And one more, you can do it! Great job, everyone. Go ahead and take a minute, have some water."

I kneeled next to Brian's gear and set down my own. He knelt beside me and reached for his canteen.

"Good morning," he said as he unscrewed the cap. "Did you sleep well?"

"Yes," I said, watching him drink. "I see you've been busy."

He nodded his head and recapped his canteen. "I'm real proud of them. They were all anxious and raring to go. They've been at it forty-five minutes now."

"Excellent work." I said and punched his shoulder.

"What's on your agenda?" Brian asked.

"I'm going to make sure Bob is doing okay with his recruitment and training and make sure he has patrols set up and schedules worked out. I have to find someone I can put in charge of supplies and medical. And I'm going take a few people on a supply run today."

"What time? I'll be ready."

I shook my head.

"Negative. You've got a lot to do with these folks and Bob's people. If there's a run on us like over at Providence, I want our people to be prepared. They need to be able to defend themselves. I want all of your attention focused on getting these boots ready."

"Yes, sir," he saluted me. "I'm going to start spending my time at the command post, so if you're looking for me, you'll probably find me there. If you have time later, check in with me and I'll show you our command structure and training schedule. I've already picked out a few of the guys here that I think would make good squad leaders."

"I'll make time. I'm looking forward to it."

We both stood and brushed grass and soil from our pants. I shouldered my gear and said, "Catch you later."

"Yeah, dude, later." After I took a few steps he called back, "Be careful, man."

"You know it."

As I passed the group who were now sitting on the grass and enjoying their break, I waved to them and they all waved back. Brian immediately fell back into drill instructor mode and ordered the boots to their feet for another round.

While he counted off more up/downs, I turned north on Crest Drive toward what would now be known as the Randall Oaks Police Department. It was only a two minute walk, and I was really enjoying the morning air.

The garage door stood open, but only one car was now parked in the driveway. The two men were still inside moving things around. I saw that they'd actually been bringing furniture out to the garage area. They now had a couple of desks, some filing cabinets, a work bench table and some chairs, turning it into a nice bullpen.

I stepped into the cool garage. "Hey fellas. How's it going?"

The small man at the desk I recognized as Dennis. He walked his dog every morning in the grassy common field outside my home. He had short cropped brown hair and bright blue eyes. We'd exchanged friendly nods or a wave from time to time, but I didn't really know him.

"Good, sir," Dennis said.

"We're fine, sir," the other man said.

I'd seen him around before, too, but I didn't know his name. He was a pretty tall and stocky fellow. Not the type of guy you'd want to meet in an alley at night.

"I'm sorry, but I don't know your name," I said to the big man.

"My name is Rory." He stuck out his hand and I shook. "Nice to meet you, sir."

"Good to meet you. Is Bob around?"

Dennis nodded and cocked a thumb toward the small door behind him. "He's inside setting things up, sir."

"Thank you, Dennis." I started to walk pass the two men and then stopped a couple of feet away. I turned around and said, "Guys, just call me Matt. Please."

Both men looked at each other for a moment and then turned to me and nodded.

"Thanks." I left them to their business.

I entered the house and stepped into the kitchen. It was empty but I could hear movement from one of the other rooms. Entering the family room, I called out, "Bob?"

"Yeah?" he responded. "Who's there?"

"It's Matt."

I leaned over and set my bag down on the sofa and leaned my SKS against the sofa arm. Bob entered the room as I stood up. He had a big smile on his face.

"Hey fearless leader," Bob said. "What a fine morning, huh?"

I couldn't help but smile at his enthusiasm. "It sure is. And it looks like you're off to a good start."

"Oh, yeah," he said. "I feel like I got so much done since last night. You know, when I was a patrolman I never realized how much work it was for the sergeants getting rosters and teams set up each morning. It takes some thought and time but I'm digging it."

"Show me what you've done, Bob." I took a seat on the sofa.

"Let me grab my stuff," he said, walking quickly back toward the room he'd been in just moments ago.

I did a sight check on my SKS while I waited for Bob to return. I had one round in the chamber and the safety was switched on; I was ready to go.

I hadn't had much time to think about last night. When we returned from Providence I was so tired I actually went to bed after a brief planning session with Brian and Bob. Now that I had a moment, I considered how many people I'd actually killed in the last couple of days. Well, they weren't exactly people, not anymore, but still, I'd killed at least seven or eight, maybe as many as ten.

I'd never hesitated. That shook me a bit. That first crazy I'd shot had been pure reaction. I didn't consider the circumstances, didn't consider the consequences, I just lined up my shot and took it.

What kind of person had I become in seventy-two hours?

Bob returned carrying a mid-size white board on a tripod and a few notebooks. He set up the board and lay the notebooks on the coffee table.

Using one of the markers as a pointer, Bob went to the board. "As you can see, I've created basically three divisions. We have administrative, patrol and sentry.

"Administrative is basically me and a couple of aides responsible for booking, paperwork, and communicating assignments as well as replacements, all that jazz.

"Right now I have Dennis and Rory but if we actually have to detain anyone, I'll have to get more help. Charlie is acting as my deputy and he'll be responsible for whatever comes up if I'm not immediately available.

"As for patrol, I have three three-man teams, each of which will have an eight-hour patrol shift. They'll use one of the vehicles to cruise around the perimeter of the community in case we're breached. I have a backup vehicle in case we need to scramble another patrol quickly.

"Sentry is pretty similar to patrol: three teams, three men per team. They'll stand guard at the main gate and alert us if anything is happening out on the street or in the vicinity. They can call on patrol for backup if need be. I'm working now on getting a reserve group that can fill in any of the areas in case someone gets sick or has to miss a shift for any reason. That's where I'm at right now."

"That's really good work, Bob."

I really was quite impressed. Both he and Brian had accomplished so much in so little time, both surpassing my expectations, and I was greatly pleased.

"You've really taken this and made it your own, Bob. This is fantastic. You should have taken that sergeant's exam a long time ago."

"Thank you," Bob said, embarrassed by my praise.

"Do you have anyone on patrol or sentry with law enforcement experience?" I asked.

Bob nodded his head. "Actually, there are two guys—Pete Gallagher and Ron Kuznicki—who were patrolmen with our local PD. They're both team leads for their respective patrols. And we have Al Sanchez who is a retired sergeant from the Chicago PD but works for the Sanitation department now. He's third patrol team leader. I'm pretty happy about that."

"What's the plan for training?" I asked.

"I'm having the men go through two training phases. First is training with the militia. I think that Brian's training will thoroughly prepare them to fight and engage any threat. They'll be able to fall into the militia if needed. The second phase of the training, which I hope happens concurrently, will be making arrests, processing and detaining individuals. That's going to be hard since we're policing our own."

"You know, Bob, I came to offer my assistance but it looks like you have things under control. I'd probably be more in the way, so I'm just gonna let you do what you need to do, and if you need anything, just let me know."

"I appreciate the vote of confidence, chief," Bob said. "I do need one thing, since you mention it."

"Name it."

"We need a couple of shotguns, don't care what kind, but pump action is preferred. We're a bit short for patrol."

"Does everyone else have a weapon?" I asked.

"There're a lot of folks that hunt deer and waterfowl, so most of them had their own shotgun and bolt action rifle." Bob laughed at the look on my face. "Why are you so surprised? This isn't the city. People here actually enjoy their constitutional rights, just like you. Well, you actually enjoy more than others... "

I laughed. "Yeah, I have this bad habit of assuming things. I just see people around the community and I don't think of them as the type to go out and shoot deer and duck."

"Now they're targeting zombies. Go figure."

I didn't correct him by telling him that zombies were arisen dead and these things were still alive; I knew what he meant, and I had other matters to attend.

"I'll get a couple of shotguns here sometime today. How are you on ammo right now?"

"I think we're okay for now. I had the guys pool their ammo. They've got quite a load of birdshot. We'll probably need some for the bolt action rifles but I haven't yet compiled a list of calibers. It would be nice if we all carried the same weapons, though."

"Well, we'll see. Maybe we can make that happen."

"Oh, yeah, more than anything else we need radios. We need to be able to communicate with patrol and vice-versa. I'd say that is even more important than ammo right now."

"Maybe we can make that happen, too. I'm going on a scavenge run later this afternoon. I'm hoping to grab some ammo somewhere, and I might get lucky and score you and your guys some matching weapons."

"That would be great. You need help?"

I shook my head. "No. I need you to keep doing what you're doing. By the way, if possible, could you send a group down to Providence to check in and make sure everything is okay? I want them to know we're concerned."

"Already did that, chief," Bob said, smiling. "If you're gonna wake up at seven in the morning, you're gonna miss a few things."

"I've been up since six-thirty, thank you very much," I said. "So what's the report?"

"They're fine. They handled the run of crazies and the rest of the night was quiet. Apparently, those things don't travel much at night.

Frank said he was surprised that the group actually showed up after dark."

I remembered what Kappy had said the morning after about the crazies sleeping through the night. He seemed to think it was when they regenerated or something. I also remembered having a run-in with some crazies during the night at the Dunkin Donuts, though. Perhaps they slept during the night unless there was something to disturb their sleep.

"That's good to know," I said. "I'll see you later, Bob."

Katherine Dudyck was a tall, leggy blonde who lived with her life partner just a few doors down from me. During Desert Storm, Kat served as supply sergeant for one of the battalions in-country.

Although she hadn't had any combat experience in the Gulf, she was qualified on the M16 rifle as well as the M9 pistol. That was as important to me as was her experience in supplying a large group of soldiers. She was the perfect choice for my supply officer, and she'd eagerly agreed to take on the role.

Kat opened the door a minute after I knocked. She was wearing a pale green bath robe and her blond hair was wet. She looked pretty as hell, too, but I admonished myself for going there.

"Hello, Matt. Sorry, I just got out of the shower. Come on in."

She stepped back to admit me and then closed and locked the door. I followed her up the small flight of steps to the main floor of the raised ranch.

"Go on in the kitchen. Sam's got coffee ready. I'll be with you shortly."

"Take your time."

I watched her walk down the hallway toward her bedroom and then poked my head into the kitchen.

"Good morning, Sam."

Samantha, or Sam to her friends, was a quite beautiful brunette. Although not as tall and graceful as Kat, Sam was very athletic and had a body to die for. My late wife had often commented that Sam was a knock-out, to which I'd always reply I hadn't noticed.

"Morning, Matt," she said. "Can I get you a cup?"

She was wearing a pair of tight gray jogging pants and a pink camisole shirt. Even without makeup she was pretty.

"Absolutely. Thanks."

I had to avert my eyes. Sammy wasn't wearing a bra and it was a bit cool in here.

"Put your stuff in the living room," Sam said as she set about the task of pouring my coffee.

I turned and stepped into the living room to lay my bag on the floor next to the sofa and leaned my SKS against it. I returned to the kitchen and sat at the table. Sam put a mug of great smelling coffee in front of me.

"So how's it going?" Sam asked as she sipped her brew.

"Everything's good this morning."

I was horrible at small talk. My wife had once told me that during our first date she thought I was completely uninterested in her and that trying to have a conversation with me was like pulling teeth.

"I heard you had a big night," Sam said. She reached across the table and touched my hand. "You weren't hurt, were you?"

"No," I said, feeling a bit uncomfortable.

When my wife was alive, we'd had Kat and Sam over a dozen of times for dinner. They were both down-to-earth girls and they were really interesting, but Sam was always a bit too touchy-feely for my taste. It's always hard for any man when a woman other than his wife gets physical, especially when his wife is in the same room.

"That's good. We need you now more than ever. We need to take real good care of you."

"You keep sweet-talking him like that, Sam, and I'm going to get real jealous," Kat said, entering the kitchen like a model strutting down the catwalk. She'd changed into dark blue jeans and a light blue crewneck sweater. Her hair was still a bit wet.

"I only have eyes for you, Kat," Sam said and then winked at me.

Kat poured a cup of coffee and sat in the chair to my left. Her shoulder brushed mine and her elbow rested up against my forearm.

She smiled. "We do need to take care our fearless leader, though."

Before I realized what was happening, she had set down her coffee and turned and wrapped her arms around me.

With her mouth against my neck she said, "I'm so sorry about Alyssa."

Sam now had my hand in both of hers and said, "Bob told us. I feel so bad. Alyssa was so sweet. She never judged us and she always had the best advice."

"And you lost those precious little babies," Kat muttered against my neck. She broke out into tears then. Her hot breath and warm tears felt like fire against my neck.

I nodded my head slightly. Kat clung to my neck for another minute and then suddenly she released me and kissed my cheek.

"Shit, I need a tissue now," she said and got up from the table.

Finally Sam let go of my hand. "Are you sure you're okay?" she asked. "You know you can let your feelings go here."

"Thank you." I was uncomfortable than ever. "I'm fine. Thank you for the offer but I've done my grieving."

Kat returned and sat back down. She put her right arm over my shoulder and then picked up her coffee with her left hand.

"Sorry about that. Girl moment. We're past it now."

I smiled at that and sipped my own coffee. "I just stopped by to see how things were going and if you needed my help with anything."

"We are ready to go operational," Kat said, perking up. "Last night Sam and I started our supply inventory. We had everyone turn over whatever extra supplies they had. Let me tell you, lots of people around here buy in bulk. Everyone was willing to pitch in and we got a pretty good stash going already. I'll have a supply list for you later this afternoon. Sam and I will also put together a necessities list, as well.

"Do you have someone who will be in charge of medical? We'll need to work with that person, I guess, to see what critical medical items they'll need."

"Not yet, but I have someone in mind. When do you think you'll have that information?" I asked. "I don't mean to rush you, but I'm making a supply run this evening, and it would be great if I had a critical list."

"What time are you leaving?" Kat asked.

"An hour after the sun sets. Let's say... seven o'clock?"

"Oh, we can have it done by then, no problem."

"You're the best, Kat," I said. "You too, Sammy."

Sam smiled. I knew she liked when I called her Sammy.

"I'll stop by the supply depot before I leave. Thank you both so much for what you're doing."

"It's the least we can do," Kat said.

"I have a lot to do, so I'm going to get going. Thank you for the coffee and for your condolences."

"Take care," Sam said.

She got up from her chair and came to me. She took both of my hands in hers and looked me in the eyes.

"Do you want to stay with us here? I know it must be hard to be alone right now. We'd love to have you."

I blushed a bit, grateful for the invite.

"I appreciate it, Sammy, but I'm not alone. My brother's with me. Although I'd definitely prefer the company of two beautiful women, he'll do."

Sammy kissed my cheek and Kat did the same. It was hard leaving the comfort of two beautiful women when all I had to look forward to was a scraggly drill sergeant living in my family room.

$$* * *$$

It was just after noon when I reached Ravi's townhome. She was alone—her roommates were willing participants in Brian's boot camp. We sat in the living room, a tray of iced tea on the coffee table.

Ravi was about five-two with black hair and a very light complexion. She resembled a vampire from a popular cable show. She was wearing khaki pants and a black cable knit sweater, and a red headband to hold her hair in place.

"Just so you know, I am not an ER nurse," Ravi said. "There are probably more things that I can't handle than I can."

"I understand, Ravi," I said.

I poured a glass of iced tea and set it on a coaster in front of me. "Even if you're not an ER nurse, you know a lot more than the rest of us. I'm sure you'll do fine."

Ravi bit her lip. She wasn't having any of it.

"This seems like such a big responsibility. I don't know if I want it."

I smiled. I knew that Ravi was a very capable nurse. As a nurse practitioner, Ravi collaborated on a daily basis with physicians, provided referrals, counseled and educated patients on health behavior, diagnosed and treated acute illnesses and injuries, ordered and performed diagnostic tests, prescribed medications, and also sutured minor wounds.

She was being more than just modest. More than anything, I think she was concerned with being the only person to make important medical decisions; she would have no doctor to concur with her diagnosis.

"Ravi, I know what nurse practitioners are capable of. And I know what you're capable of. If I didn't think you could handle it, I wouldn't ask you."

"Thank you for your confidence, but it's not the same. At the hospital I have equipment, I have medications and colleagues, we have schedules and rotations. Without that there would be too much confusion."

"Well that's what I need from you, Ravi. Create schedules and rotations. Help train people and create your own colleagues. I'll try to get equipment and medications for you. I'll get you some help, too. I know that David Green was a corpsman in the navy. He can help you deal with severe traumas, God forbid. I really need you to do this, Ravi. We all need you to do this."

Ravi was silent for a moment, biting her lip. She rubbed her hands together, realized what she was doing, and shoved her hands into her pockets.

"What's really wrong, Ravi?" I asked. I got up from the sofa, moved to her, and sat beside her on the love seat. "What can I say to get you on board with us?"

She looked at me for a moment and then said, "I'm afraid to make a mistake. I'm afraid to let anyone down. And I am definitely not a leader."

I took a deep breath, beginning to lose my patience.

"Look, Ravi, you're the most qualified person we have to be the administrator for our medical unit. You've got the experience and the know-how. But I'm not going to force you to do anything you're not comfortable with. I'll find another way."

When she didn't respond I stood up and walked back to the sofa. I slung my bag over my shoulder and hefted the SKS.

"If you change your mind, let me know. We'd love to have your help."

Ravi continued to bite her lip and she wouldn't meet my stare. I walked slowly toward the door and opened it.

Before I crossed the threshold I said, "Kat and Sam are probably going to stop by soon. Would you mind giving them a list of what you feel are critical medications and supplies to have on hand? That would be a big help."

She didn't say anything, but she nodded.

"Thank you, Ravi. See you around."

I closed the door behind me and walked slowly down the three concrete stairs. The morning had been going so well, it was merely a matter of time before I'd suffer a setback.

Although we had three very important divisions up and operational, having a competent medical unit would become extremely important. Winter was on the way and common colds and illnesses were bound to rip through the community if we remained under lockdown. And as we started going on more supply missions, there was always the risk of severe injury from the crazies we might come into contact with during our foray.

Well, I still had Dave Green I could tap into. As a medical corpsman, he'd certainly have experience with the latter of our problems. We'd just have to hope that through sanitation and limited exposure to outside parties that we'd experience only mild illness through the winter months.

As the sun reached its midday peak, I headed out to pick my group for the supply mission I had planned. I wanted at least several hours to work through a plan, some basic tactics, weaponry and transportation before we went out. I also had to map our course and select stores and shops that were not too far away and would yield the best supplies.

I was actually looking forward to getting out on the road again. Maybe by luck I'd run into the crazy that infected my wife. Although that seemed impossible given I had no idea what that thing looked like, it was still a comfort to think about it.

CHAPTER 12:
BEST LAID PLANS

The rest of my afternoon was busy. I planned on meeting with Dave Green to discuss his role as administrator and facilitator of the Randall Oaks Medical Unit, but by one o'clock it was clear I wasn't going to have time today.

After leaving Ravi's house my first order of business was to secure transportation for my supply run. Since this was our first run I wanted to be as light as possible, but at the same time be able to transport as much as possible. I had no idea if we'd be able to make additional supply runs, so we needed to take as much as we could on this trip.

It was a pretty nice day, so I pulled my 10-speed down from the hooks on my garage wall and took a ride around the community. I was looking out for vehicles that I thought would serve my purpose; when I found something to my liking I would kindly commandeer the vehicle in the name of community security.

After riding around the west half of our community my options appeared pretty slim and I was a bit disappointed. I counted six mini vans and two panel vans but nothing larger.

I discounted all of the SUV's because they did not allow enough cargo space. I didn't even consider a coupe, sport or sedan.

The mini vans could work if we drove more than one, but I was leery about splitting up the group or supplies. I had no idea how dangerous it might be out there and I would feel safer if we all stayed together and I could better control movement and action.

My dissatisfaction did not last long. After leaving the west side I pedaled my bike down Cameroon Drive with the goal of passing our north wall—the less populated area of our community—and checking out the field house security post Bob planned to have set up.

As I came around the bend where Cameroon swung around and opened up to the playground, I saw the UPS truck parked in the small visitor's parking section to the west of the playground. I had no idea why it was there or how I'd missed it earlier but it was exactly what I was looking for.

It took more than an hour to track down the driver. I had a couple of Bob's men help me go door-to-door but that didn't yield any relevant information. Almost everyone was either out with the militia or doing something else.

After we gave up knocking on doors, I let Bob's men go back to their duties. I made my way over to where Bri and the militia were currently working out squad assignments.

I pulled Bri aside. "I need to make a quick announcement."

"What's up?" he asked.

"I need to find out who drives the UPS truck that's parked out by the playground."

He nodded his head and turned to his company.

"Listen up!" he shouted. The group stopped what they were doing and turned in our direction. "They're all yours," he said.

"Good afternoon," I said.

I felt like I was back at work addressing a group of potential college students in my current life or green recruits in my former.

"I'm trying to find the driver of the UPS truck parked by the playground. Anyone know anything about it?"

I saw a hand come up from one of the squads to our left. I waved my hand and motioned for the man to come over to me.

A plump man wearing a grey jogging outfit steadily made his way through the group. He wore a Cubs baseball cap over his greasy brown hair, sporting a thick beard and mustache that he continuously scratched unconsciously as he approached.

"That's my truck," he said. He stopped a couple of feet in front of me and stuck out his hand. "Alex Baldwin."

"Hello, Alex," I said and shook. "I'd like to borrow your truck. I'm going to make a supply run and your truck is the biggest thing I can find to hold a group of men and a large number of supplies. Is that okay with you?"

Alex nodded his head and scratched his beard again. "Can I come with? I'll drive."

I considered this a moment. I didn't know Alex, so obviously he wasn't on the list of men I'd already chosen for the job. Since my life was going to be in the hands of these men, I'd been very particular about my selection. I had concerns about Alex joining us.

"You are aware that we're going to be going out there, right?" gesturing in the direction of our gates.

"Yes," Alex said.

"There's a chance that we're going to run into those crazies out there. Maybe a whole lot of them. This could be dangerous. Are you okay with that?"

"Yes."

"Can you handle a gun, Alex?" I asked.

Alex nodded again. "I hunt duck. I'm really familiar with shotguns."

"Can you handle a pump-action?"

"Sure." There he was scratching that beard again.

"Why do you want to go with us, Alex?" I asked.

"Aside from it being my truck? Do you have someone that can handle it? I've been driving that truck for seven years in all kinds of weather, in all kinds of traffic. No one is going to drive that better than me. I think I'm your best chance of making it there and back in one piece. At least while you're in my truck."

I looked at Bri who shrugged and raised his eyebrows in a look that said 'why not'?

I turned back to Alex. "Okay, you're on the crew. Report to the command post in one hour. I'll brief the team and we're going to spend the last hours of daylight drilling. Bring your shotgun with you."

Alex smiled. "Well alright."

"Thanks, Bri," I said.

I got on my bike and started to ride back toward the command post.

Behind me I heard Brian say, "Get back to your squad. Fall in! Double time it, Baldwin!"

I grinned. Brian always was a ballbuster.

No decorating work was done at the command post. Brian had his hands full trying to get the militia underway and I was busy with my own projects. For the time being, the staging furniture would do.

I sat at the dining room table with my notebook in front of me, creating a list that consisted of the seven men that would be accompanying me on our supply mission and what job each would be responsible for doing.

Alex would be driving the UPS truck and providing vehicle security with Hector while the rest of the group scavenged. The scavenge teams would be split into two: Ken and John would be on my team. Charlie would lead Mike and Ignatius.

All of the men I selected were capable of handling a firearm and all were single, which was my preference for this mission. I refused to be responsible for a family losing a father.

Although I did not plan on losing any of the men, we all had to be prepared should the situation arise. I briefly considered finding David Green and having him come along as our medic but I couldn't justify leaving the community without medical assistance in case of an emergency.

I'd have to tap into my basic training if anyone was wounded. I'd have to remember to pack my aid kit and do my best to stabilize until we could get further medical assistance. I hoped it wouldn't come to that.

From my shirt pocket I pulled out the two sheets of paper that Kat had given me about an hour ago. One was her supply list, which I had to admit was quite hefty. When I returned to her house to collect Ravi's request, we'd spent about fifteen minutes trying to whittle the list down a bit but Kat was adamant about having everything.

Eventually I gave up and promised I'd do my best to get everything she asked for.

The second sheet of paper was Ravi's critical supplies list. Although Ravi would not commit to a leadership role for our medical center she did promise to compose the list. Most of the items listed were not going to be easy to get. Some stuff I might find at the local Walgreen's or CVS, but for many of the mechanical items we'd need to raid St. Ann's hospital, which I wasn't looking forward to breaking into. I had no idea what to expect. Surely the hospital staff would not have left and abandoned their patients. There were bound to also be others who would be in search of the same medical supplies and I wanted to avoid any skirmishes with humans.

I had started to write out a list of possible stores that we would hit when I heard the garage door open. A moment later Brian came up the stairs; fresh sweat dripped down his face and his long hair was plastered against his neck and forehead. He went to the mini fridge and opened it.

"Want water?" he asked as he bent and grabbed a bottle.

"No thanks," I said.

I pushed the notebook into the middle of the table and put my face into my hands.

Brian pulled up a seat next to me, cracked open the bottle of water and drank it down, belched loudly, then tossed the empty plastic bottled into the open trash can with a hook shot.

"Two points." He looked at me and asked, "What's up with you?"

I looked at him between my fingers and then took my hands away from my face. I slid the notebook toward him and waited while he looked it over.

"Well?" I prodded.

He was quiet for a moment and then he got up and went to the refrigerator. He returned with another bottle of water in his hand. When he sat down he asked, "You sure you want to do this?"

"I have to," I responded, perhaps a bit too defensively.

"You don't have to do anything," Brian said. He opened the water and took a long swig.

"They made me their leader and they're expecting me to take care of them."

"Yeah, but they're not expecting you to do that by going out there into crazy-infected streets to get toilet paper and Band Aids."

I shook my head. It was always hard arguing with Brian because, although he looked like a wasted rocker, he was actually a pretty smart guy. Often his arguments were too logical and difficult to debate.

"I'm doing this," I said. "What I'm asking you is what you think about the people I'm bringing and the places I plan on hitting."

He picked up the notebook and looked at it again. Without taking his eyes off the paper he asked, "Do you really want to take these guys out there right now? I mean, none of them has any training. They're liable to either shoot each other or freeze right in the middle of a fire-fight."

"You have a better suggestion?"

"Hell, yeah. Why not just take me and Bob, and maybe Charlie? We made a good group yesterday and you know you can trust us."

"I trust you guys, sure, but I can't leave the community without some people who know what they're doing."

"Then leave Bob and take me."

I let out a deep sigh.

"Look, man. I need you here and that's final. Bob's a good guy but he's still too unsure of himself. He already willingly turned over leader-ship remember?"

"We'll be back in a few hours, dude. He can handle it."

"Bri, enough. You're not going."

"I'm the big brother here," Brian said. He slammed down the water bottle.

"I'm not going to argue with you." I stood up from the table. Before I could leave he grabbed my arm and pulled me back into the chair.

"Just tell me why you're acting like a pussy. What's the problem? Why don't you really want me to go?"

I turned on him then and we both stood face to face. It had been a long time since my brother and I had a physical fight with each other. During our teen years we'd come to blows over stupid things, but as adults we'd been able to talk things out without fists. At the moment, however, all of the pressures I had felt building up got the better of me. All of the anger and rage I'd been keeping bottled up inside over the loss of my wife and children surfaced.

I grabbed him by the shirt and shoved him backward. His legs hit the chair he'd been sitting on and he fell backward, trying to catch himself before he actually fell, but failing to do so.

"You want to know why? I'll tell you! You're all I have left. My wife is dead. My children are dead. You're the only family I have left and I am not going to risk losing you!"

Surprised by my sudden fury, Brian did not react as I expected. Instead of getting to his feet and knocking me on my ass, he sat down in his chair and pulled in close to the table.

"Sit down," he said. When I didn't move, he looked up at me. I saw no anger in his eyes, only sadness. "Dude, sit down."

My breathing was labored and I could feel my arms and hands shaking. Adrenaline was coursing through my veins. I sat in my chair and tried to calm my breathing. I could feel a tension headache coming on. My temples throbbed, I must have been grinding my teeth again, a sure sign that I was angry, my wife would say.

Brain picked up Kat's list again and without looking at me he said, "You have to cut this down by a lot. You wouldn't fit more than half of this into that UPS truck. And half of this isn't important yet anyway."

As was his way, Brian chose to ignore our argument and move on as though nothing happened. I'd always admired the fact that he didn't hold grudges and could easily brush things off. On the other hand, I could hold a grudge like no one's business.

Apologies did not come easily for me. I don't know why but for some reason an apology seemed like a sign of weakness to me.

Rather than apologize I said, "Kat's not going to be happy if I edit her list."

Finally turning to me Brian said, "Who cares what Kat thinks? She's not the one going out there and risking her life for toilet paper.

You asked for her opinion and now it's your job to make the final decision."

I nodded my head, again finding it difficult to argue with his logic. I took a pen from my shirt pocket and tossed it across the table to him. "Start lining out."

Brian lifted the pen. He continued to look at me. I could see he wanted to say something, but it had always been difficult for him to express his feelings.

I knew my brother better than anyone else. In truth, he was a bit bipolar with extreme sociopathic tendencies. Over the last few days I'd noticed changes in him, but whether or not these changes were for the better remained to be seen.

After a moment he turned away and got to work on the list. While he started scratching items off I turned back to my own list of stores and shops I planned to raid. Some of the things Brian said made me reconsider my original plan.

I realized I was being too optimistic. Hell, from the beginning of this whole mess I never let the seriousness of our situation actually sink in. I'd purposefully been trying not to think too seriously about things because then I'd think about my children, and then I'd think about my wife, and then I'd break down.

Even now just thinking about them made my eyes water. My family was my life and now they were gone. Not only had they passed, but they'd died in a terrible way. As a husband, as a father, and as a man, I was supposed to protect my family. In this, I had failed miserably.

I put my face in my hands and cried silently. It was all I could think to do besides grabbing my gun and seeking revenge, which I wanted so badly to do. I knew, though, that killing those pathetic creatures would not bring my family back to me. And I also knew that my wife would not like the person I'd become if I let my dark side take control.

It would be easier to just let myself go, to drink myself into a stupor and go all terminator on the first group of crazies I made contact with. It would be easier to just forget about everyone else and their survival and just allow myself to rage and let my anger burn white-hot.

Yet what is easiest is not always best. I needed to put my personal feelings aside.

Although I had not been able to save my family, I could make a difference for others. Instead of throwing what was left of my life away and going down in a blaze of glory, I could actually do some good. I could honor my family and their memory by helping those that needed me now.

I leaned back in my chair and took my hands from my eyes. The cool air struck my face and was welcome. I wiped away hot tears with my sleeve, and when I finally looked at Brian, he pretended to be focused on his task.

I went to the refrigerator and got a bottle of water, drank half of it down, and put it back in.

At the sink, I splashed tepid water on my face and dried off with a paper towel. I stood with my hands on the counter and looked over at Brian in the dining room.

He was right. This group of guys I'd selected weren't exactly the ideal bunch for this mission. I don't know what I was thinking. I expected to be able to spend a few hours running over tactics, movement and fire drills before we struck out.

When I was a platoon leader, this planning would have made sense because I would have been working with trained soldiers and we'd have just been going over details.

Was I going to get these guys killed?

I couldn't answer that question honestly right now. But whether it was now or later, everyone was going to find themselves in danger.

The crazies were definitely spreading, and if this event continued without cease, things were going to get worse by the day. Although I was their leader and would do everything in my power to protect them and help them survive, they would need to learn to fend for themselves. I might not always be here for them.

I had to believe that these men would realize the seriousness of our situation and would understand the seriousness of their actions. I needed to rely on Charlie to help me make sure that we'd all be safe and in control. And I'd be in a better state of mind knowing that Brian was here safe and should anything happen to me, the rest of the community would be in good hands.

Back in the dining room I picked up my notebook and looked it over again. Looking at things through different eyes, I started to cross out most of the stores and shops I originally planned to visit. Most of them were too far away and I had to assume that many of them would have already been picked over by people who realized earlier on how serious things might become.

It took about an hour but Brian and I managed to edit our lists and come up with a more realistic set of items. In another fifteen minutes we'd meet with the men I selected and do our best to train them. Hopefully, it would be enough.

Brian and I spent the last several hours preparing my team as best we could. For the most part, it wasn't as bad as we expected. All of the men were familiar with firearms and most were used to being in the field with friends while hunting and the need to constantly check your fields of fire. Being aware of the location of others was not a new idea for them.

Although we did not practice live-fire exercises, we made the training as realistic as possible. We devoted a large part of our time to training in and around the vehicle as we expected that if we were attacked the vehicle would be our rally point and we needed to defend our cargo at all costs.

We spent some time on movement as a squad as well as in smaller teams. We drilled on clearing close quarters battle and situational awareness.

It was just after seven in the evening that I decided we were as ready as we could be when we first heard an alarm sound. I had no idea that Bob had managed to find an old hand-cranked air raid siren that he set up at the sentry post. It was loud and scared the hell out of us.

When the alarm sounded, Alex was behind the wheel of the UPS truck with an M9 pistol while Ken, John and I were providing vehicle security. Charlie and his team were 10 yards away practicing fire and maneuver drills.

"What the fuck?" Brian shouted over the alarm. "What is that?"

"I have no idea," I said.

I moved away from the truck and looked up Cameron Drive toward our front gate. Even from this distance I could see there was a commotion, although I couldn't determine the cause.

Before I could react I saw both of Bob's designated patrol vehicles fly past, Bob bouncing in the front seat of the lead vehicle.

"Something's happening at the gate," Charlie said.

"Fall in!" Brian shouted. "Fall in! Move!"

And within seconds both teams had formed up at the truck and started to pile in. When all men were in the cargo area I slammed the side door closed and jumped into the front with Alex.

"Go!"

Alex popped the clutch and already had the truck moving before I was able to close the side door.

"Careful with your weapons," I heard Brian saying in the back. "Keep them pointed at the floor and keep your damn fingers off the triggers. Check your safeties."

Within half a minute we traveled down Cameron Drive and came up to the T-section that led to our main gate, where a crowd had already gathered. Bob's patrol cars were already there and Bob was out of the vehicle waving his arms signaling people to move back.

Alex blew his horn and shouted for people to get out of the way. After maneuvering around another vehicle that was blocking our way, the truck jumped the curb and plowed through the grass and brush, sliding to a stop just feet away from Bob's lead patrol.

Turning and facing the rear I said, "Brian, Charlie, get that crowd organized before someone gets hurt. I saw some folks with guns over there."

"On it," Brian said. "Charlie, on me." The two of them were out of the vehicle and moving toward their objective.

"Alex and Ken, stay with the truck. The rest of you with me," I said and we jumped out of the vehicle.

I went straight to Bob and his group, who were already gathered around the front gate. Just before I reached them, I saw them all jump back as if something had charged them.

When I was about ten feet from Bob I heard him roar, "Turn that damn alarm off already Ted!"

Ted, a veteran of the Korean War and our oldest resident at Randall Oaks, immediately stopped cranking his machine. His face was red and so drenched with sweat that I thought he might fall over from exertion at any moment.

I reached Bob and touched his shoulder. "What the hell's going on?"

Instead of answering he merely pointed his finger. I looked forward in the direction he pointed and saw a group of six or so crazies pushing against the gate.

"They don't look like zombies," one of Bob's men said.

"How long have they been here?" I asked the men who were on guard duty.

Kendall, a young man in his mid- twenties, tore his eyes away from the crazies long enough to look at me and say, "Just a few minutes ago. We saw them in the field across the way. As soon as Teddy there started cranking that alarm they rushed us."

"I almost pissed my pants," Martin said.

He stood next to Kendall. Both men held shotguns with barrels pointed at the sky.

"You didn't think about shooting them before they got right up against the gate?" I asked.

Martin looked surprised and Kendall looked back at the group of crazies. I turned to Bob who just shook his head and said, "We're working on it."

I sighed.

"What do you want to do?" Bob asked.

I turned to him now but didn't immediately respond.

The group of crazies pushed against the gate again and rattled the thick chain and padlock, but it held. I focused my attention on them for a moment. Although I'd seen plenty of them over the last few days, some up close and personal, I'd not had the chance to study them up until now.

Of the six that pushed against the gate, two were women. One of them I recognized as the woman who got taken down the night before at Providence.

Why they hadn't killed her before she changed was beyond me. How she made it out of Providence before she joined the ranks of the crazies was puzzling.

Their eyes were wild and dull at the same time. You could tell there wasn't much thought going on in their brains. Their bellies were hungry. They saw us and we looked like food. Grunts and meaningless words escaped from their lips as they continued to push up against the gate.

Their movement seemed monotonous. None of them screamed or howled. They just made their noises and reached into the gates and rocked against it trying to get their hands on a meal.

"What should we do?" Bob asked again.

I shook myself out of my daze. "Get everybody back from here. We don't know how infection spreads and everyone here could be getting exposed."

Bob and his men immediately turned and started to direct the crowd back.

"Get them at least thirty yards back, Bob!" I called out.

I turned to John, Mike, and Ignatius—Iggy to his friends—who stood beside me waiting for their orders.

"I want you all to line up in front of the gate here and take about ten steps back."

The men all looked at each other for a moment and then John started to move. The rest of them followed and formed up a line as I'd asked.

"Are we going to shoot them?" Iggy asked.

"Yes," I said, looking at Iggy to take in his facial expression.

Iggy looked at the crazies at the gate and then down at the turkey gun he held in his hands. "This is going to get messy."

I smiled. That's the spirit.

I was thrilled to see that he was more concerned about the mess we were going to make than the fact that he was going to shoot things that were once human beings.

I looked at the rest of the men and all of them were stone-faced and resolute. Ken racked the slide on his shotgun and pulled a couple of shells from his pants pocket to load his scattergun. As I watched, the rest of the men followed suit.

Taking my cue from my men, I thumbed a stripper clip into my SKS and released the charging handle. I stood in line next to Ken and leveled my weapon.

"I want everyone to fire two rounds on my mark. Aim for the head only."

Turning to my left I looked down the row at the men assembled. Each had their weapon raised and their eyes focused ahead at the crazies who'd been human not too long ago. In just seconds I would turn these men into killers.

"Fire!" I shouted and squeezed the trigger.

The blast of multiple scatterguns was much louder than expected. All of our shots were true and each of the crazies crumpled to the ground in a heap of dead flesh. Iggy was right; it was messy.

Not wanting to lose our momentum we'd built with training and our unexpected live-fire exercise, I signaled for my men to gather around me. I also motioned for Brian and Bob to join us.

When the men huddled around me I turned to Bob. "We need volunteers to clean up that mess but we need to take precautions. They need to cover their mouths and noses and try not to get any of the blood on their skin."

To Brian I said, "Grab some of those guys with guns and set up security for the clean-up crew. We don't know what sort of attention that alarm attracted but we need to be prepared."

"We'll be ready," Brian assured me.

"Good. And if your men have to engage, it's best if they can engage at a distance. Don't let them waste ammo, though."

"And us?" Charlie asked.

"Everyone else check ammo and reload if necessary. Training is over. We're mission ready. Load up and let's get moving."

"Alright," Alex said, bolting for his truck.

After reloading my SKS I started toward the UPS truck. Brian grabbed my arm and halted me. "Good luck, bro," he said. After a brief pause he gave me a quick hug. "Bring back some smokes if you can. I'm fucking dying here."

I smiled at my brother. That was the Brian I knew. It was the end of the world for all we knew and he was still concerned about his nicotine fix.

Within ten minutes the gates were opened and the clean-up crew began their gruesome task. I'd have to create a sanitation group when I returned. If this latest attack at our gates was any indication of what we could expect in the future, we needed to be prepared to clean it up. Although no one seemed particularly affected by the sight of the dead bodies, after a while they would begin to stink and draw unwanted attention.

Brian had a squad of eight men standing security for the clean-up crew. With his STG at the ready in his right hand, with his left he waved Alex forward. The UPS truck pulled onto the Route 20. I was on the road again and for some strange reason it felt good.

CHAPTER 13: SUPPLY

I buckled my seatbelt and slid forward in the passenger's seat of the UPS truck as we approached the Providence roadblock. My SKS stood between my legs with the muzzle pointed toward the roof of the vehicle.

"Slow down, Alex," I said.

There was a lot of activity at the roadblock, more than I'd seen the few times I'd been there. As we slowly approached on the eastbound lane, a man flagged us and motioned for us to stop.

"What is all this?" Alex asked.

"Don't know."

A line of three trucks of various sizes and make lined up on the westbound side of Route 20, just the other side of the roadblock. A group of men approached the first vehicle, talked to the driver for a minute and then directed the truck to move onto the Providence access road.

As the truck turned left into the complex I saw Phil talking to another group of men on our side of the roadblock. After a moment he looked in our direction. He held up a finger in a wait gesture and I nodded my head.

I was surprised to see Phil at the roadblock but I was also relieved. I expected Comedian again. Although the last time I interacted with Comedian he'd been docile, I knew that wasn't his normal attitude, especially toward folks from the Randall Oaks Community. I had no idea what we'd done to piss him off, but he certainly had no love for us.

"Are we okay?" Charlie asked from the rear.

I turned to look at him. He stood in the small space between our two seats. I saw concern on his face.

"No problem," I said.

I turned forward again and was relieved when I heard Charlie turn and move further back into the cargo area. What I just witnessed with those trucks made me nervous for reasons I didn't want to share with these men. At least not now.

Phil approached us finally, and as he made his way toward my side of the truck I turned to Alex and said, "Let me do the talking."

"Sure, it's your show." He looked away then and pretended to busy himself with checking the fuel gauge. He looked out his window and absently scratched at his beard.

I slid my door open as Phil jumped onto the first step of the truck and pulled himself up.

"Hello, Randall Oaks," Phil said. He smiled at me."Nice ride you have here. Even during the apocalypse, Brown delivers, huh?"

"Thanks," Alex said and rolled his eyes. He'd probably heard just about every UPS joke out there.

"Hey, Phil," I said and shook his hand. "What's up?"

He looked back over his shoulder for a moment and then back to me. His eyes wandered over toward Alex for a second and then back to me. "Can I talk to you a minute?"

"Sure." I released myself from the safety belt and jumped down onto the street, taking my SKS in hand as I went.

"Where are you headed?" Phil asked.

He was fidgety, which wasn't his usual manner. I'd only met him a few times but I felt I had a pretty good gauge of his personality, and this wasn't like him. Something was obviously on his mind.

"Supply run."

I liked Phil but I had to remind myself not to give too much information. Something about those trucks stopped at the roadblock and the one being diverted had my guard up.

"You and everyone else," Phil said.

He put his hand in his pocket, pulled out a stick of gum, and offered me one, which I accepted.

"Seems like I'm late to the game again," I said.

Phil nodded. "Kind of late in the day, too. It's not a good idea to travel during the night."

I shrugged. "I heard those things sleep in the night. Seems safer to me to travel when they're slumbering."

He nodded again. He looked down at his shoes and then at my SKS. When he spoke, he didn't look at me.

"Those things sleep during the night, sure. But at night you have to watch for people. They're getting desperate and they'll do anything to get their hands on supplies. We heard stories of people being ambushed by groups of marauders."

"Shit." I shifted my SKS to my other hand. "Have you guys lost anyone to ambush?"

He looked at me now and said, "A few. We lost more this afternoon on our second run. Frank is pretty upset about it."

"I imagine he would be."

We were both silent for a moment. I still didn't understand why he wanted to talk to me privately. He was avoiding eye contact with me, too.

"We really should be on our way," I said, breaking the silence.

"Yeah." Phil spit his gum out, lifted the baseball cap he wore and ran a hand over his thick hair before snugging the cap back down.

I turned and took a few steps when Phil said, "Randall Road has pretty much been picked clean as far as South Elgin. Don't waste your time there."

"What about further down Route 20?" I asked.

He shrugged. "Not too sure, but that's probably a better idea. I haven't heard much news from that direction."

I paused a moment and shifted my SKS again. Finally I asked, "Are those your trucks?"

Phil was silent. He dug into his pocket and pulled out his gum, deliberately unwrapping a stick. "Most of them. We've been at it all day."

"And the others?" I asked.

He shrugged again. "Neighbors."

I nodded. When he didn't elaborate I turned away. I jumped up onto the truck and set the SKS down beside my seat. I sat down and then turned so I could see Phil.

"Take it easy, Phil," I said and waved.

"You, too."

I watched him walk back toward the roadblock. When he was about ten feet away, he whistled and made a motion with his hand. A moment later the vehicle that blocked our path drove forward onto the Providence access road and cleared a path for us.

Phil waved us forward.

"Let's go," I said to Alex. Turning slightly in my seat I called to the guys in the back, "We're moving, gentlemen."

We drove past Providence and we were on our way again. I looked one last time at the truck that had been redirected. The driver was sitting on the floor beside his cab while a few other men were sorting through the cargo. I had a bad feeling that I really couldn't explain.

"Change of plan," I said to Alex as we approached the Randall exit. "Stay on East 20."

Alex nodded. After a moment he said, "What was that all about?"

"Supplies. It's all about supplies."

⋆ ⋆ ⋆

I was surprised that so much of Route 20 had been cleared of the vehicles that blocked much of the road only a few days ago when I navigated it in Kappy's Jeep.

On both sides, east and west, vehicles that once clogged the blacktop were now either pushed off into the ditch or the emergency lane in many places. Where the ditches and emergency lanes were filled, cars and trucks were flipped onto their sides in an attempt to clear the road.

I wasn't sure what to make of this development. What would prompt people to come out onto the road and take the time and effort to move the vehicles?

I guess it could suggest that people realized how important quick travel into neighboring communities could be. According to Phil, it could also be dangerous.

The night that I returned home and encountered the Providence roadblock came back to me. If I hadn't been a resident of their neighboring community, what would they have done? Sent me away? Worse?

That had been just a day after this whole snafu had begun. Given the developments of the last few days, I shuddered to think what those at Providence would do to anyone they considered unfriendly or hostile now that the world had changed.

The road was intermittently lit with the occasional street lamp but I could see Alex was watching the road and his surroundings intently. As we passed the first exit ramp after leaving Randall Road behind us I noticed Alex's grip tighten on the wheel and he increased his speed, putting a potential ambush point quickly behind us.

I don't think he was on edge because he'd heard any of the conversation with Phil but more the fact that we were out at night in potentially dangerous surroundings for the first time since the crazies appeared. Those things were still mysteries to us.

After twenty minutes of driving without incident we all started to relax a bit. We'd passed downtown Elgin which I felt was the biggest threat. If there were marauders who were indeed preying on road travelers, I expected ambush points at the main interchanges of Route 25 and 31.

I saw Kappy's restaurant about a quarter mile ahead of us because his sign was on, shining like a beacon in the night. I hadn't thought much of Kappy because I'd been so busy. It was only days ago that he saved my life, but it seemed like much longer.

"Alex, stop at that restaurant there on the right," I said.

Although this was certainly not a planned stop, there was no way I could pass Kappy's without stopping in to see him. I owed him. And I wondered if he'd accept another invitation to join me and become a member of our community. He had to be lonely in there.

"You hungry?" Alex raised an eyebrow. And there he went scratching his beard. He hadn't done that in the last twenty minutes and now it aggravated me.

"I need to see a friend," I said.

Alex slowed the UPS truck as we neared and came to a stop at the entrance to Kappy's. He did not pull in; we sat idle.

"This place is lit up like a Christmas tree. Is he trying to attract them things?" Alex said.

Charlie crouched beside me again. "What's going on, boss?"

"I need to check on someone," I said.

Alex was right. Kappy had every light in the place on, including the massive sign. I wasn't sure what to make of that. I surveyed the parking lot. The John Deere I'd rode on still sat against the sign post where I'd crashed. The heap of dead crazies that I'd picked off from Kappy's roof littered the ground around the green machine.

A light blue sedan was angled in front of Kappy's place about ten feet away from the door. The driver's door stood open. From this distance the car appeared empty. A man's body slumped over the hood of the vehicle. I couldn't tell if it was human.

More bodies lay together on the west side of the building next to the dumpster and grease trap. The way they huddled made me think of images I'd seen of concentration camps during World War II. I hoped those were crazies piled up out there and not people.

"What the hell happened here?" Charlie asked.

I glanced at him and saw that the rest of the men had gathered around him and were trying to get a look out the window. Their eyes were wide and I saw concern on their faces. This worried me because I knew what fear could do to men in combat.

"I don't know yet."

I asked Alex to pull the truck in closer to the blue car. I wanted to get a better look. The man slumped over the hood of the car was definitely a crazy. His skin was filthy with dried blood. His left hand was severed at the wrist and his pants were filthy with excrement and urine. He was still alive; his body rose slightly each time he took a breath.

"Jesus Christ," Alex breathed.

Aside from those crazies we'd executed at the front gates less than an hour ago, none of these men had come face to face with the abominations. They certainly hadn't seen any in this sort of condition.

Sliding the door open as quietly as I could, I stepped out of the truck, snagged my go bag and slid it over my neck and shoulder. Taking up my SKS I said, "I want Iggy to come with me. Charlie, I want you and Ken to come out here and keep a look out. The rest of you stay in the vehicle."

"What are we doing?" Alex asked, subconsciously scratching his beard again.

"I have to go inside for a minute," I said.

"Is that a good idea?" Charlie asked.

Charlie and Ken exited the truck and now stood beside me. When I looked at Charlie his eyes were locked on the pile of bodies to the west.

"No, but I have to do it anyway. Are you going to be okay out here?"

He looked at me now. "Yeah, I'm good, boss."

I stared at him.

"Seriously, I'm good. Do what you need to do."

I nodded my head. I had no doubt he could handle this.

"Listen to me good, gentlemen. Keep your eyes and ears open. If anything happens out here, blow the horn and I'll come running. Don't hesitate to use your guns, and if any of these fucking things moves, shoot. I mean it. Am I clear?"

Heads nodded. I was sure Charlie would do what he needed to but I had reservations about the others. They were not tested and I hoped they wouldn't have to be tonight.

"Watch the road, too. These things aren't the only things we have to worry about," I said.

"What does that mean?" Iggy asked. His large brown eyes bore into me.

"People. They may want what we have."

"Are you serious?" he asked.

"I'm dead serious. If anyone else comes into this place you set up a defensive perimeter around this vehicle and don't let them come close. I don't care what their intentions are."

I stepped in front of Iggy and made sure we had eye contact. "I need to know I can trust you, Iggy. I need to know that you're not going to freeze up if something happens. I can't have you hesitating if confronted by a threat, whether it's human or not. Can I count on you?"

He swallowed hard. "You can," he said after only a brief hesitation.

"Good," I said, although not convinced. "And I meant that for all of you. This isn't a game. Things can get serious real quick. Take a life to save your own."

They were all silent, taking that in. I had no idea what they were all thinking, but I was pretty sure I'd made my point. I expected trouble and we needed to be prepared.

"How come they haven't gotten up?" Alex asked. He came out of the driver's side to stretch.

"I don't really know. I think they…regenerate or something while they sleep. But they will wake if they hear a loud noise."

I remembered the alarm at the Dunkin' Donuts. The alarm had brought them running, just like a dinner bell.

"Should we kill them now, while they're sleeping?" Charlie asked.

I had already considered this. My concern was that a gunshot would wake the others and possibly draw further unwanted attention. I didn't want to make trouble; we wanted to avoid it if possible.

I shook my head. "Not unless we have to. Keep your eyes on them. Iggy, let's go."

"With you," Iggy said.

He carried his shotgun at the ready and followed, staying several steps behind and to my right. That was a good sign. He wasn't crowding me and he kept his gun pointed safely away from me.

As we passed the blue vehicle, giving the crazy on the hood a wide berth, I focused my attention on the front of Kappy's place. All of the lights burned brightly but the shades were pulled down. I could see clearly enough through the smoky plastic film to verify that no one moved around inside.

The front door was unlocked and that surprised me. Kappy had been vigilant and never would have left the door unlocked. I remembered him checking the lock often; something was definitely wrong.

"Keep your eyes open," I told Iggy.

I pushed open the second interior door and stepped into the place. Iggy and I both stood still and looked around. The place definitely appeared empty. I listened carefully trying to capture any sound that might betray someone or something lying in wait, but I heard nothing.

"This is creepy," Iggy said.

I didn't say anything but I was thinking the same thing.

We crossed the main dining area and made our way toward the kitchen. My eyes kept moving from booth to booth, expecting someone or something to emerge from the confined space. Nothing did.

We stopped in the small corridor that led to the kitchen to our left. On our right were three doors—two restrooms and Kappy's office—and straight ahead was the rear entrance.

I pointed toward Kappy's office first and Iggy nodded his head. We moved together and I was happy to see that Iggy naturally turned to keep an eye on our six.

I pushed the door open slowly and entered the office. It was empty. Although a bit disorganized, everything seemed to be in order. Kappy's personal bathroom was also empty.

Back in the hall we checked the bathrooms; both were empty. The smell of pine was strong. Kappy must have recently cleaned them.

Together we moved into the kitchen. The bright fluorescent lights gleaned off the stainless surfaces.

I found Kappy spread out on the green tiled floor, his back against one of the huge refrigerators. Dried blood covered his lips, chin, and neck, and his white apron was stained with it as well.

"No, Kappy," I said.

I set my bag down on a chopping block and set my SKS beside it. Slowly I approached my friend and knelt down beside him.

"What are you doing?" Iggy whispered.

"Be quiet."

Kappy was definitely infected. His eyes were closed but they moved quickly beneath his thin lids. He was dreaming. A long scar branded his neck from ear to shoulder, a dark scab formed around yellow pus. I was assaulted by the smell of feces and urine.

There was no way to know when Kappy had turned. It could have been after I'd left or it could have been much more recently. He didn't appear to have any other marks on his body. Perhaps the scratch on his neck was the initiation point. My wife had been scratched by one of those things, too, and had become infected soon after.

"We should go," Iggy said nervously.

He moved from side to side like a child who had to use the bathroom.

"Stop doing the pee-pee dance and call Charlie in here," I said. I didn't turn to see if Iggy obeyed my order. I heard the kitchen door swish open and then closed again. Now I was alone with Kappy. Well, I was alone with the thing that had once been a good friend to me.

"I'm so sorry, Kappy."

I should have made him come with me. He'd be alive right now. Rage built up inside me and I did my best to push it away. Kappy had saved my life. He gave me food and shelter, gave me his damn Jeep. And then one of those Godforsaken things took his life.

I wanted something to strike. I wanted to step outside and lay waste to all of the crazies that slept outside, regenerating their rotten bodies. But those actions would not bring Kappy back. And I would probably end up getting someone hurt, or worse, dead.

The kitchen door swished open and I stood. Charlie stopped just within the threshold. His eyes were glued to Kappy.

"Don't worry about him," I said.

I walked over to the butcher block and leaned against the thick wood. Charlie continued to stare at Kappy for a moment longer and then he looked at me. "What are we doing, boss?"

"We're going to take what we can from here. Kappy has a fat pantry and I know he wouldn't mind if we borrowed some supplies."

"Who's Kappy?" Charlie asked.

I ignored his question. "Tell Iggy and Ken to join me in here. Have Alex and the rest of them get the truck ready to load. I want you on watch."

"Whatever you say, boss."

He remained in the kitchen a moment longer. His eyes went back to Kappy. "What about him?"

"I'll take care of him. Do what I asked, Charlie."

Without another word Charlie backed out of the kitchen and the door swished almost noiselessly in his wake.

While he was gone I started to go through Kappy's kitchen and take inventory. There were two large pantries stacked high with canned and boxed goods. On stainless steel shelves stood huge jars of mayonnaise and mustard, enormous cans of tomato sauce and Ketchup. I might as well have been at my local Meijer.

I pulled open the walk-in freezer and stood speechless. The stainless steel walls gleamed under the light. The black metal shelves were piled with boxes of lamb, beef, pork and chicken. There were crates of fish, shrimp and shellfish on beds of ice. I saw several white five gallon buckets, plastic containers filled with pre-made sauces, sliced vegetables and stocks. This was much more than I expected to find and quite a wonderful surprise.

Iggy and Ken returned a short time later with a two-wheeler in tow. Under my direction the two men started stacking and porting supplies from Kappy's kitchen back out to the UPS truck. I noted the pleasure in their eyes when I started pointing out boxes I wanted them to take.

We worked for the next twenty minutes in relative silence so that we would not wake the sleeping Kappy. It was a bit difficult maneuvering around his body but Iggy helped Ken move the butcher block and one of the other shelving units once we'd cleared it of its contents and that gave us the room we needed to avoid Kappy easily.

Once we had most of the dried goods carted away and stacked in the truck we started on the meats in the freezer. Iggy and Ken had just left to unload their haul of meats when I heard the horn blare sharply three times. I dropped the case of pork chops and sucked in a surprised breath.

Turning quickly, I ran from the freezer and stopped in my tracks. Kappy's eyes were open and he stared straight ahead. As he turned his head to look at me I heard the first gunshot outside, followed closely by a series of shots.

Kappy looked at me with that dull look but his face didn't change like the rest of them when they saw fresh meat. I don't know if he recognized me; I thought that was pretty doubtful, but I held out hope.

"Kappy?"

At the sound of my voice Kappy's eyes changed and he rolled sideways onto his knees. More gunfire erupted outside. I had no time for feelings right now.

"I'm sorry, Kappy."

I pulled my 1911 from my hip holster and shot him twice in the top of his head. His body fell forward and I cringed at the cold, wet smacking sound his face made as his flesh struck the tile.

Without looking at my friend, I holstered the 1911, grabbed my go bag and SKS, and made for the parking lot, shouldering my bag. A moment later I slammed out the front door.

A shotgun blast to my immediate left drew my attention first. Charlie stood with his 870 and shot again from the hip as a group of four crazies rushed him. They'd been piled up next to the dumpster but now they rose up like an angry mob. Charlie shot again as I shouldered the SKS and started to fire into the approaching group.

Our shots were wild and within seconds the creatures were upon us. I had just enough time to watch Charlie slam the butt of the 870 into the jaw of one of the crazies before I had my own troubles to worry about.

Shifting my grip on the SKS, I grabbed the barrel and swung my rifle like a baseball bat, connecting with my assailant's face. The ugly bastard's jaw shifted, hanging askew. He took two awkward steps backward but that gave me just enough time to pull my 1911 and fire two more shots into his brain.

I turned back to the group and fired the remainder of my rounds from the 1911. Two more went down and didn't get back up.

Suddenly my body was jarred to the right as one of the dumpster monsters tackled me like a professional linebacker. I hit the ground forcefully, bit my tongue hard enough to draw blood, and smacked the side of my head against the black top. Although I'd lost my breath I had the presence of mind to grab the thing's neck, just barely stopping it from taking a bite out of my face.

With all the strength I could muster, I choked the thing and pushed his head back at the same time. His eyes glared at me from behind thick, greasy bangs. His face was blood splattered and his breath stank like rotten meat. His teeth gnashed and clattered and he grunted as he fought against my death grip. My arms were aching and would fail me soon.

Although I was focused on my attacker I could hear other scuffles around me as my men fought for their lives. I thought I heard Iggy shout in pain. I even thought I heard a child crying out. I had to help them.

Yellow spit dripped down from the crazy's lips and splashed on my neck. My stomach churned but I fought the urge to vomit.

With one last surge of adrenaline I dug down deep and pushed like I was bench pressing weights. I heard a deep grunt issue from down in my belly. I tried to twist to my side, hoping gravity would help get him off me but he was immovable.

Just as my grip loosened on his neck, the monster was tackled off me. Two bodies rolled to my right. I rolled with them, got to my knees quicker than I thought I was capable. Charlie had managed to get on the thing's back, hooked it with a choke hold, and it was trying to stand.

Getting to my feet I yelled, "Get off, Charlie!"

He looked at me with wild eyes that seemed to ask 'are you crazy?' but he let go after only a moment's hesitation. He obviously had no idea of my intentions.

As the crazy turned on Charlie, I loosed a war cry and charged the monster. I built as much speed as I could in the short distance, tucked my shoulder at just the right moment and slammed into him. We both left the ground for a moment, carried by the force of momentum. The dirty thing flew into the blue sedan, bounced off the right fender and rolled to the side.

Although I stumbled, through luck or the graces of some unknown deity, I managed to keep my feet under me. In one fluid movement, more graceful than I thought myself capable of, I took a giant jump step and kicked the thing as hard as I could. I felt his ribs crack against my shin and pain reverberated up my knee, into my thigh.

The thing rolled and I kicked him again and again. I went for the head next, punted him between the eyes. His neck snapped back by the force of the blow but still he was breathing. Out of breath now, but my rage still burning, I grabbed it by its filthy jacket and pulled him to his feet. I swung him with all my force, really putting my body weight into it, and slammed him headfirst into the grille of the sedan.

Grunting like one of the crazies, I pulled him back, ready for another round. I saw that the skin of his forehead had peeled back, and white bone poked through. His left eye was a bloody mess. I was out of control and I couldn't stop myself. And then Charlie rescued me again. He grabbed me from behind and held tight even as I tried to throw him off.

"It's me boss," he yelled. "It's Charlie!"

I ignored him. When he'd first jumped me, my grip had loosened on the crazy. The thing was now trying to crawl away from me. I reached out and snaked one of its ankles and tried to pull him back.

Charlie got his arm around me in a chokehold. He was still screaming in my ear, "Stop it, Matt, let him go!"

I fought to keep hold of the thing but I was winded and my body was too exhausted to cooperate. Finally, I went to my knees and then bent forward on my hands.

I sucked in great gobs of air, and I felt Charlie's arms unlock.

"Mike, kill that," Charlie ordered. On his knees next to me he squeezed my shoulder and said, "Take it easy, boss. We got them. Just relax."

I pushed him away. "Watch the road." My voice was thick and my throat burned something fierce.

Charlie hesitated and then got to his feet. He said, "Iggy, watch the road. Ken, you and Mike check our perimeter and make sure we're clear."

I tried to stand but my legs were shaky. When Charlie offered me help, instead of childishly pushing him away again, I let him steady me.

I took another deep breath and walked over to where my weapons lay on the ground. I picked up the 1911 and popped in a new magazine before holstering it. I tossed the empty into my go bag and snatched up my SKS.

My body swooned a bit. My face was hot, sweat dripped down from my temples and neck, my legs ached, and every time I took a breath, a stitch tore at my left flank. I rubbed my eyes with my forearm and finally took a look around.

Dead bodies littered Kappy's parking lot. By my count, at least twelve crazies were finally put to rest, including our friend who'd been sleeping on the hood of the sedan.

"Sound off," I said, my voice a bit too loud.

"Iggy okay."

"Charlie okay."

"Mike okay."

"Ken okay."

"John okay."

"Alex, all good."

I nodded my head. All of my men were unscathed. A shaky sigh escaped me. Still trying to get myself under control, I walked over toward the truck.

To Charlie I said, "What happened?"

Charlie shot Alex a dirty look before finally turning to me. "I was helping load the truck and John shouted that someone was coming. I dropped what I was doing and I saw those people approaching."

Charlie nodded to my right and I looked in that direction. I hadn't seen them until now. A man, woman and young boy sat on the ground next to a tipped shopping cart. The boy was huddled against the woman. The man was holding a dirty piece of cloth against his head. They all looked at me with fear in their eyes.

Charlie continued. "I shouted for them to stop and not come closer. They kept coming anyway. I hit the guy to let him know I was serious. I had it under control. Then this…guy over here starts blowing the horn and woke the dead."

"He told us to blow the horn if we saw anything," Alex said, jumping down from the truck. His face was pale and his hands were shaking.

"I told you I had this under control," Charlie said turning on the man. Although Alex was bigger than Charlie, I saw fear in Alex's eyes.

"Okay, okay, guys, cool it," I said. "We'll talk about this later. Right now we need to get this truck loaded and moving. Charlie, send Iggy, Mike and John to get the rest of that meat loaded. Alex, make sure our load is evenly distributed."

After staring daggers at Alex for another few seconds, Charlie turned away. Alex stood where he was, absently scratching his beard.

"Go on, Alex," I said. As he started to move I called to him, "And do me a favor?"

He turned back expectantly. "Sure."

"Shave that damn beard."

After a second his hand slowly dropped to his side and he smiled. "Yes, dear," he said and went on about his assigned task.

I dug into my bag and pulled out a bottle of Mountain Spring water and approached the trio. They were obviously scared and I tried my best not to look menacing. I kneeled in front of them and held out the bottle of water to the child. He was about six or seven years old, just about my daughter's age. His dirty blond bangs hung down over his brown eyes, which shifted to his mother for a moment and then locked on mine.

"It's okay," I urged gently. "Take it."

I smiled at him as his hand slowly reached out and took it. He tried to open it and after a few seconds his mother reached down and helped him.

To the man I said, "Where did you come from?"

He pulled the cloth away from his forehead exposing a cut above his right eye where Charlie had struck him. "We came from Route 59."

I looked at the shopping cart. It was from Wal-Mart. "You came from the mall?"

The man nodded. He prodded his cut again with the cloth and then finally put the dirty rag into his coat pocket.

"Are there still supplies there?" I asked.

He shook his head.

"We're not going to hurt you."

The man just looked at me.

"What's your name?"

He hesitated. "Ron."

"And what's your name, buddy?" I asked the boy. He held the water bottle close to him as if it could protect him.

"Wesley," he said in a small voice that reminded me of my son Mark.

God, I missed Mark's little voice so much.

"You're a brave kid, Wesley." I smiled at him. I wanted to hug him and tell him I'd protect him, that I wouldn't let the bad things get him.

He's not Mark, I told myself.

"And your name?" I asked the woman.

"I'm Anna." She hugged Wesley closer to her bosom.

I turned back to question the man. "Okay, Ron. May I ask why you approached my men?"

Again he hesitated. Before he could respond Anna said, "We're hungry."

Ron glared at her.

"Why are you wandering out here?" I asked. "It's dangerous, as you can see."

Anna ignored her husband's angry eyes and said, "We were visiting from Wisconsin. We…lost our car. We haven't eaten in a while now. We just want to go home."

I felt sad for these people. I remembered how I felt when this all started. I'd been away from my family, away from home. All I could think about was getting back to them and getting home. I'd made it, although my family had not.

These people had no shot at getting back to their home. Although the roads were clear on Route 20, I very much doubted the highways would be. And Wisconsin was a long way away.

Standing up, I righted the shopping cart and started to pick up the few supplies they had and put them back in. The man stood, too, but he only watched me with weary eyes.

When I was finished I said, "Why don't you go inside? There's food in there."

They all just looked at me as if they didn't comprehend my words.

I held out my hand to the boy. I said, "Come on." To my surprise he took my hand. As we walked I looked over my shoulder to see that Mom and Dad were following. Charlie looked at me curiously as we passed him and entered Kappy's. I winked at him to let him know everything was okay.

I herded them into one of the booths that Kappy and I had sat in a few days before. Under the bright lights I could see that the family was exhausted. I had no idea how long they'd been out on the road but that sort of living had taken its toll on them, for sure.

"Ron, come with me a second," I said.

He slid out of the booth and followed me toward the kitchen. Mike and John passed us with a stacked two-wheeler. Iggy must be in the kitchen deciding what to load up next.

We stopped at one of the tables closest to the kitchen and sat down. Ron was nervous and he had every right to be. He'd risked his family by revealing themselves to a group of armed men. He had to have been desperate, though, or his better senses would have kept them behind cover until we'd gone.

"How long has it been since you've eaten?" I asked.

Ron shrugged his shoulders and looked down at the table.

"Tell me how long, Ron."

He looked up at me. "Three days now. I think."

I let out my breath between clenched teeth. I knew what I had to do here.

"Ron, would you and your family like to come with us?"

His eyes shifted to his family, then back to me and then down at the table. His breathing increased and I could see his wheels were turning. He had shown poor judgment in exposing his family to me and my men, and he probably didn't want to make that mistake again.

"What do I have to give in return?" he asked finally.

"You'll have to contribute to the community," I said.

He eyed me cautiously. "Would my family be safe?"

"As safe as the rest of us." I didn't understand his question.

His eyes squinted and his forehead creased. "The men won't hurt my wife? They won't touch Wesley?"

"No, of course not."

My stomach churned at the man's implications. I was almost insulted, but the guy had been through a lot and I immediately forgave him.

"Ron, I don't know what you've been through but we're not that kind of people. I personally guarantee you that no one will hurt your family. You'll have a place to live and food to eat. All we ask in return is that you stand with us and defend the community."

Tears started to fall from his eyes. His hands clasped each other. He was clearly a man without options; his fate, as well as that of his wife and child, was now in the hands of strangers.

"Are there other families there?" Ron asked finally. Tears continued to roll down his cheeks.

"Yes," I said. "There are a few kids Wesley's age. I know some people who will gladly take you in, two nice women who will be happy if you and your family stayed with them."

I truly had no idea how Kat and Sam would feel about me volunteering them to adopt this family but I strongly suspected they'd be open to the idea. I knew I could find other alternatives if they weren't. Whatever it took, we needed to help these people.

"Why are you doing this?" Ron asked.

He wiped the tears from his cheeks and looked into my eyes. For the first time I saw something other than fear in his eyes. Perhaps a glimmer of hope.

"I had a family, too," I said. "I lost them to those things out there. I know that my wife and my children would want me to do this because it's the right thing to do."

Ron reached across the table and grabbed my hand. Dirt and grime covered his thin fingers but his grip was strong.

"You are an angel," he said.

I shook my head. "I'm just a man who believes in doing what's right."

I stood up from the table and Ron got to his feet as well.

"Come on in the kitchen and get something to eat for your family and think about my offer. I really hope you come with us, Ron."

He followed me into the kitchen and spent the next few minutes in the refrigerators preparing a quick meal for his family while I spent the next half hour checking on the loading process and generally making sure things were going smoothly.

Charlie had taken up sentry duty. He wandered over toward the old John Deere, clearly still upset with Alex. Although we'd made it through unharmed, things could just as easily have gone the other way. I knew that bothered him. I decided he needed some time alone so I let him be.

Alex took to his task of organizing the load. His years of experience certainly paid off. We'd hit the mother lode at Kappy's. As more and more boxes were rolled out I started to worry we'd run out of space. But with simple reorganization, Alex easily cleared up the space we needed.

Kappy's had not been on my list of places to visit on our supply run, but now that we were here it certainly changed my plans. I had once said I was optimistic, but I realized now that I'd been too unrealistic. Originally I thought we'd make one good supply run and get enough supplies to last us for a while, maybe until this damn thing was over. I saw now that we'd have to make a series of supply runs over the next couple of weeks if we were even going to put a dent in the lists that Kat and Ravi put together.

We were fairly well off on our food supply now, thanks to Kappy, but we had no medical supplies. I also promised Bob I'd look into some weapons and ammo but that had to be scratched. There was no room for anything else and I didn't want to test my luck on Route 59 tonight.

I'd also have to figure a way to get some larger vehicles to haul our supplies, too. Thinking back to the trucks I'd seen at the Providence roadblock we were again woefully underprepared, and that fact reflected poorly on me. I was their leader and I needed to get my shit together and start thinking more clearly. This shit was really happening and things were going to get worse before they got better. This shit was real.

About two hours after leaving our home, we were ready to head back. Our supply run, although not a complete success, was far from a failure. There was that.

I was happy to see that Ron and family had gathered their meager belongings and sat waiting for me by the blue sedan. When I approached, Ron put down the bag he'd been holding and came forward to meet me.

"We'd like to come, if your offer still stands," he said.

I smiled. "Of course. We're glad to have you."

He got choked up again and tears formed in the corner of his eyes. Before he broke down I grabbed his shoulder and gave it a good squeeze.

"Don't give it any more thought. Be strong for your boy. You'll be helping us as much as we're helping you."

Now he smiled for the first time. When he smiled, his whole face lit up and did my heart some good.

"Get them in the truck," I said to him. I turned around and addressed the men. "Listen up everyone. This is Ron, Anna, and that handsome little fellow there is Wesley. They're going to be joining us. Make them feel welcome."

The men clapped them on the back and gave Wesley high fives as the family made their way to the UPS truck. Once they were in, the rest of my guys clambered in after them. It was a tight fit with all of the supplies but they managed.

Before I stepped up into the truck Charlie touched my elbow. I turned to face him.

"Sorry I let things get out of control, boss."

"Don't apologize, Charlie. You were great. Even when things fell apart you handled it well. You got the job done. You saved my ass."

"You saved mine first," he said.

"Then we're even."

His eyes glanced over toward the new members of our community that now sat in the back of the truck. When he looked at me again, he said, "I think you did a good thing, boss."

"You too, Charlie. You didn't shoot them."

Soon we were on the road again. As Alex drove us down the all-too-quiet Route 20, Ron told us about his experience with a group of men who'd blocked Route 20 where it intersected with Route 59. He told us they'd taken his car and supplies and that he and his family barely escaped. The men had tried to have their way with Anna.

As he spoke, I felt anger again creeping up inside and I cursed myself for feeling this way. I had never felt hatred so strongly in all my life.

Since my wife had died and my children had been torn apart by their teacher, my view of the world had changed. So had my emotions. I didn't like the person I had become.

CHAPTER 14: DEMAND

Comedian stood in front of us with both hands raised and outstretched. He stood about fifteen feet ahead of the Providence roadblock and he didn't look pleased to see us. Two men stood behind him on either side. Both men had AR-15 carbines but Comedian seemed to be unarmed.

Although the roadblock had been busy earlier just before we'd left, it was deserted now. The three large SUV's cut across Route 20, blocking the entrance to Providence's main access road as well as access to our own community.

There was no way around, at least not by vehicle. On foot you'd have to navigate thick trees and ponds. If you did make it to Randall Oaks, you'd have to scale the eight foot brick fence that surrounded our community.

"What the hell is he doing?" Alex asked. He slowed the UPS truck to about five miles an hour before finally coming to a stop just a few yards from where the men stood.

"I don't know," I said.

I had an idea, though, and I didn't like it.

All evening something had bothered me about the way they'd lined up the trucks and then diverted them onto the access road. Phil had been cryptic in his answer, but he confirmed that they had not all been Providence vehicles.

He'd said they were 'neighbors'.

I slid the panel door open on my side and locked it into place. Before I stepped out I asked quietly so those in the back could not hear, "Alex do you think this truck can ram that roadblock?"

He looked at me for a moment and when he realized I was serious he looked back ahead at the vehicles that blocked the road. He studied them for a few seconds and then said, "I don't think so. Why do you ask?

"Stay calm but alert," I said ignoring his question. "Charlie, come up here."

Charlie appeared in the small space between our two front seats. "What's up, boss?"

"Come with me."

"Okay."

We both swung down from the truck and approached Comedian and company. His arms were down at his side now and his face was stern. I knew he didn't like us, and I could see the disgust on his face as we approached.

"We're from Randall Oaks," I said when I stopped in front of him.

He rolled his eyes. "I know who you are. What do you have in the truck?"

I looked at Charlie who shrugged. I guess it was an honest question to ask.

"Some supplies. Food mostly," I replied.

Comedian nodded his head. "We're going to need to look inside. Open the rear doors."

"What?" I asked, not sure I'd heard him clearly.

"I said open it up." His eyes squinted as he stared at me. He had the look of a man who was used to getting what he wanted, and what he wanted most was trouble.

"Just let us through," I said. "We're tired and we don't have time for games."

Comedian took a step forward so that he was just inches away from me. I could smell his cheap aftershave and booze on his breath. His eyes were rimmed red. When he spoke, his voice was loud and authoritative.

"By order of Frank Senior, all vehicles entering will be searched and Providence is entitled to half of all supplies. Please step out of the truck and open it up for our inspection."

"You're nuts," I said. "I want to talk to Phil."

"Phil ain't here," he said with menace in his voice, "and I'm not going to ask you again. Open the truck. Whatever you have in there, we're taking half."

Anger filtered through my veins. My breathing grew rapid and my hands clenched my SKS tightly. After what we'd just been through, my adrenaline was already up and I was in a fighting mood.

Apparently Charlie could see from my body language that I was about to cause trouble. He took a step forward and said, "Easy fellas."

Before I knew what was happening, Comedian drew a revolver from his hip. He aimed it at Charlie and said, "No one's talking to you, asshole."

The gunshot temporarily deafened me and I cringed, my left hand automatically going to my ear. I crouched instinctively and at the same time turned toward Charlie. He stood about three feet to my left and about a foot behind me. His eyes were wide and his face shocked. Both of his hands clutched his abdomen where the bullet had torn his flesh.

I turned back to Comedian, who looked as shocked as Charlie.

"Oh, shit," he said, just as I smashed the butt stock of my SKS into his face.

Everything happened quickly, I'm sure, but to me, time seemed to have slowed to a crawl. My vision tunneled in on Comedian and for a moment only he existed.

He stumbled backward a few steps from the force of the blow and both of his hands went up to his face. He still held the pistol in one hand and I think he was screaming.

Holding the SKS out in front of me I charged the bastard and pushed him the rest of the way until he slammed up against one of the SUVs that blocked the road. I don't remember losing hold of the SKS, but I had, because both my hands were wrapped around the bastard's throat, squeezing with every ounce of strength I possessed. Tears streamed from his eyes and his face was contorted into a mask of fear.

I felt hands desperately pulling at my arms and then fists pelted my shoulders and back. I felt my grip slipping on Comedian. I rammed a knee into his crotch and he slid to the ground.

Phil whirled me around and held his hands out in a non-threatening way when I shoved him back.

"Take it easy, Matt," he said. "Everybody just calm down, damn it."

"He shot Charlie!" I yelled at Phil and pushed him again. His movement was halted when he struck the side of the Escalade.

"I know, I know. I'm sorry, but calm down before this turns into a bloodbath here."

I knew he was right. We had to rein things in, get some control. I saw Charlie lying on the ground and Alex kneeling beside him with his T-shirt wadded up, applying pressure to his wound. John and Iggy stood nearby; they'd been tussling with the other Providence men who'd been trying to pull me off Comedian.

"Move this truck," I ordered Phil, and pushed past him. To John and Iggy I said, "Help Alex with Charlie. Get him into the truck. We have to go. Move!"

Phil grabbed my arm and halted me. When I faced him he handed me my SKS and said, "Look, we're under orders here, and I really can't let you go without taking half of whatever you have there."

"Orders from who? Frank Senior? He has no authority over me or my community. He doesn't own the road. Now get the hell out of my way, Phil."

"Matt, I understand you're angry, but listen to what I'm saying. Providence has been keeping this road safe; we've been keeping those crazy things from your doorstep. You owe us."

"You're crazy. We don't owe you a damn thing. And if Senior has a problem with that, he knows where to find me. And this is the last time I'm going to ask you to move that truck, Phil. If Charlie dies here, I guarantee Comedian follows. Right here and right now."

Phil stared at me for a long moment, our eyes never leaving each others'.

Finally he said, "This isn't going to end well for either of our communities." He turned away from me and yelled, "Open it up!"

Comedian was on his knees. Blood trickled down from his mouth and his nose was already starting to swell. He looked at me with half closed eyes as I walked up to him. His hands went up instinctively to block his face.

"You'd better hope I never see you again," I said. I kicked him in the ribs and he fell onto his right side.

"What the hell?" the man next to Comedian said.

I looked him in the eyes and said, "I better not see you either."

Charlie had already been moved into the truck when I swung up into the passenger's seat. I could see Charlie wasn't doing well. He'd lost all color from his face, and the shirt Alex used to compress the wound was soaked with blood. Iggy continued to compress the wound with his T-shirt against Charlie's abdomen. He looked up at me with horror in his eyes.

"Hang in there, Charlie, we're gonna get you some help." To Alex I said, "Come on, move this thing."

We blew past the Providence roadblock and within minutes we were at our own gates. Alex slammed the truck to a stop and laid on the horn until the men on sentry scurried over and opened them.

A crowd had already gathered on the main access road and they were clapping and cheering as Alex navigated the brown truck.

I hung out the side door shouting, "Get out of the way! Make a hole!"

At the T-intersection Alex turned right and then made a quick left, heading toward the command post. In the side mirror I saw a crowd of people following down the street.

Bob and Brian stood on the small porch of the command post and they both approached with smiles on their faces. When I jumped out of the vehicle and pulled open the side door their smiles faded. Bob looked like he'd been hit in the gut. He stopped in his tracks, frozen or in shock, I couldn't tell which. Brian came forward at a trot. I could see he was upset. He had that set to his walk and his fists clenched at his sides.

As Iggy, John and I lifted Charlie and started to carry him toward the CP, I said, "Bob wake the hell up! I need David Green and Ravi at the CP now! Tell them we have a gunshot wound. Hurry!"

Without asking questions, but with a stunned look still on his face, Bob shook himself out of his stupor and took off running.

The crowd started to catch up to us. I didn't want them to see Charlie like this. "Move faster! Get the door open for Christ's sake!" I yelled.

"What the hell happened?" Brian asked. He matched our pace as we carried Charlie into the CP. "How did this happen?"

"Not now," I said. "Get the door open already!"

"Where's he hit?" Brian asked. "Charlie, who did this?"

Not thinking but just reacting, I shoved Brian away with my right hand. "Back off! Why don't you get those damn people out of here?"

Brian stopped but we kept moving. I didn't have time to worry about his feelings. And I certainly didn't need to hear him say 'I told you so'.

Within seconds we were up the short set of steps and moving into the command post. We cut quickly through the living room and into the dining room.

"Get him on the table," I said. "Someone get some pillows from the sofa. Move!"

The three of us gently lay Charlie onto the dining room table. He was still conscious, but just barely. His face was absolutely colorless. I grabbed his right hand and it was cold as ice.

He moaned a bit and tried to turn his body, but Iggy and John stabilized him. "Hold still, buddy," Iggy said.

Brushing his wet hair away from his forehead, I leaned in close to Charlie and whispered, "We're going to take care of you, Charlie. You hang in there, man. Ravi's coming."

He didn't respond, not even a moan. I moved around to the left side of the table and bumped Iggy out of the way.

"Iggy, see if you can find some towels or sheets. Lots of them." To John I said, "Go into the kitchen and get as many pots of water as you can on the stove and start boiling. Hurry!"

The two men moved off to do as they were told. The minutes seemed to be ticking away and with every second Charlie's life was slipping away with them. I took his hand and squeezed it gently.

"Please hang in there, man."

I heard breathing behind me and turned to find my brother standing there. I hadn't heard him enter.

"He doesn't look good."

I shook my head.

Brian stepped forward and stood next to me. With the tips of his fingers he pinched the T-shirt and lifted it, exposing the gunshot wound. Blood bubbled up from the torn flesh and spilled down Charlie's flank.

"Bleeding's not stopping," Brian said and put pressure on the wound.

"Bob's taking too long." I turned away and started toward the door with the intention of tracking down Bob and Ravi when Brian called out to me.

When I turned back Brian shook his head. He slowly unzipped his fleece sweater, and with a gentleness I did not know he possessed, he draped the sweater over Charlie's torso and head.

"No," I said. I moved forward stiffly and stopped about three feet away from the table. "Please, no."

Bob, Ravi and David Green hustled into the room but stopped in their tracks just inside the door. I saw John standing silently in the kitchen doorway and Iggy stood behind Brian with an arm full of sheets. The room was silent. All eyes moved to Charlie's lifeless body. We all stood that way for the next few minutes before I finally turned and walked away.

* * *

I stepped out of the house and onto the front stoop. I put my face into my hands, doing my best not to break down. Charlie was a good man. He'd watched my back at Providence when we fended off an attack of crazies who'd breached their borders, he'd saved my life at Kappy's just an hour ago, and he'd tried to quell the situation at the Providence border and it gotten him killed.

I wanted to take time to grieve Charlie properly but I had a truck full of meat and supplies that needed to be attended to, I had a family of refugees that needed to be situated, and I had to arrange for Charlie's funeral.

I stood up and brushed the seat of my pants, inhaled deeply, and looked around.

Several groups of people had gathered outside the command post, most congregated around Alex and his UPS truck. They gave the command post a wide berth. Whether or not they actually knew what happened, they at least sensed there was tension here and they gave us space.

Katherine and Sam stood nearby and I made eye contact with them. I made my way to them and I could see they were both scared and confused.

"Is Charlie really dead?" Kat asked.

I nodded and took her hand.

"Kat, I really need you to have Alex and whoever else you can find get those supplies stored away. I have two freezers in my garage. You'll need them."

"Are you going to be okay?" she asked.

"Yes. I'm fine. I'll be better when the 500 pounds of meat isn't defrosting in the truck," I said.

Kat hesitated a moment more and then turned to go about her task. Sam moved to follow, but I halted her by taking her hand.

"I need your help with something else, Sam."

She nodded and stared at me with sad eyes.

Holding her hand, I led her toward the UPS truck. A small group of folks were gathered around a tall, balding man. He wore khaki pants and a pale pastel checkered shirt. His name was Reginald Osgood, known to most of us as Reverend Reggy.

Reverend Reggy held mass at the Randall Oaks Church and Center for Arts located just to our west, outside the walls that surrounded our community. Although I was not a member of his congregation, I had no doubt that Reverend Reggy would honor my request.

Sam and I stopped beside the small group and Reggy, who had been in the middle of discussion, stepped forward and embraced me.

"My condolences, brother," he said.

"Thanks, Rev," I said. I nodded to the rest of the group and then asked, "May I have a word with you?"

Reggy nodded and excused himself. Together the three of us stepped away from the rest of the group and huddled together.

"Things are kind of crazy right now, Rev, and I was hoping I could count on you to take care of the arrangements for Charlie. I'd like to have something for him today and I don't care how late it is. I'd like to lay him to rest on Harper's Knoll."

"Absolutely," Reggy said. "I'll handle all of the arrangements. Don't fret. Go on and take care of what you need to take care of. Charlie will be in good hands."

"I know he will," I said and hugged the reverend.

He moved off quickly and stopped at his small congregation, probably seeking assistance for the task at hand.

I turned my attention back to Sam. "While we were out there we came across a family that's been stranded here while visiting from Wisconsin. They had a tough time out there and I've offered them sanctuary here. Right now I have no idea what to do with them and I was hoping that they could stay with you and Kat until I can find a place for them."

"Is that the couple with the little boy over there?" Sam asked, nodding her head toward Alex's truck.

Turning in that direction, I saw Ron and his family huddled together on the curb. Someone had brought out a blanket and wrapped it around Wesley's shoulders.

"That's them," I said. "I know I'm asking a lot but I could really use your help with this."

"Consider it done," Sam said.

"Do you want to make sure it's okay with Kat?"

Sam shook her head. "Kat will be thrilled. Don't worry about that, just introduce me to them."

I smiled. "Thank you, Sam." I hugged her.

"Any time."

Together we approached the Randall Oak refugees. As we drew near, Ron stood up and took a few steps forward to meet us.

"I heard your man didn't make it," he said. "I'm really sorry. He seemed like a nice guy, even if he did hit me with his gun."

"He was a nice guy," I replied, "and I'm glad he didn't shoot first and ask questions later."

We were all silent for a moment, each of us awkward in our emotions. After an uncomfortable fifteen seconds I said, "Ron, this is Samantha. She and her friend Katherine have graciously agreed to give your family temporary shelter while we try to find something more permanent. I hope that's okay with you."

Ron was silent for a moment and I could see he was fighting back tears. He nodded his head vigorously and reached out for Sam's hand.

"Thank you so much." Ron's voice cracked and his eyes watered. "This means so much to us."

"It's our pleasure," Sam said. I could see that she, too, was greatly affected by this family's situation. "Come on, introduce me to your family and then let's go home."

As Ron turned away, I grabbed Sam's elbow. "I owe you both," I said.

"I'll collect sometime," Sam said and winked at me. "You just better be willing pay up, mister."

I returned to the command post and stood in the doorway of the living room. Charlie's body lay on top of white sheets and a white pillow case covered his private area. Reverend Reggy and a woman I didn't know were using wet cloths to clean the blood from Charlie's torso. Reggy dipped his hands into a pot of water and softly used his fingers to comb back Charlie's hair. I had to look away.

Iggy and John sat on the living room sofa and were staring off at nothing. They both looked exhausted and Iggy looked as though he'd been crying.

Moving quietly across the carpet from the dining room to the living room, I knelt down in front of the two men, placing the SKS on the coffee table.

"How are you guys doing?" I asked.

John's eyes shifted toward me and he said, "We're okay, boss."

Iggy closed his eyes for a moment and then opened them. He didn't look at me but said, "I'll be okay."

I took in a deep breath and exhaled. Iggy looked like he was about to fall over. His eyes were sunken and red from crying, his breathing was labored. When I touched his forehead it was hot against my skin.

"Look, you guys have done enough for today. Go on home and get some rest."

Finally Iggy turned and looked at me. "What about Charlie?"

I looked over my shoulder. Reverend Reggy and team were still cleaning Charlie's body, gently wiping away dirt, grime and dried blood.

"In a couple of hours we're going to have a service for Charlie. We're going to bury him at Harper's Knoll."

Iggy and John both nodded their heads.

"Go on home now, guys," I said. "I'll send someone to wake you when we're ready for Charlie. Get some rest. You both deserve it. Come on now, move out."

Both men slowly rose from the sofa, and with downcast eyes they moved past me. After a brief pause to look over at their friend, they left the command post.

I rose from my crouch. My legs felt cramped and sore and my back ached something fierce. Instead of standing, I slid onto the sofa and leaned back into it. I sank comfortably into the soft fabric and allowed myself to close my eyes for a second.

Although I'd lost my watch during my scuffle with the crazies, I knew it was just after midnight. In fact, it was probably closer to one in the morning. It had been an extremely long day and I was beginning to feel exhaustion set in.

With all that was going on, I probably wouldn't get back to my house and into bed for a long time. I figured I could get a little nap for a few minutes. Reverend Reggy would wake me when he was ready.

I closed my eyes and actually started to doze off when I heard Brian ask, "Are you really sleeping?"

My eyes sprung open. "What's wrong?"

Brian was standing just a few feet away from me. His arms were crossed at his chest and I could tell immediately by the look on his face that he wasn't here for friendly conversation.

"What the hell happened out there?" he asked.

I sighed and wriggled up off the sofa. "I'm not in a mood to go through this right now, Bri."

"Well get in the mood," he insisted. His hands dropped to his sides and his stance widened. "I want to know why Charlie died."

"What difference will it make?" I asked. "He'll still be dead."

"Why didn't you listen to me? I told you to take me and Bob, but no, you had to take a bunch of green men out there. Charlie's dead because you fucked up."

I admit that hurt, but I wasn't going to get sucked into this conversation with my brother and I certainly did not feel the need to justify my actions.

"I'm going home." I reached down to grab my SKS but Brian kicked the coffee table sending the SKS onto the floor and the table up against the sofa.

He advanced on me, covering the distance quickly. Before I could react, my brother struck. His fist slammed into my chest. I stumbled back a step, the crook of my knees hit the sofa, and I fell back onto it.

"Are you fucking kidding me?" I asked.

I expected Brian to be upset, but I never expected him to turn on me and physically assault me. "You got Charlie killed. You better wake the fuck up and start taking things seriously."

As much as I tried, I could no longer contain my temper. Not only had my brother struck me, but was he really accusing me of getting a man killed because I was just fooling around, playing leader? Did he really think I wasn't taking this situation seriously?

I launched myself from the sofa and charged Brian. He was ready and countered my move by sidestepping and allowing my momentum to take me to the ground. In a moment, he was on my back trying to put me into a sleeper hold.

From my hands and knees position I tried to turn my head and tuck my chin, to get under his grip. From my peripheral I could see Reverend Reggy was looking at us, stunned. I think he was saying something, but I couldn't hear. My blood rushed to my ears and I could only hear my pulse throbbing.

"You always have to be the boss, right?" Brian shouted into my ear as he tried to choke me out. "You always have to be in charge, always have to make the decisions. Well you made the wrong one this time."

I got one of my hands on Brian's forearm and started to work my fingers to loosen his grip.

"I told you this was too dangerous!" Brian shouted. "I told you to take me with you!"

I shifted on my knees a bit to get better leverage. With my left hand I took hold of his bicep and dug my fingers into his flesh, desperately trying to get purchase. I was starting to feel lightheaded now, and I needed to break his grip.

"You better wise up or you're going to get us all killed," Brian said. "Do you understand?"

I dipped my chin even further and with one quick fluid motion, I threw my head backward and connected solidly with Brian's nose.

"Son of a bitch!" he said and his grip loosened.

Taking advantage, I threw a left elbow around and hit him in the side of the head and thrust my weight forward, breaking completely out of his hold.

With adrenaline coursing through my veins, my brain switched to survival mode. I turned quickly and thrust myself at Brian before he could get to his feet. I bowled him over and got on top of him, pinning his arms down with my knees. I punched my brother with a right and then a left, watching as blood burst from his lips when I mashed them back against his teeth. I hit him again with a right, and then again, and a fourth time before someone grabbed me and pulled me off.

Struggling to break free, I heard Bob yelling, "Quit it goddamn it! We have trouble outside, now cut it out!"

Reverend Reggy was on the floor next to Brian helping him sit up. Using one of the damp cloths he had in his hand, Reggy pressed it against Brian's lips to stem the flow of blood.

Behind me, Bob had me in a death grip. I stopped struggling with him and said, "Okay, okay, Bob, let me go."

"Are you going to behave?" Bob asked.

"I'm good, Bob. Let go."

He thought about it for a moment. "Okay," he said, and freed me.

I got slowly to my feet and stood for a moment trying to catch my breath. I saw Brian doing the same. We both eyed each other from across the room but we said nothing.

"Are you guys done here?" Bob asked. "We have trouble at the gate. Get your shit together and meet me outside. Fast."

I grabbed up my SKS and started after Bob, who had already made his way across the living room and was heading out. I stopped next to Brian and looked at him.

"Let's go," I said.

"After you," he said.

★ ★ ★

As I approached the gates, my first thought was, Thank God they didn't sound that stupid alarm. My second thought, upon seeing who was at the gate, was, Oh shit.

At this time of night, I was surprised to see so many people awake and about in the community. I guess I should have expected this, though. With all the excitement when our team returned, I suspected it would be difficult for anyone to sleep. Aside from the men who were actually posted as sentries at the gate, I spotted about ten or twelve others who were huddled around one of the patrol vehicles.

I drew nearer the gate and stopped suddenly. Bob and Brian halted, both turning to cast an inquisitive glance.

"I would have let them in, but Iggy saw them on his way home and was adamant that they stay out," Bob said. "He didn't say why, he just said to get you, quick."

Looking beyond those gathered around the patrol cars, I saw our visitors: Senior, Frank, Phil and an unknown man from Providence leaned against our gate.

I swallowed hard and felt my hands began to tremble slightly. I didn't need more trouble right now—I had my hands full. I didn't think I could take on anymore.

"Iggy was right," was all I could manage for the moment.

"You okay?" Bob asked.

"Yeah," I said.

Mentally, I got my shit under control for the moment. I got us into this mess and I knew I would have to get us out.

I took a couple of more steps forward and then stopped again. "Bob, can we get everyone to back away from the gates? Anyone who's not on patrol needs to be off the street."

Bob looked a bit perplexed but he followed my order, calling out to his men currently on patrol, and they immediately started ushering people back further into the community.

"Are you going to tell me what the hell is going on?" Brian asked.

Turning to him, I sighed deeply. "Providence is taking supplies, like a toll. Anyone who wants to pass the roadblock has to give half of their haul."

"That's bullshit," Brian said. "You didn't give them anything, right?"

"No."

"Is that how Charlie died?" Brian asked.

"I had a heated exchange with Comedian about letting us through without giving up our supplies. Charlie tried to calm us both down and Comedian shot him. I don't think he meant to, I think his finger just slipped, but he shot Charlie just the same."

"Bastards," Brian spat, and turned quickly, stomping toward the gates. I grabbed his arm and halted him before he did something we'd all regret later.

"I'm going to handle this," I said, stepping in front of him. "Let me do this my way."

"No way they get away with killing Charlie," Brian said. "I'll kill every last one of them right here."

"They're not getting away with anything, Brian, but now is not the time for revenge. Just let me handle this. I promise Comedian will get what he deserves soon enough."

"Don't mess with me," Brian said. "You better be serious about that. I want that bastard dead. And I want to be the one to do it."

"I promise we'll avenge Charlie," I said. I squeezed his arm tighter. "You'll be the one that does it. I mean it."

His eyes bore into mine for a moment and then finally he shook his head. "Handle it your way."

"Thank you," I said.

"Don't forget your promise. I sure won't."

I nodded my head.

Together Brian and I approached the gate. Bob and his men had gotten everyone back behind the patrol vehicles, but didn't manage to get many to go home. That was fine, as long as they could not hear our conversation. I didn't want panic or outrage to sweep through the community, as both emotions could be extremely dangerous.

As we drew near, Senior spoke. "Sorry to show up unannounced and at such a late hour, but we have business that can't wait."

I ignored Brian's grunt and said, "What might that be?"

Senior smiled knowingly. He put one meaty hand on the bars of our gate and leaned in close. His bearded face loomed in the darkness. I wanted to smash his nose with my fist.

"I believe you have some supplies and we're due half," Senior said. "We can arrange for pick-up in, oh, about ten or twenty minutes."

"We made a supply run," I said, "but we don't owe you anything. We took the risks and we reap the rewards."

Frank stood behind his father, watching the big man with great scrutiny. I could not tell if he agreed with his father's attempt to bully our community, but he was backing his father's play. To Senior's right stood Phil. His eyes focused on a spot on the ground and never lifted, like he couldn't bear to look at me.

Senior smiled again, a wolf's smile. "Our roadblock keeps those crazy things away from your front doorstep. That kind of security ain't cheap. It can cost lives, and we're not working for free."

"I didn't ask for your roadblock. And in case you hadn't noticed, we have a pretty defendable community. Open the roads and let the crazies in. We'll take care of ourselves."

Now Senior's face changed, his smile replaced with a frown, and a deep furrow creased his brow. "You're obviously not thinking clearly right now, but you'll want to start. You need our roadblock, we need supplies. I think this is an equitable tradeoff."

"Fuck your roadblock and fuck you."

"Damn! In your face, you fat fuck," Brian said.

Senior flinched as though slapped, but to his credit he kept his cool.

"Don't forget, Senior," I said, "that we helped you fend off crazies in your own community. And your roadblock cost us the life of a friend. So we don't owe you shit. You want half of our supplies? The only way you're going to get them is if you turn over Comedian to stand trial for what he did."

Senior scowled. "Who the hell is 'Comedian'?"

"He means Andy," Phil said, still not looking at us.

"I'm not turning over anyone," Senior said. "And let me tell you, son, turning him over ain't the only way to get those supplies. We can take them by force, and I have the means to do just that."

"Take your chances, fat boy," Brian taunted.

Frank, who had been quiet during our exchange finally showed a spark of life. He launched himself forward, pushing past his father and slammed up against the gate.

"Come out here and I'll teach you some respect," Frank said to Brian.

Brian laughed and kicked the gate.

"Get your dog on a leash," Senior said to me. "You're just digging your hole deeper."

"I think we're done here," I said.

Putting a hand on his son's shoulder to calm him, Senior said to me, "You're obviously not thinking clearly. You lost your friend and I guess I can understand the way you're feeling, but you're not thinking about your people. What about them?"

I only stared at him. There was truth in what he said; I knew it and Brian knew it, but I just couldn't let this bastard bully our community into turning over supplies that we'd need to get us through until this craziness blew over.

"Don't make a decision based on your emotions," Senior continued. "Any good leader would be able to put their emotions aside and make a decision with the wellbeing of their community in mind, not revenge."

"Go home, Senior," I said. "I have nothing left to say to you."

"How are you going to get more supplies? This is the only road that leads to anywhere. Do you think we're going to let you through our roadblocks? You're condemning these people because of your pighead-edness! Don't be a fool."

"Providence killed my man and now you're trying to extort us. How am I being a fool? No. We're not going to give in. We're not going to give you those supplies, or any others, no matter what."

I turned away from the men and started to walk away. I did not stop to see if Brian followed. Behind me, Senior continued to raise his voice.

"I'm going to let cooler heads prevail here," he shouted. "I'm going to forget about the supplies you owe us, because you lost a man. And I'm not going to send my people to war over your lust for revenge."

As Brian and I neared the patrol car where Bob waited, Senior said, "But don't mistake my kindness or my generosity. If we see you or your men at our roadblock again we will shoot on sight. Don't let it come to that. Dissolving our alliance won't end well for either of us, you know."

I was dead on my feet and I couldn't take any more. This had been the longest day and I just wanted it to end. I went home and slept for an hour before Reverend Reggy shook me awake.

CHAPTER 15: FALLEN

I opened my eyes to bright sunlight that cut through the slits in the blinds. I'd fallen asleep on the living room sofa again. I couldn't bear to sleep in my room anymore, ever since my brother shot my wife there. It was a mercy killing, as much for me as my wife, but I could not look at the barren spot where the bloodstained carpet had been removed.

Reverend Reggy loomed over me. The morning light shone over him, illuminating him like an angel. The image was both surreal and calming.

"It is time," he said. "Our brother Charlie is ready to be laid to rest." He hesitated. "I didn't know him very well... I was hoping that you'd say a few words."

"Yeah, sure, no problem, Rev."

I swung my legs off the sofa and sat up. My back cried out and every bone and muscle in my body screamed out in agony. I cursed myself again for becoming so out of shape and complacent.

Trying to mask my pain from Reggy, I said, "I'll be down shortly. Just let me clean up a bit and get dressed."

"Of course, that will give me time to gather the rest of the community. I'll see you shortly."

"Thank you, Rev," I said as he made his way toward the steps that would lead him out the front door.

"It is the least I can do." He bowed his head slightly and disappeared, the door closed softly behind him.

I stood and stretched, grimacing at my aches and pains. Walking with my hands pressed firmly against the small of my back, I made my way to the bathroom and started to wash up in the sink.

The cold water felt good against my skin and revived me a bit. The mirror revealed a few new abrasions and cuts on my forehead and cheek from our run-ins with either the crazies or the bastards from Providence. I didn't have time to give the wounds proper cleaning and disinfecting. I made do with some Dial soap, working the cuts and abrasions softly with my fingertips.

Back in my room, making a wide berth around the hole in the carpet where my wife's blood once stained the light tan fibers, I went into my closet and sorted through my clothing. In the end, I pulled down a simple black suit with a dark maroon tie and dressed in silence.

I wasn't sure if Brian had come home during the night. When I last saw him he was headed back to the CP to oversee Charlie's preparations. I think he also wanted to hang around should the Providence folks come back.

I grabbed a banana for breakfast when I made my way downstairs. Taking a bite, I poked my head into the family room, which doubled as Brian's bedroom, but he wasn't there. He wasn't in my office or the armory. He was probably already out at Harper's Knoll.

Tossing the banana peel into the trash can in the downstairs powder room, I finally left the house. Standing on the front porch under the brilliant sun, breathing in the tang of cold November air, made me feel vibrant. For the moment, I almost forgot about my tender flesh.

I made my way to the sidewalk, pausing to glance at my wife's rose garden, her current resting place. I sighed deeply and made the sign of the cross.

"I miss you so much, Alyssa. And I miss our babies, too." Again I wished I'd been able to bring them home to rest with their mother.

I made my way down the slight incline toward Harper's Knoll. It was a bit brisk, and I found myself wishing I'd grabbed an overcoat. I hadn't really noticed the cold last night; I was a bit pumped up on adrenaline I suppose.

I waved across the street to a group of people who were making their way to the knoll. I spotted Ravi, dressed in a black dress. She wore black gloves and had a navy blue scarf wrapped snuggly around her neck. I also spotted Iggy and John making their way with the crowd. Iggy looked a bit under the weather—he seemed to be dragging behind the group, clutching the collar of his shirt against the cold day. John on the other hand seemed in good spirits. He clapped his friend on the back and smiled at Ravi as the two exchanged pleasantries. I was glad to see that yesterday's events hadn't had a lasting impact on these men.

I stopped at the corner of Churchill and Pinehurst, shocked and awed by how beautiful Harper's Knoll looked. Reverend Reggy and his crew had certainly taken their task to heart.

Normally, Harper's Knoll was nothing more than a small field blanketed in lush green grass, with a slight incline on the west side. Now, it looked like the setting for an outdoor wedding for the rich and famous. White fabric covered the grass, rows of wooden chairs were set up just east of the knoll, facing the incline, and white streamers were intertwined in the tree branches and raised like thousands of waving arms when the wind blew. A small stage and podium, also covered with white fabric, sat atop the incline. In the few hours they'd had to prepare, some exceptionally skilled member of our community had fashioned from wood a beautiful resting place for our poor Charlie. His coffin stood next to the podium atop more white fabric.

I started to move again, honored by how the members of the community had come together to create such a sendoff for one of their fallen brothers. I felt warm tears on my cheeks and wiped them away with my sore hands.

Many of the seats were already occupied and I could see that I and the group across the street were among the last to arrive. As it turned out, the entire community gathered on this brisk morning. I wondered if any of them had slept, or if I'd been the only one to indulge.

I met up with Ravi as her group crossed the street. She took my arm in her own and without a word we crossed the blacktop and stepped onto the grass, then up onto the beautiful white fabric. At the front row of seats we parted and I continued past my friends to meet with Reverend Reggy at the base of the knoll while Ravi moved off to find a seat and be among her friends.

Reggy wore his black clerical with white neckband and black trousers. I'd been too groggy at home and I hadn't realized he'd changed into his formal attire. I was pleased with the formality and I knew Charlie would be, too.

"Rev, this is beautiful," I said in greeting, and shook his hand. "This is far more than I expected. I'm speechless."

"It is the least we can do for our brother." I could tell he was uncomfortable with my praise.

"Will you lead with a prayer, Reverend?"

"Of course," he said.

Together we walked up the incline and took our places at the podium. Reverend Reggy stood front and center and I stood slightly behind him and to the left.

"Brothers and sisters," he began, "please rise."

All at once, with fluidity that reminded me of a school of fish, our community rose to their feet. They stood with their backs to the morning sun, highlighted against the cold morning sky.

"In the name of the father, the son, and the holy spirit," Reverend Reggy said as he crossed himself.

As he prayed, I looked out over our people, watching as they bowed their heads. Some held each other's hands while others prayed alone.

"Almighty God, You love everything You have made and judge us with infinite mercy and justice. We rejoice in Your promises of pardon, joy and peace to all those who love You. In Your mercy turn the darkness of death into the dawn of new life, and the sorrow of parting into the joy of heaven; through our Savior Jesus Christ, who died, rose again, and lives forevermore. May You grant our brother Charlie everlasting eternity. Amen."

Reverend Reggy turned to me and I nodded to him, dismissing him from his perceived obligation of presiding over Charlie's funeral. I stepped forward and cleared my throat. The sun was bright and I squinted my eyes against its brilliance. The cold air nipped at my ears and found its way down the collar of my shirt.

"Thank you all for coming."

I put my hands in my pockets and then pulled them out quickly and clasped them in front of me. I was nervous. This was the first time I had to say words at a funeral with so many people looking at me. In the Army, when I lost a man, I wrote a letter. I did not have to feel the weight of the eyes of the bereaved on me.

"Like most of you, I didn't know Charlie very well before…well, before this all started. He was a pretty quiet guy and he usually kept to himself."

I took a few steps to my left and stood beside the coffin. I put a hand against the cold wood.

"If you asked me just a week ago if I would ever consider Charlie a hero, I probably would have said no. I've known heroes in my time, believe me. But after last night, if you were to ask me, I'd say different. I know now that Charlie was a hero."

I looked out over the gathered. Their eyes were upon me, enthralled by my words. "Charlie saved my life. In fact, he saved me twice. He gave his life for me just as he gave his life for all of you. And he did it willingly, with love in his heart and courage in his soul."

Putting both hands on the coffin, I bent forward and put my lips against the cold wood.

"You will be missed," I said. "May God have mercy on your soul, Charlie."

Stepping away from the coffin, I came down from the knoll and stood before my friends, choosing my next words carefully.

"I fear that this will not be the last time we gather here, on this knoll, for this purpose. The world as we know it has changed. There are things out there now that want to kill us. They want to infect us and bite our flesh."

Suddenly I felt warm. A bead of sweat trickled down my right temple. I unbuttoned my suit jacket and loosened my tie. The eyes of a hundred people were still upon me.

"Those crazies out there, those poor infected souls, are not the only ones that would do us harm. Our own neighbors seek to take what is ours."

I let those words sink in for a moment. Now those hundred eyes turned away, looked at each other. I heard murmurs float to me on the cool breeze.

"If we're going to survive, we have to work together. We're all family now. We are all each other have left in this world. Charlie understood, and he fought to his death to protect us from what lies outside those walls."

"This is only the beginning. I can't lie to you. Our situation is going to get worse before it gets better. We're going to be tested to our limits. We're going to see things we never thought we'd witness and do things we never thought ourselves capable of doing. And you're going to do these things for the person to your right, to your left."

They turned to each other again, looking upon their new family with new eyes. The fear was clear on their faces, but I could tell that defeat was not in their hearts. Although unsure about what was coming, I knew that they all wanted to survive.

"I will do my best to help you all live through the coming months, but I can't do it alone. I need your help. This is your home and you will protect it and your family from anyone or anything that tries to harm us or take what is ours."

Sweating now, I took off my suit coat and let it drop to the grass. I wiped sweat from my brow and at the same time shivered with pleasure as the cool air found my damp skin.

"Who will fight with me?" I asked. "Who will stand with me to protect our home and these people?"

In the front row, I saw Brian stand and beside him Bob also rose to his feet. And one by one, each man, woman and child stood, one after another until all were on their feet.

"Thank you," I said. "Let not Charlie's death be for nothing. Let not his sacrifice be for nothing! Who will help me lay our brother to rest?"

Men and women stepped forward, more than was needed, but I let them come. They came together, crossing the distance to the knoll. I watched as they gathered around the coffin and lifted it with strong hands.

Reverend Reggy led them. At the north base of the knoll they carried Charlie to the neatly dug grave. I watched while the men and women lowered the coffin into the hole. I noticed that from my deck I would be able to look out across the field and see the very spot where my friend would lay at rest.

As they stood looking down, I stepped up beside my neighbors. Crouching down, I scooped up the loose soil in my right hand. Standing again, I let the earth fall between my fingers. Tears began to well in my eyes again as the dirt fell upon the wood.

"Be at peace, Charlie," I said.

Brian followed suit, dropping a handful of cold earth into the grave. He walked away, and then Bob was there, and John. Alex and Ravi each took their turn and moved on. For the next few moments I watched as each member of our community bent for the loose soil and let it slip between their fingers and silently moved on.

I was so hypnotized by the monotonous motion of the silent men and women as they paid their last respects that I didn't at first notice the commotion. I didn't look away from the grave until I heard a woman's ear-piercing scream.

Instinctively, I reached down to grab my SKS before I realized I'd left the house unarmed.

Pushing past those gathered in front of me, trying my best to contain the fear that suddenly rose like bile in my throat, I drew closer and saw that something was happening in the third or fourth row of seats. My view was blocked by bodies crowding together, unconsciously flocking toward the activity rather than moving away.

Then I saw people turn with horror and shock on their faces. They started to run. A moment later I heard a gunshot.

I shouted as I slammed into the crowd and pushed my way through. My pulse beat so heavily I felt it in my ears. "Move! Get out of the way!"

I pushed and pulled, struggling to find a way past the crowd of people who were making their mass exodus, as well as those who stood too shocked to move. After what seemed an eternity but was actually less than half a minute, I broke through to the center of the commotion.

Chairs were tumbled and thrown haphazardly in all directions. A woman I didn't know lay on the ground screaming, both of her hands covering her neck and the gaping wound that bled freely. Her feet tangled in the white fabric and pulled it askew. On the ground beside her, his blood staining the white fabric, lay Iggy. The side of his head was blown open.

I fell to one knee beside him and reached out to lift him.

"Don't touch him," Brian said coolly.

I looked up and saw him with his Glock.

"Why?" I asked.

"He was infected," Brian said. "He turned." Before I could react, he pointed the Glock at the screaming woman and pulled the trigger.

Charlie was the first of our fallen buried on Harper's Knoll, but he was not the last. Mad Swine had come to Randall Oaks, and with it came death.

EPILOGUE: VENGEANCE

We moved silently across the field, heading toward the extreme west side of Providence's property line. After much deliberation, this spot had been chosen because it was furthest from the community's center, was lightly guarded, and would prove to be their most vulnerable point.

For the last half hour, we moved stealthily through the field, taking caution in the dark. It was difficult to see on this moonless night and I was very worried that in our haste we might stumble upon one of the sleeping *things* that had taken up residence among the maize. The dampness of the cool, moist soil permeated my black jeans. My knees grew numb with the cold. The chill of the early morning air continued to sting my face; the black greasepaint offered no protection from the elements. This was a damn cold November and it made me worry about the coming winter.

The soft rustle and whisper of the dying stalks as our bodies brushed against them became monotonous and I found myself breathing in time with our movement. Crawl and breathe. Crawl and breathe. The silence of the deep morning and my breathing was hypnotic and my mind slowly turned itself to autopilot.

Brian suddenly halted in front of me. I knew he stopped not because I saw him—in the oil black darkness of the morning I could barely see him against the dark soil of the earth—but because of the cessation of his sound. The whispering cornstalks fell silent and I immediately held my position. I shifted my SKS to a more comfortable position on one knee as I listened intently. Almost instinctively I turned away from my brother and checked our rear before finally moving forward as silently as possible to where Brian crouched. When I reached him, my eyes followed Brian's pointing finger toward what looked like a mound of earth but turned out to be the sleeping body of one of *them*. With little ambient light, it was difficult to make out the details without a much closer inspection.

I shifted onto both knees now and leaned forward, keeping a tight grip on my SKS. From my slightly improved position I could see it was a man...or used to be. Straining my eyes in the dark, I leaned even closer and looked him over. He appeared to be in his early twenties, perhaps no older than twenty-five. He wore dark jeans, light colored work boots and a bright orange T-shirt. The fact that he looked normal, save for the tell-tale sign of bloodstained lips and mouth, told me this poor guy was recently changed. Still examining him, I wondered if he'd been a resident of Providence or if he'd come from somewhere further away. We'd been experiencing more wandering traffic on Route 20 coming from the west where farmland and small roads which were rarely traveled ruled. Where he came from didn't matter, of course, but I was curious. Against my better judgment I almost felt sorry for the man before me. I checked myself. I had to remind myself that this wasn't a man any longer, and emotions were best left at home. Emotions could be dangerous in the field.

Looking up, I made eye contact with Brian and ran a finger across my exposed neckline, silently querying my brother whether we should kill the creature. Surprisingly, Brian shook his head distinctly—his long hair held tightly against his skull by a black cap—and motioned me forward with the flick of his gloved hand.

I hated the idea of leaving this sleeping lion at my unprotected back. My instincts told me to I should pull out my knife and end the suffering of the poor soul, and at the same time eliminating a possible threat to our escape route. But this was Brian's mission and I agreed that I would only play a back-up role. Perhaps that had been a mistake, but I would have to live with that decision.

Shaking my head, acting against my better judgment, I started to move again, as silently as possible, and followed my brother. The whispers rose up against the cold night as he moved to the east. I took one look to the north, toward Randall Oaks, its property line merely a deeper shadow among shadows. Our community was dark and our residents were in slumber, unaware that its leaders were moving them silently—unwillingly—toward a new destiny.

Our mission must be completed before daylight broke across the eastern sky. At dawn, the crazies would rise from their coma-like sleep and so would the slumbering residents of Randall Oaks. No one knew about our mission—not even Bob—and we wanted to keep it that way. No one could know what we were planning to do this night. As it would turn out, this mission would divide my brother and I, and things at Randall Oaks would soon take a turn for the worse.

The western border of the Providence property line stretched out for more than two miles from north to south, but that stretch of unprotected property was covered by only two security outposts, each manned by two armed residents. Providence would soon learn their lesson and fill in the gap in their line. But tonight, we used this to our advantage.

For three consecutive nights following Charlie's funeral, Brian and I had crawled across the field that bordered our two communities. We hastily set up an observation post from within what was left of the grain silo at the abandoned barn—the property had sold to land developers who intended to build another community on it before the whole financial system collapsed on us—and surveyed the movements of these security details. For six hours each night, we made notes on their shift changes and personnel and weaponry.

The first security outpost to the north was of no interest to us and we casually observed it for the sake of thoroughness. Instead, we focused much of our surveillance on the southern outpost, where Comedian had been reassigned from his original post at the Providence roadblock. He was our mission.

Like clockwork, the security shifts ended at 3:30am and the four men who manned the outposts—two to the north and two to the south—were relieved by fresh security teams. By 3:31am each morning, Comedian would be on his way to his home on the extreme southwest end of Providence.

Now, consulting my watch I noted the time was 3:52am. Comedian should be home by now, hopefully his sleep plagued by nightmares of Charlie and the undead.

With the stealth of ninjas, my brother and I made our way from the fields to the edge of the Providence property line unnoticed, using the cover of the low rolling hills and shadows cast by the large homes. If our intelligence was sound, which it was, we knew exactly where we needed to go. Without pause we crossed dewy grass, which we exchanged for damp pavement, and moved silently toward the pale blue single-family home where Comedian resided.

Leaning against the wood siding trying to catch my breath, I could feel the cool night air against my damp pants. My knees and thighs puckered with gooseflesh. Plumes of vapor escaped through my slightly parted lips with each exhale. I could feel Brian's body next to mine as I surveyed our immediate surroundings. At this time of the morning, all was silent. Street lamps burned brightly but we lurked silently in the shadows cast by the attached garage against which we leaned.

Brian started to move again when I tapped his shoulder with my left hand. Walking backward, SKS pointed at the street and shoulder sliding softly against the structure, I made my way toward the rear of the home. The one story ranch-style home backed up to a large pond flanked with tall witch grass and cattails that bent slightly against the cold breeze. The water looked like a pool of shadows. I don't know why, but I suddenly wondered if those creatures could survive in the water. I started to imagine one of them lying in the pond, just below the surface, watching us as we stealthily moved across the wet grass.

Brian halted his movement, pulling me from my dangerous daydream. I took to a knee and looked around. A medium sized wood deck spread out behind the home. I stood as Brian signaled and we crossed the creaking planks to the patio doors. Long vertical blinds blocked our view of the interior. At the patio door, Brian leaned his M4 against the wall and removed his gloves. Stuffing them into his right jacket pocket, he reached into an interior pocket and pulled out a small black zippered case. Gingerly, he removed two of the thin metal tools. He knelt beside the door and using the tools, went to work.

His nose was red from the cold but he was completely oblivious of the November air. I could tell from each exhale of vapor that his breathing was steady. Brian was calm. Working quickly but quietly, he picked the flimsy lock of the patio door. Within seconds he finished his task. As I watched, he returned his tools to the zippered case, which disappeared into his pocket. He tugged his gloves back on and took up his carbine. Brian turned toward me and I gave him a thumb up to let him know we were still unnoticed. Nodding his head, he put his right hand on the handle and slid the patio door open with a harsh hush.

Fortunately for us, Comedian did not block the base of the patio doors with a bit of pipe or wedge, and within seconds we entered his home like thieves in the night. The living room or family room—I couldn't tell which—spread out before us in a rather spacious open floor plan. The back of a dark leather sofa greeted us as we entered, just a few feet in front of the patio door. A large flat screen TV stared back at us with its blank face. Our footsteps betrayed us briefly as the rubber soles of our boots squeaked against the wood floors. We both paused and crouched instinctively. Brian looked at me with wide eyes and then faced the direction of the hallway we'd been heading toward, expecting Comedian to emerge in his pajamas, wondering about the strange sounds.

A few moments of intense silence passed as we waited to be discovered. Setting my SKS against the sofa, I began to untie my boots. Without hesitation, Brian followed suit. In seconds we stood in our stocking feet and grabbed up our weapons. With my left hand I indicated our path to the right and together we moved further into the home.

We crossed through the open living room, passed the galley kitchen, and continued through the combination dining room to the short corridor to our right. There were three doors along this twelve foot hall. We stopped at the first on the right; it opened into a full bathroom. Brian closed the door softly and moved to the next door on the right. It stood open halfway and nothing but darkness greeted us through the void. Using the barrel of his carbine, Brian nudged it open and took a step inside. He used the flashlight mounted to his gun and thumbed a quick flare of light into the room. The bedroom was empty.

Leaving the door open behind, we moved on, stopping behind the closed door on our left. Brian stood to the left of the frame and I moved to the right. We pressed our backs to the wall and gave ourselves a moment to get our breathing under control. Brian gripped the doorknob with his left hand and his eyes locked on mine. We stood that way, eyes locked, for a long moment.

Although this was his mission, I knew that he was awaiting my approval. We both knew that what we were about to do would not only impact us, but also the entire community. We were just seconds away from crossing a line over which we could not step back once our action was complete.

With fear gnawing at my belly, I nodded my head.

After the slightest pause, Brian turned the knob and slowly pushed the door open. Stepping into the room, we slowly traversed the cold floor toward the bed, our stockinged feet just whispers against the teak wood. Beneath a single sheet, Comedian lay on his back. His dirty stubble played tricks on my eyes, deforming his lower jaw in the dark room, giving him a haunted scarecrow look. For a moment, I thought he was one of those things...that he had turned. A slight movement of shadows from outside the window changed his face and it was just Comedian again.

Brian and I watched him sleep for a moment. The man's lips trembled as he exhaled. I could smell the liquor on his breath. His eyelids twitched a moment, as did his right cheek, an involuntary movement in sleep. He had gone to bed in his clothes, not even removing his boots before sagging into his bed. His body odor was pungent, like the smell of bad garlic.

Brian was watching me, perhaps for signs that I had changed my mind. His questioning eyes bore into me. Again, I simply nodded my consent. After holding me with his eyes a few seconds longer, Brian finally reached out with his gloved hand and held Comedian's nose closed for a few seconds, cutting off the man's breathing. Comedian's eyes sprung wide open in shocked surprise. He tried to sit up in bed, sputtering and fighting for air, but Brian stunned him with a quick jab to his mouth, knocking him back down into the mattress.

This time I flicked on my flashlight, hooding it with my left hand to diffuse some of the crisp white light. I could not suppress my smile. Comedian's eyes were as wide as he could manage to open them in his drunken state. His face contorted with terror giving him an almost comic countenance when he recognized who was in the room with him. A thin line of blood spread across his front teeth and down the side of his lip. His tousled hair poked out in every direction.

"Hello, douchebag," Brian smirked.

"God, please," Comedian said.

His voice was not slurred as I'd expected. Perhaps the shock and terror that slammed adrenaline into his blood stream had sobered him. He tried clumsily to sit up again, to get into a more prepared position, but Brian shoved him back down roughly.

"God can't save you from me," Brian said.

"It was a mistake," Comedian said. "I didn't mean to kill that guy. You have to believe me."

"That 'guy' had a name. Charlie." Brian said. "And begging won't help. But keep going if you want. I might enjoy this more if you cry like a little girl."

Realizing that his pleas would not work with my brother, he turned his wide eyes toward me, the perceived reasonable one. His perceptions were off-base.

"Please don't let him kill me. *Please*," Comedian begged.

Comedian's voice rose in pitch and his eyes grew glassy until tears formed. He sat up, this time with no resistance from Brian. He got on to one knee beside the bed. The top three buttons of his shirt had broken loose, perhaps when Brian shoved him down. In the shadows of the room his face again took on the look of one of the changed.

"Please, you have to forgive me. *I didn't mean to shoot him!*"

"You can ask Charlie to forgive you," I said coldly. "But I don't think you'll see him where you're going, you son-of-a-bitch."

I stood there a moment longer and watched as tears rolled down Comedian's bristled cheeks. A thick phlegm-like sound escaped his throat and horrible sobs wracked his body. His chest heaved and shuddered and thick mucus oozed down from his nose. Finally, his thin body slid to the floor, curled like a fetus, trembling like a shivering dog. Before my conscience got the better of me, I simply turned, and with a quick nod to my brother I left the room.

In the hall now, I closed the bedroom door softly behind me until I heard the audible click of the bolt latching securely. With my back against the wall to the left of the door frame, I slid to the cold wood floor. My SKS rested on my knees and moved up and down slightly because my knees trembled. From behind the thin wood door I heard Comedian's first muffled screams. I had no idea what Brian did in there and I didn't want to know. But the muffled screams lasted for more than thirty minutes.

To be continued in:

MAD SWINE

DEAD WINTER

Coming Soon...

ABOUT THE AUTHOR

Steven Pajak was born in Chicago and raised in the city's Near Northwest Community. He also lived in Wartrace, Tennessee and Dallas, Texas before moving back to Illinois where he now resides in a Chicagoland suburb.

Visit Steven's official website at www.stevenpajak.com.

For information about the Mad Swine series visit the official Facebook page at www.facebook.com/MadSwine.

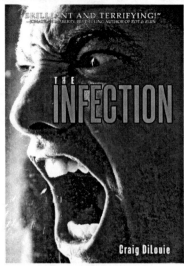
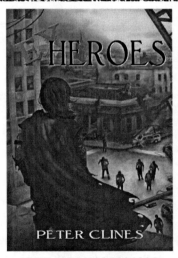

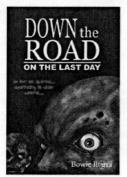

EDEN

A ZOMBIE NOVEL BY TONY MONCHINSKI

Seemingly overnight the world transforms into a barren wasteland ravaged by plague and overrun by hordes of flesh-eating zombies. A small band of desperate men and women stand their ground in a fortified compound in what had been Queens, New York. They've named their sanctuary Eden.

Harris—the unusual honest man in this dead world—races against time to solve a murder while maintaining his own humanity. Because the danger posed by the dead and diseased mass clawing at Eden's walls pales in comparison to the deceit and treachery Harris faces within.

ISBN: 978-1934861172

CRUSADE

A ZOMBIE NOVEL BY TONY MONCHINSKI

The world is dead, and millions of flesh-hungry zombies roam the land. Refugees from Eden seek a better place. They face adversaries living and dead, and befriend new survivors, whose sole hope lies is the complete annihilation of the undead. The only chance humanity has is a total war against the zombie hordes, and only one side can emerge victorious!

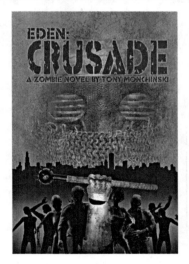

ISBN: 978-1934861332

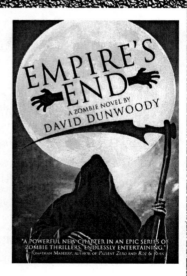

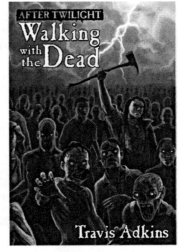

DEAD EARTH: THE GREEN DAWN

Something bad has happened in Nevada. Rumors fly about plagues and secret government experiments. In Serenity, New Mexico, Deputy Sheriff Jubal Slate has his hands full. It seems that half the town, including his mother and his boss, are sick from an unusual malady. Even more worrisome is the oddly-colored dawn sky. Soon, the townspeople start dying. And they won't dead.

MARK JUSTICE AND DAVID T WILBANKS

eBook Only

DEAD EARTH: THE VENGEANCE ROAD

Invaders from another world have used demonic technology to raise an unholy conquering army of the living dead. These necros destroyed Jubal Slate's home and everyone he loved. Now the only thing left for Slate is payback. No matter how far he has to go or how many undead warriors he must slaughter, Slate and his motley band of followers will stop at nothing to end the reign of the aliens.

MARK JUSTICE AND DAVID T WILBANKS

ISBN: 978-1934861561

MORE DETAILS, EXCERPTS, AND PURCHASE INFORMATION AT
www.permutedpress.com

AUTOBIOGRAPHY OF A WEREWOLF HUNTER

After his mother is butchered by a werewolf, Sylvester James is taken in by a Cheyenne mystic. The boy trains to be a werewolf hunter, learning to block out pain, stalk, fight, and kill. As Sylvester sacrifices himself to the hunt, his hatred has become a monster all its own. As he follows his vendetta into the outlands of the occult, he learns it takes more than silver bullets to kill a werewolf.

BY BRIAN P EASTON

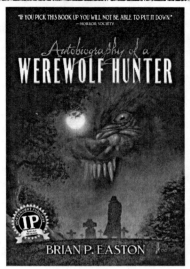

ISBN: 978-1934861295

HEART OF SCARS

The Beast has taken just about every-thing it can from Sylvester Logan James, and for twenty years he has waged his war with silver bullets and a perfect willingness to die. But fighting monsters poses danger beyond death. He contends with not just the ancient werewolf Peter Stubbe, the cannibalis-tic demon Windigo, and secret cartels, but with his own newfound fear of damnation.

BY BRIAN P EASTON

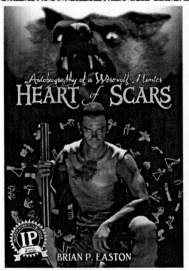

ISBN: 978-1934861639

MORE DETAILS, EXCERPTS, AND PURCHASE INFORMATION AT
www.permutedpress.com

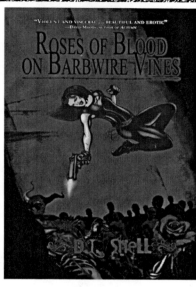

CPSIA information can be obtained at www.ICGtesting.com
Printed in the USA
LVOW08s1635310314

379675LV00002B/661/P